CONTINGENT UPON
MAGENTA

CONTINGENT UPON
MAGENTA

by
C.Drying
cdrying.com

San Jose, California

For permission requests, contact the publisher.

Gothlick
1750 Lundy Ave.
P.O. Box 610071
San Jose CA 95161
gothlick.com
gothlick@gothlick.com

ISBN 9781946935007
ISBN 9781946935014 (electronic copy)

Library of Congress Control Number (LCCN): 2017936229

This book is a work of fiction. Names, characters, places, and incidents are either the product of the author's imagination or are used fictionally. Any resemblance to actual persons, living or dead, or to actual events or locales is entirely coincidental.

Cover design by Cakamura Art Studio

ACKNOWLEDGMENTS:

Thank you—Su, Pam, and Diana—for proofreading my manuscript. Also, thank you to Teresa for suggesting the phrase "a little lilac."

To mothers who love their daughters,
especially Billie and Su.

CHAPTER 1:
BUTTERFLY

BUTTERFLY'S LAUGHTER and zeal for riding down stairs on cardboard will kill me later. I'll not be able to suppress the memories of this moment after I leave tonight.

"Mom! Why are you staring at me? C'mon, let's go again."

Taking two steps at a time, I bolted up the stairs. "Why am I waiting?" I yelled from the top.

She darted up, tripping on each step in her haste.

"You're name is Butterfly, but you sure don't fly like one," I told her and laughed. We rode down the carpeted stairway again and again. My sister cringed each time we hit the landing.

WHEN BUTTERFLY was finally tired, I put her to bed. "Don't forget this moment," I told her.

"Why?" she asked.

"Because I love you."

I heard my ride pull into the driveway and kissed Butterfly goodbye. Out of habit, I looked for my knapsack but realized I wouldn't need anything to bring with me tonight.

My sister stood at the bottom of the stairs, gazing at me with a slushy stare.

"Joan—"

"Don't speak," I said and then saluted her and exited the house.

WILLIAM AND PORTER greeted me as I arrived at Moffett Field. Moisture from the south end of the San Francisco Bay chilled the evening air. We boarded a C-40 Clipper along with a dozen other military and government officials. We sat at the back of the plane, separated from the other passengers by thin curtains. A few barreled through the sheers to shake our hands and bestow praise upon us.

"You are brave souls, you are," said one.

"Godspeed," said another.

William, Porter, and I tried to relax. We didn't speak much. Naturally, thoughts of Butterfly landed just behind my eyelids, so I forced myself to be present in the moment, which was no easy task since the two men accompanying me were very likely deeply engrossed in mentally replaying their farewell sex sessions. Over the last few days, their wives probably fulfilled every sexual fantasy they ever had. Perhaps I should have had farewell sex too, but I had no spouse or lover because I was married to my career. Butterfly was a direct product of my marriage as I agreed to be artificially inseminated based on the belief that the experience of growing and carrying a human being for nine months and enduring the intense pain of delivering it was unmatched by any other experience a man could ever have, making a woman soldier exceptionally superior to her male counterparts. Ok, the military would never acknowledge female superiority, but it's true that a woman who has borne a child surpasses those who have not. But childbearing weakened me too because of love. A mother's love can all too readily trump her individual will.

WE MADE IT to Hickam Field, landing in the fading light of dusk. While stepping down the C-40's rear set of airstairs, I felt the sweet Honolulu air envelop me. William paused at the bottom to demonstrate his chivalry by offering me his hand as I descended. That told me the media were present, so I scanned the airport grounds. Spotting them, I decided to do a forward-flip dismount off the stairs. No, I didn't really, but I've always found it funny how the media can inspire a circus.

After we deplaned, we were transported to a nearby banquet building in a black sedan, which had darkened windows.

Once inside, we were taken to a small locker room, a dressing facility where we undressed then re-dressed into suits made of Kevlar-like material. Mine was bright yellow. Porter's and William's were magenta and resembled Densip Pi's uniform. Densip Pi was the last Magentan to come through the Magentan Interrealm Conduit, which we simply called the MIC. Before we knew it was of Magentan origin, we called it the Pacific Ocean Atmospheric Cord or the POAC for short.

"Brown! Jones!" William called.

Porter and I hurried over to Lieutenant Colonel William Jeff, saluted and stood at attention.

"I realize it is redundant at this point for me to remind you of our specific mission plans and goals, but it's my duty to do it yet again."

"Yes, sir," we replied in unison.

"After the ceremony, we will deploy to the MIC platform, so this review is our last. Be at ease and have a seat," the Lieutenant Colonel ordered.

We sat upon wooden locker benches under flickering long-tube fluorescent lights as he rolled a portable whiteboard over to us.

"We will eject from the Magentan end of the MIC almost simultaneously. Jones will be in front." He drew an ellipse to indicate the MIC opening then drew three separate circles representing each one of us. "The frequency-emitting suit that Jones is wearing will immediately attract hostile fire." He marked my circle with tens of dashes and dots to show the inevitable bullets, projectiles—and who knows what else, maybe high-energy laser beams—that would strike me. "Our stealth-enabled suits," he gestured between him and Porter, "will allow us to seek cover undetected." He drew single dotted lines from the center of his and Porter's circles, illustrating movement away from the MIC edge and away from the circle that represented me. "Jones, what's next?"

"Sir, contingent upon my suit holding up, I will survive an onslaught of heavy fire, and this will provide an opportunity for the Magentans to identify me as female. Per our prediction, upon this discovery, they will cease fire, sir."

"And if your suit fails, Jones?"

"I will die, sir," I said proudly, feeling a pang of inevitable finality.

"What happens after the Magentan soldiers cease fire and *seize you*?"

"My aim, sir, is to get as close to the Magentan ruler, Maerora Ma, as possible to kill her at first opportunity by way of breaking her neck."

"And after you're successful, Jones?"

"I will most likely be killed, sir."

"But if you are *not* killed, Jones, what will you do?"

"I will kill until I'm killed, sir."

The lieutenant colonel then turned to Porter. "Brown, what is your role in this mission?"

"Sir, my role is to ensure Captain Jones accomplishes the mission objective and to adjust for contingencies," Porter said and then glanced at me as if to remind me he's no slacker and won't be part of a failed mission. But then I was no slacker either. I was the only woman in the world who could break the necks of three consecutive men in less than thirty-six seconds, based on simulation of course. It so bugged me that Porter needed to give me an admonishing look. There was no one more capable and committed to this mission than me.

"Now, let's hope to God the Magentans will believe Joan is a woman," the lieutenant colonel said jokingly.

"Should we add a little padding?" Porter gestured at my breasts.

I laughed knowing full well my breasts were of ample size. This joke was getting old, but it was effective in delivering the relief we needed. We had our egos that both enabled our incredible abilities and complicated many a moment, but I had no doubt we were a rock-solid force.

The ceremony was already underway when we made our entrance. A group of less than a hundred men and women from several nations stood up from their metal folding chairs to applaud us.

"Captain Joan Jones," the MC announced, "Captain Porter Brown, and the leader of this mission, Lieutenant Colonel William Jeff."

We walked down the middle aisle in single file and then stepped up a small set of stairs to the stage and sat side by side at a curtain-draped table on which three evenly spaced microphones were mounted. We would be responding to questions from the audience after the senator from Hawaii delivered an historical perspective of the mission. He was already standing at a podium to our left.

"Thank you for your representation here this evening. We now hereby proceed forth with an official recording of the embarkation of this mission for posterity. Whether the mission fails or succeeds," stated the senator, "the very electing to serve in this mission automatically deems these three officers as the most laudable men and woman among us here in this building this evening."

As the senator spoke, images of Butterfly fluttered about my vision. I imagined how she might be as an adult, thinking about her long-gone mother, sharing a kinship with other families of fallen heroes, expressing the pride of her lineage with her own young daughter, and speaking to national crowds every Veteran's Day in the future.

"Twenty years ago, the POAC was discovered by the U.S. Air Force who recognized it to be a global common, a phenomenon that belonged to the inhabitants of Earth. Some ten years later, a hostile incident of extraterrestrial origin occurred at the site of the POAC. A small army of purple, humanoid aliens discharged from the mouth of the POAC and killed over three-hundred men and women, civilian and military, who had built platforms for peaceable study cooperatives to research the POAC phenomenon. Subsequently, the U.S. government claimed jurisdiction over the region to ensure global safety and security."

The senator paused to sip from his bottle of water, and in an attempt to block more thoughts of Butterfly, I engaged in mental practice of snapping the necks of the people around me. It was something I did every day, and no one was off limits except for Butterfly. All my mental conditioning, probably more than anything else, perfected my skill.

"A little over a year ago, we were once again visited by a purple person. His name was Densip Pi, and he informed us of a warring world led by a vicious ruler who is hell bent on destroying Earth. He warned us and advised us, and we heeded his advice. The mission that we acknowledge execution of this evening is, in fact, based wholly on the instruction of Densip Pi. He taught us about the Magentan world, their beliefs, their traditions, and their Earthly origins. Densip Pi wasn't long for this world. Unfortunately, he only lasted a couple of days, but his sacrifice will not go unforgotten, for I am proud and honored to reveal the official appellation of this mission—the Densip Pi Mission." The senator pulled a drape off an easel that stood behind him to reveal the mission's commemorative plaque, marking the end of the senator's speech and segueing into the question-and-answer period.

I was still obsessively breaking the necks of the ceremony attendees, preventing Butterfly from flitting about in my head when the realization that I would be on the MIC platform in just an hour accelerated my heart rate, which caused me to inhale deeply a few times. Porter noticed, so I broke his neck repeatedly.

"We now turn over the microphone to the audience. Please feel free to ask our brave officers any question, and remember you were invited here tonight to help document this mission for posterity. We invited only academic representatives in hopes that the knowledge exchanged this evening will be done so at a high level of discourse. Also, please don't languish at the mic or contribute to disruption of the productive exchange of information. We're allowing only one question per person, and please state your name and affiliation. Thank you so very much for your cooperation," said the MC.

"Hello, my name is Doreen Townsend, I am an anthropologist from the college in Weston-super Mare in England, and my question is for Captain Joan Jones. Since the public has not been entirely privy to all the intelligence disclosed by Densip Pi, would you be able to share perhaps a spot of a hint as to what significance a female human being *is* to the Magentan world?"

"Thank you, Ms. Townsend, for the question. As we understand it, Magenta is a world dominated by a matriarchal society, and we believe Magentans will relate more positively to an Earth woman rather than to a man," I said.

"But, of course, you're not *leading* the mission, are you, Captain?"

"Obviously, we don't live in a matriarchal society here on Earth, do we?" I quipped, and the audience chuckled.

"Only one question per person, please, thank you. Can we have the next question, please?" said the MC.

"I am from Israel, and my name is Dara Haim. Captain Jones, in the Hawaiian Senator's speech, he mentioned the vicious ruler of Magenta is 'hell bent on destroying Earth,' and since you have revealed that Magenta is matriarchal, I will have to assume that this threatening ruler is female, so, then, is it your mission to kill her or reason with her?"

Preempting my answer, William quickly scooted up to his microphone and responded. "We like to believe we're on a benevolent mission."

"Forgive me, Mr. Jeff, sir, I did not ask *you* the question—"

"*Please* only one question per person. Come on, let's have the next questioner," ordered the MC.

"*Olá*, I am Mariana Maldonado from the South American Academic Collective located in *Brasília*. My question is for Joan Jones. *Senhorita* Jones, is it a mission to *reconnaissansa* or *destroyo*?"

William leaned forward quickly to answer yet another question intended for me. "This is not an offensive mission, but it is a dangerous one."

"Can we have some questions for the gentlemen, please?" The MC asked.

"Hey, yeah, thanks so much—all three of you—for your, uh,

bravery and *especially* Captain Jones. She's awesome, and—"

"Sir, please state your name and affiliation and ask your question," said the MC.

"Oh, yeah, um, I'm Dirk Jennings from the School of Humanities at Summertown University in California. Misses, oh, uh, I mean *Mizz* Jones. Uh, when you go to Magenta, could you, like, check out the art and all, you know, like statues and paintings and things?

Funny how William didn't jump to answer this one. "Dirk, thank you for your gratitude and for your question. I will most definitely observe the Magentan artwork to the best of my abilities."

"Thanks, Misses Jones, oh, I mean—"

"Next person, please," said the MC.

"Hello, I am Monisha Durga from the North-Eastern Hill University in Shillong, India. Since before the POAC was discovered, we have had many in our state believing in a maroon-colored Goddess. She is very much beloved by Her people and cherished for Her maternalism and feared by those who would decry Her all-encompassing governance. We strongly believe Densip Pi brings validity to the existence of our Goddess, and instead of a question, I will simply say that we *implore* you to refrain from aggression and to *honor* this so-called fierce and vicious ruler who is supposedly set on destroying us. You, Ms. Captain Jones, will be The Great Liaison between Her and Her people. We are Her people, so please proceed forth with feminine wisdom."

"Well, Ms. Durga, I'm fascinated by the information you've shared with us. When we return from our mission, I'd like to learn more about your goddess culture," I replied.

"Since there's an imbalance of questions here, I will ask the gentlemen a few of my own," said the MC. "Captain Brown—"

"Yes, sir," Porter said.

"Captain Brown, can you tell us more about your actual mission role, sir?"

"I am responsible for adjusting for contingencies, which

means if things don't go as planned, I must make the most of the situation and advise Lieutenant Colonel Jeff. He, in turn, will execute orders based on my input."

"Wholly impressive," said the MC. "Lieutenant Colonel Jeff, can you tell me more about the training and preparation for this mission?"

"Very happy to . . . ," William said, and as he explained our grueling mission training in minute detail, I allowed myself one more thought of Butterfly and hoped it wouldn't make me cry.

I was ordinarily quite stoic, but when I thought about Butterfly, I melted like butter. Isn't that why I called her Butterfly? Oh, how that girl loves to play, and her greatest thrill seemed to be when I played with her. I reassured myself that my sister would play with her, and I then held onto Butterfly laughing as my sustaining image of her.

"All right, thank you, Lieutenant Colonel Jeff, for your well detailed explanation," said the MC. "Now, can we have the next question from the audience, please?"

"Hello, my name is Dr. Timothy Rumple. I'm Canadian and have a question for Colonel Jeff—"

"Bravo!" said the MC.

"Uh, yes, my question is about previous missions. I realize all of them have been covert operations, for some reason, until now, but can you shed any light on the history of previous missions?"

"Actually, no, I cannot," said William.

For one, not even he knew the details about those missions, and, two, all *we* knew is that no one ever returned, which meant most likely we would not return either. According to the Densip Pi transcripts, however, previous troops who made it through to Magenta were all killed because they consisted of men and that by virtue of sending a female, access beyond the mouth of the MIC would be possible.

The MC announced the official end of the ceremony, and very quickly four soldiers presented themselves to escort the three of us from the hall. As we walked to the exit, my eyes met with the Indian woman who had mentioned the goddess culture that had arisen after (or was it before?) the discovery of the POAC. She nodded, and I smiled back at her. I had it in my head that she was just a woo-woo holdover from the New Age movement, but I was struck by how close the magenta color of her sari was to Porter's and William's mission uniforms.

WE REACHED THE AIRPORT apron where a Coast Guard helicopter waited to take us to the MIC platform. Two Apache Guardians started up nearby and would be flying in escort formation with us. It seemed each branch of the armed forces was granted a role in this mission. I felt the soft humidity of the Hawaiian Islands on my face as we dashed to the helicopter. Dusk was long gone. The four attendant soldiers assisted us onto the helicopter but did not board themselves. Our nighttime departure was a deliberate tactic to avoid giving the mainstream press a chance to sensationalize our mission.

It was too dark to see the entire area, but I had been to the MIC platform many times to know what was below us. There was a little ghost town of platforms. After the Magentan attack, the U.S. military forbade access to the area, but before that, it was teaming with research institutions. Some limited commercial tourism had even begun.

The whole world was horrified by the Magentan invasion, perhaps not so much because people were killed (because people are killed all the time in skirmishes between warring nations, tribes, and gangs, and we've all grown accustomed to such violence) but because of the realization that hostile extraterrestrials really did exist after all, and what was particularly worrisome was since their technology was advanced enough to get them here, we had to conclude that their weaponry must have far exceeded anything we had in our own arsenal. Some insisted that their technological advancement was accompanied by mental and emotional superiority as well, so we had nothing to worry

C.DRYING

about, but that notion didn't reconcile with the fact that they attacked us for no good reason, which had only left us in constant fear of more Magentans spewing out of the MIC. Personally, I didn't think there was any mental and emotional superiority in it, but in terms of psychological warfare, it might have been a strategy.

I strapped myself into the coarse-canvas bucket, which was attached to the cable of the Coast Guard's helicopter. The winch then lowered me down. Flood lamps drenched the platform with cold-white light. Porter came down then William. Brackish seawater sprayed all over us from the stir of the helicopters' rotary blades. Platform technicians handed us our helmets, which were relatively small low-profile type helmets that were designed mostly for deflecting bullets, not for protecting the skull from being crushed. Once our helmets were on, the technicians grabbed us and placed us in a human-sized egg tray. The helicopters quickly departed. I was placed above William and Porter unstrapped and unattached with my legs set into and held onto by both men. Before I tucked my arms under my breasts, William grabbed for my hand as I reached down for his. He squeezed it tightly then let it go.

"Ashes to ashes," said one of the technicians.

"Star dust to star dust," replied William.

"Goodbye, Butterfly," I whispered. Four technicians stretched the opening of the MIC fabric and pulled it over the pile of us.

SWOOOSH!

11

CHAPTER 2:
TRAVELING

The mother of invention is a very well-endowed woman, and she has been suckling technology forever at her perpetually full breasts.
—Eldora Ma

ELDORA MA HAD A DESIRE, a *strong* desire that swelled tremendously within her. In fact, it grew too big for comfort, and it became quite a threat to her well-being, so much so that it became a necessity to deliver it by way of fulfillment. Thus, she invented the MIC, which consisted of six elements: the Earth-side sack, the transport sphere, the Earth-side reduction sequence, the realm-barrier transfer, the Magenta-side enlargement sequence, and the Magenta-side sack.

Captain Jones, Captain Brown, and Lieutenant Colonel Jeff were midway through the Earth-side reduction sequence wherein they were shrinking in size. Infinite division was not the means used in the MIC. Instead, it employed infinite proportional-size reduction in which the cells of the body reduced in size, and molecules within the cells drew smaller, and atoms comprising the molecules also decreased in size as well as the protons and neutrons and the hadrons within them, and the quarks within the hadrons also proportionately became smaller.

"Small is infinite." That's what she said, Eldora Ma, when she proposed her ideas to the collection of the greatest minds she had brought together for the erection of the MIC.

Joan, Porter, and William were inside a semi-rigid spherical enclosure, which had accumulated around them as they were siphoned up through the Earth-side sack. The Earth-side sack was suspended in Earth's atmosphere and consisted of a translucent fabric, which had a less-than-one nanometer mesh. The Earth-side sack was the only portion of the MIC visible to those on Earth, though it was not readily observable by the naked eye. One had to concentrate his or her focus tremendously to see the very long and narrow empty upside-down bag, which was in geosynchronous orbit around Earth. Nevertheless, the Earth-side sack was chock full of technology and raw material necessary to maintain orbit and to enable fabrication and decomposition of the transport sphere.

The transport sphere was the working mechanism that enabled the proportional-size reduction based on a calculation of rotation rate, speed, and distance applicable to the locality of natural laws. When the Joan-Porter-William bearing sphere will have reached the optimal size, it will have encountered the realm barrier, known to Earth humans as the edge of the observable Universe.

Transport through the barrier itself will be achieved by virtue of miniscule size. Crossing through it had previously been a literally mind-blowing experience before the understanding that the barrier was comprised of pure consciousness. During testing trials of the then newly constructed MIC, countless volunteers lost their minds after passing through the barrier. Since Eldora Ma had died before the completion of the MIC, her daughter Amora Ma carried on the effort and postulated that absorption of individual consciousness was occurring inside the barrier. She, thus, ordered technology to be installed in the transport sphere that would amplify—by way of excitation—the matter and energy constituents of individual consciousness. Consequently, a hyper-psychic effect results during passage and has been likened to an extreme experience of narcissism or solipsism.

After passage through the realm barrier, the sphere will have begun to enlarge as it will go through the Magenta-side enlargement sequence. Two-way travel was made possible by the MIC's complementary reduction and enlargement sequences that straddled the realm barrier. Once the sphere will have reached its normal size, a simple homing mechanism will then direct it to the Magenta-side sack where it will settle into a meniscus atop the sack, and the meniscus will become increasingly unshallow, lowering the sphere to a point at which its contents will then be expelled. The sphere itself will then be re-absorbed by the translucent fabric.

Previously, the Magenta-side sack had a landing pad to dampen impact of the expelled contents. However, it was redesigned by order of Maerora Ma such that the pad would be optionally placed for planned arrivals and otherwise absent for unplanned arrivals. This was one of Maerora Ma's measures to thwart Earth-originated missions. Sphere passengers landing sans pad would perish or at least become significantly impaired.

I LOST CONSCIOUSNESS and regained it in a place where all I could see was amorphous white. I couldn't orient myself because my proprioception was shot. I didn't know if William and Porter were with me or not. There were no shapes or forms or textures. I think I was at the point of transit Densip Pi referred to as the realm barrier.

I couldn't recognize whether or not I had arms or legs. Thinking about them made me feel sick, but I had no stomach to be sick. I wasn't walking. I wasn't floating. I wasn't moving, but I wasn't stationary.

Thinking was all there was, so like René Descartes I concluded that I was existing because I was thinking. Surprisingly, the endless whiteness was familiar to me. It reminded me of how I had imagined the edge of the Universe would look. I had travelled there in my mind many times when I was a teenager, and it was always eternally white right after I managed to hop over the moment of the Big Bang. Probably my imagination used white as a placeholder until I could develop another idea about it, but I never did. I just left it white, white like Heaven.

Perhaps I was actually inside my very own imagination, not just picturing my thoughts, but really being inside them. What a frightening idea especially if I were to think not of me accidentally. I mean, that could end me here and now because there's nothing here but me in an infinite loop of my existence within an eternal white backdrop of myself.

CHAPTER 3:
MAGENTA

THAT BLESSED awareness of my body and limbs returned, but it was accompanied by the distinct sensation of falling headfirst really fast, and, of course, I couldn't see much, just maroon-tinted darkness. I became aware of William and Porter as their grips tightened around my thighs. A modicum of relief swept through me, and then we hit the solid ground hard. I instantly felt the force of William and Porter land on my lower back. They then launched from me with their heels digging into my sides. Immediately, shelling began, and I was relentlessly sprayed. Round after round fired on me. My suit was effectively absorbing the shelling, but it hurt like hell each time a bullet hit the high tensile-strength fabric of my suit, displacing my flesh at impact a few centimeters all over my body at a high rapidity rate.

I tried ever so hard to roll onto my back to expose my front in hopes the Magentans would recognize me as female, just as Densip Pi had advised, but my arms and legs seemed disconnected from me. I strained and pushed with all my might to give them my frontal view. However, I could only manage a partial turn.

The terror of the moment was nothing like the agony of the intense burning, stabbing, and stinging sensations pervading my body. Can a human being withstand this much pain? I felt defeated, but this was the plan, wasn't it? A thick fluid then filled my right palm, and I figured my suit had failed me. "Oh, God," I whimpered aloud. Porter would have to start his contingency calculations right away. "Butterfly . . . I . . . love . . . ."

MAERORA MA sat at her console in her station within the enormous cylindrical-shaped hall, which stood many stories high. Large translucent planes comprised the upper levels, revealing spectacular views of the Magentan sky.

The Magentan ruler spent much of her time in the hall, controlling the realm from her console. She referred to it as her general headquarters wherein no fewer than one-thousand Magentans scurried about, supporting surveillance, data analysis, and Maerora Ma herself, and all of them sported pan-omni glasses, which were devices that provided audio and visual communication as well as access to a database of everything. The glasses were designed to detect neural undulations (i.e., brainwaves) through numerous sensors embedded within the frames of the glasses, and brainwaves were then translated into machine code. This eliminated the need to type on a keyboard or verbally speak instructions. All one merely had to do was mentally visualize his or her commands to access and to interact with information and to communicate with others as well.

A large balcony projected forth from just under Maerora Ma's station and was connected to a dwelling that Maerora Ma's two daughters resided in throughout the day. It was a Magentan tradition for mothers to be near their daughters. Katydid, the younger of the two, raced from one end of the balcony to the other kicking a mechanized ball that was designed to anticipate her movements and persistently entice her into a long play period. Mălĭn, the older daughter, stood in the doorway of the balcony. She was engaged in remote conversation through her pan-omni glasses. A little floating ball carrying a camera hovered in front of her, enabling her distant interlocutor to see her.

As sounds from the hall's activities constantly echoed upward in a low invariable drone, Maerora Ma spoke to the chief science officer from the nearby planet Oaktobron. The two spoke through pan-omni glasses in Magentan, the *lingua franca* of the realm.

"But we *have* pursued the technology, Maerora Ma, and it is ready," whined the scientist. "To refuse use, is to refuse progress."

"Progress is not alone a matter of technology," Maerora Ma said, looking directly into the camera of the small ball floating in front of her, "and it is not wise to go about poking holes in realm barriers, Quercus."

"Well, *you* did."

"And we paid a dear price for it," Maerora Ma growled.

"Well, *we* seek *higher* realms, not lower ones."

"That makes it all the more perilous. Do you not understand?"

"Of course, as if Oaktobrons are not as brilliant as Magentans."

"You see, Quercus, by that very reply, I'm reminded of the long-standing ambivalence Magentans have for Oaktobrons. Oaktobrons are brilliant, almost to a fault, but you're hasty and petulant to no end."

As Maerora Ma and Quercus argued, Katydid, who was still on the balcony below, appeared to lose interest in pursuing the intelligent ball. She tried to ignore it but couldn't refrain from giving it sidelong glances, and each time she saw it, it wiggled and rolled towards her. Finally, however, she stomped away appearing quite miffed by it and then hunted for her set of pan-omni glasses to call Maerora Ma's chief personal assistant, Yaylor Pi.

"Yaylor Pi! Yaylor Pi, where are you?"

"I'm here, little one, next to your mother," he answered.

"Why do we have to stay so late? When can we go home? I'm getting *very* tired. Please tell Mama I want to go home." The two spoke to a floating camera ball that streamed their images to each other.

"Your mother's almost finished," he said.

All pan-omni glasses within the headquarters hall then flashed a visual warning, and a soft horn-like sound filled the air. However, no one seemed overly fazed or stopped their activity. The bustling hall's residents went on hustling. Maerora Ma's eyes, nonetheless, exhibited a faint element of consternation when she shifted her glance to Yaylor Pi. Yaylor Pi looked back at her with widened eyes but no other physical indication that anything was amiss. Katydid entered the station and ran up to Yaylor Pi. He knelt down to greet her.

The warning indicated that MIC activity had been detected,

which meant a sky object may have collided with the Magenta-side sack or the alarm system was being tested or some malfunction had occurred or humans from Earth were sending a mission team to Magenta. In any case, Maerora Ma had not paused from her conversation with the Oaktobron.

"Quercus, realm barriers exist for a reason. I won't allow an unplanned, unauthorized experiment to be conducted. It's too dangerous. Is this not plain enough for you to understand?"

"Maerora Ma, you'll regret your fascist ways," Quercus said.

"Fascist?" She chuckled and then launched into a full hearty laugh. Quercus terminated the communication session.

Seeing that her mother's conversation had ended, Katydid quickly set herself into her mother's lap, forcing Maerora Ma to adjust her position to accommodate her.

"Yaylor Pi, what's happening at the MIC?" Maerora Ma asked.

"There's no word yet," he answered. The soft horn ceased sounding.

"Katydid, where's your sister?" Maerora Ma asked.

Katydid just shrugged her shoulders, so Maerora Ma called Mălīn with her pan-omni glasses but to no avail. She gently tapped Katydid to get off her lap and then sprang forward to go search for Mălīn herself. Yaylor Pi leaped to accompany her and pulled Katydid along. They descended into the dwelling below, and Maerora Ma hunted high and low. They then headed down to a large internal ledge that ringed the building.

"We can monitor an entire realm, yet my *daughter* is no-where to be found," Maerora Ma stated, and then, through her glasses, she called Vysender, the highest-ranking military leader in all the realm. "Vysender."

"Yes, Ma'am, we have an intruder from Earth being elimi-nated at this very minute," Vysender said.

"Ok, good. Take care of it, but I'm calling about Mălīn. She's not accounted for here. Please find her."

"Yes, of course, Ma'am," acknowledged Vysender.

"Ma'am, Quercus is calling back. Shall I forward him to you?" asked Yaylor Pi.

"Ha! He's desperate to apologize. Yes, forward him and continue to search for Mălīn," Maerora Ma ordered. "Katydid, come along with me," she said, holding her hand out for the little girl to take. They walked back to Maerora Ma's station while Maerora Ma spoke to Quercus en route. The camera ball silently flew along in pace with Maerora Ma's stride.

"Quercus, my dear, it has been such a *long* time," said Maerora Ma.

"Sarcasm, my mother used to tell me, is the protest of a feeble mind," Quercus mumbled.

"Ah, yes, I'm certain your mother knew that all too well," Maerora Ma said, and upon arriving at her station, she let go of Katydid's hand and sat at her console. Katydid picked up a smooth, shiny obelisk-shaped ornament from her mother's station and analyzed it.

"Look, Maerora Ma, there is no denying that Oaktobrons are a bit impatient and prickly, if you will, but we are a vibrant and productive people too—"

"Quercus—"

"Must you interrupt me?" he whined.

"Quercus—"

"You just can't bear for me to carry on with anything positive about Oaktobrons, can you, Maerora Ma?"

"Quercus, there will be no upward barrier busting until the first realm is assimilated with the second," she stated.

"Fine!"

"It's late and my daughters are still up. Are we finished?"

"Look, Maerora Ma, the reason I called you back is to invite you to a celebration we're having to commemorate a recent breakthrough we've achieved?

"'Breakthrough?'"

"Don't fret. We didn't break through the realm barrier . . . *yet*. We overcame a technological challenge, and that's why we think it would be beneficial for you to be present to acknowledge our technological excellence and to see the device first hand."

"All right, Quercus, I'll marvel at your doohickey, but I dread addressing your crowd. 'Behold. How grand this technology is that we shall now mothball forever,'" she mocked.

"Yes, it doesn't make sense whatsoever, does it? If you would only be open to the possibilities," he grumbled.

"*Possibilities* tend to writhe and twist about in the minds of the discontented among us. You won't be able to secure your technology from them," she warned. "It's better concealed than revealed."

"I wish you were more like your mother. Ah, yes, this realm would be happier, and the happiness would stimulate advancement and there would be no discontent . . . none. No, instead you are so stiflingly totalitarian in your approach."

"If that were the case, Quercus, you would never have been able to make that technological breakthrough that you're itching to publicize nor would you even dare express your contemptuous sentiment." A strained silence ensued.

"Oaktobrons are a spirited people, Ma'am," he said.

"We call it petulant."

"Well, there are worse ways to describe us I suppose."

"I have no doubt," she said. "Go ahead and contact Yaylor Pi. He'll make the arrangements for my visit to Oaktobron." After the communication session had ended, she pulled off her glasses, reclined in her seat, and gazed through one of the hall's large viewing planes at the ever-present huge dying star that dominated the Magentan sky. It was a dark sphere on which small lines of dim luminosity shimmered through. On average, it was a tiny star but because of proximity, it appeared large in the sky.

"Mama, can we go home now? Katydid asked, still holding the long ornament she had picked up from her mother's console.

"Not until we find Mǎlīn," Maerora Ma said.

"Maybe Mǎlīn is at home," whined Katydid, tugging at her mother's arm. Maerora Ma then picked her up and set her on her lap. The ornament was still in Katydid's hand.

"Do you know what that is?" asked Maerora Ma.

Katydid shook her head.

"It's a miniature replica of the Washington Monument."

Katydid simply smiled and ran the object through the centers of her mother's spirals of hair. Maerora Ma then kissed her daughter on the top of her head.

Just then, Mălīn entered the station accompanied by DeNitor, a young, good-looking military officer. Maerora Ma quickly put Katydid down and arose to hug Mălīn. She held her tightly, but Mălīn curtailed the would-be long embrace and excitedly spoke to her mother.

"Mama, an Earth woman has arrived. Can you believe it? In all these years, we've never had a woman come through the MIC. Are you not thrilled, Mama?" Mălīn asked.

"Amazed," answered Maerora Ma. "Is she alive? I can't imagine she would be intact after coming through the MIC without the landing pad in place, let alone enduring the automated shelling," Maerora Ma said.

"Ma'am, we disabled the shelling," DeNitor said, "as soon as we recognized she was female. I apologize for the violation of protocol. We wanted to give you the opportunity to meet with her. Naturally, we can carry through with her elimination on your command."

"No," Maerora Ma said.

"The truth is the Earth woman did actually die, and the team saved her. They were able to revive her, but she remains unconscious," DeNitor said.

"Hmm, I didn't think our medical teams were capable of such feats. What's the prognosis?"

"Positive," he answered.

"Mama, when she wakes up, you must meet her," Mălīn said.

"How long is her *full* recovery expected to take?" Maerora Ma asked.

"I don't really know," answered DeNitor, "she may never *fully* recover."

Yaylor Pi snuck into the station. Katydid noticed him and ran over to him. He patted her on the head.

"Mama, I can't wait for you to meet the Earth woman," Mălīn said. "As soon as she awakens, you should meet her."

"No," Maerora Ma said, "I shall wait for her to completely recover. I must meet her in earnest. She should not feel disadvantaged in any way."

"But, Mama—"

"Mălīn!" Maerora Ma shouted, startling all in the vicinity. "What do they say on Earth about patience, Mălīn?"

"Patience is a virtue," she answered in English.

"Where were you when the MIC alarm sounded?" Maerora Ma asked abruptly.

"I was trying to reach DeNitor to find out what was happening."

"*Your* place is at *my* side when there's MIC activity. Don't attempt to fertilize my horrible memories."

"I'm sorry, Mama."

"At the least, Mălīn, you should ensure your tracking mode is on."

"Ok, Mama."

"Take my daughters home, DeNitor. I intend to stay here for a while," Maerora Ma said as she put on her glasses and turned towards Yaylor Pi to usher him down to an anteroom away from all the activities of the open hall.

Once inside the room, Maerora Ma secured the door and asked, "Is there a way we can accelerate the Earth woman's complete recovery?"

"I believe the Oaktobrons have developed a rapid-healing system," Yaylor Pi said.

"It figures," Maerora Ma said.

"Shall I arrange—"

"Yes, right away."

"Yes, Ma'am," he said and processed the request through his glasses while Maerora Ma began to pace the length of the small room.

"Oh, Yaylor Pi," she said, sighing heavily, "I admit that I've blundered our affairs with Earth. Perhaps I let my zeal for retribution disable all reason in me."

"No, I don't think so," he said quietly.

She then turned away from him. "My mother and her mother would be utterly horrified at what I've done."

"You did what was right," he said.

"The agony of regret, Yaylor Pi, it bleeds through the scratches left behind by doubt."

Yaylor Pi moved closely behind her and gently placed his hand on her back. "You did what was right."

Maerora Ma turned around to face him. "No, I won't rationalize it any other way than what it is, and it is vengeance. Vengeance courted me, and like a wanton—"

"Ma'am," Yaylor Pi interrupted assertively, "have you forgotten the sequence of events? You responded to Earth-initiated aggression. You made the right decision to deter them from further aggression. You only feel regret now because you have a conscience."

"Ah, yes, 'conscience,'" she said in English, "'does make cowards of us all.' Isn't that what they say?"

"That I would not know," he said.

"How I cultivate relations with this Earth woman could restore the damage I've done," she said.

"Ma'am—"

"Let's stop talking about it please. Did Quercus contact you?"

"Yes, I've scheduled a trip to Oaktobron to correspond with a death-acknowledgement visit," he said, reaching out to touch her.

"I'm not feeling right about a death-acknowledgement visit," she said, backing away from him.

"Be it far from me to advise you on such matters, but death-acknowledgment visits are your inherited obligation."

"Yaylor Pi, advise me not," she said, heading towards the door.

"Yes, Ma'am, but I will tell you the people love death-acknowledgement visits. They crave your presence. Even Oaktobrons like death-acknowledgment visits."

Maerora Ma stopped at the door. "Do they really?" she asked, turning around.

"Did not hundreds of Oaktobrons die as a result of the

construction of the MIC? Your grandmother insisted that *no* family—no matter of what origin—would go unacknowledged for their sacrifices," he said. "Your very own mother spent her entire life visiting families throughout the realm almost every day—often in risky environments for Magentans," he said, moving towards her.

"Yes, Amora Ma was relentless that way, wasn't she?"

"Yes, she was."

"I suppose that's why the Oaktobrons liked her so much more than they do me," she said. "Yaylor Pi, please take an assessment on the contentment of the people of Oaktobron before we leave."

"Of course, that's standard operating procedure."

"Is it? I've lost touch with the Oaktobrons, and that is a very dangerous thing for a leader to lose. They're the most inharmonious creatures in the realm with one-track minds aimed at penetrating the outer realm barrier. I have difficulties with them."

"I know."

"Thank you, Yaylor," she said and then kissed him on the lips.

He set his hands on her waist, and she then pushed them off and exited the room.

WISPS OF CONSCIOUSNESS were encircling me like silent hawks high in the sky. A long quietude elapsed, and I was once again gone.

A STEADY HUM grew present in my mind, and I tried to determine whether or not I was alive. I couldn't move my arms; I couldn't move my legs; and I couldn't open my eyes. I just had the involuntary sense of hearing and hung onto it in a very voluntary way, but ultimately I couldn't hold on.

THE WEIGHT of my eyelids was so heavy, I stopped trying to open them, but if I could have seen out of my eyes and I were wearing a HUD, the words "Kill Maerora Ma" would be entering my field of vision, for I realized I was on a mission, and I *had* to believe all was going according to plan, but I needed rest, and so I let myself go again.

THE HAWKS of consciousness finally landed, and I could open my eyes, and when I did, the place I was in was a monochrome world. Everything was conducted in one color—magenta.

"Hello, I am Bonson," said a small maroon-colored man who kindly hovered over my face to ensure eye contact with me.

"I can't move," I said.

"Yes, we suspected as much."

"What do you mean?" I asked.

"You fell from very high in the sky. No one lands from such heights without impairment."

The dread of what I heard devastated me. How would I be able to fulfill my mission? Would William and Porter complete it? Would the Magentan's end up dissecting me? Dying there at the MIC would have been better than impairment. I did notice, however, that I could feel the existence of my arms and legs, unless I was feeling phantom limbs. Phantom or not, a tremendous weight seemed to be holding them down.

"Am I shackled?"

"Yes," he answered and smiled sheepishly.

"Why?"

"We have determined that you are dangerous," he said.

Well, *I am*, I told myself but maybe not anymore. I thought about William and Porter and wanted to believe they survived the fall since they landed on top of me.

"How can I be dangerous if I'm paralyzed?" I asked.

"It's best for you to remain immobile," he replied, still arching over me.

"Can't your advanced technology cure me?"

"All is inconclusive at the moment," he said.

"So, I may be beyond repair then. Is that right?"

"I do not think you suffer from anything that time cannot heal."

"Time?" What did he think I had a broken heart? "Don't you have wonder drugs or laser things that instantly repair?" I asked.

"The best medicine right now is for you to rest, Captain Joan Jones," he said and then put on a pair of glasses and stared straight ahead.

"Bonson?" I called.

"Yes, Captain Joan Jones?"

I desperately wanted to ask him if William and Porter had been found and if they were ok, but I knew better than to reveal their existence. I wondered about them and hoped they weren't suffering like me.

"Yes, Captain Joan Jones, do you have a question for me?"

"I'm sorry. I've forgotten what I was going to say."

"That is most understandable. You certainly have undergone great physical injury."

I hated hearing that. It made me want to cry, so I tried to change the subject. "I'm glad you speak English. I mean, you speak it really well," I said.

"Yes, I do speak Earth English quite well," he said. "I ought to since I was taught by the absolute authority and preeminent Earth scholar herself—Maerora Ma."

"Did you say 'Maerora Ma'?" I asked.

"Yes! Of course! Do you doubt me?" he challenged.

"No, not at all," I said.

"Maerora Ma has never admitted it, but I believe she knows I am—by far—the best speaker of Earth English on Magenta. That's how we earn our rank around here, you know. Maerora Ma will randomly stop you in the hall and quiz you about Earth. Those who pass rise; those who fail fall, and she most definitely will want to meet *you*," he said and then stood straight again, put on his glasses, and exited the room.

So, gaining proximity to Maerora Ma would be quite

convenient, but actually breaking her neck would be contingent upon my full recovery. Why didn't Densip Pi prepare us better for the landing?

"KAYTID, PLEASE go to bed before Mama comes home," Mălīn ordered.

The little girl appeared more than happy to go to bed and headed to her room, leaving Mălīn alone with DeNitor. He didn't waste any time in grabbing Maerora Ma's beautiful daughter by the waist and squeezing her tightly against his body. She reciprocated his advance by moving her hands down the outside of his pants to his crotch. After a moment, they pushed apart to talk.

"Everything seems to be going as planned," Mălīn said.

"Yeah, but we almost lost the Earth woman," DeNitor said.

"Well, it was impossible for us to have had the landing pad in place. It would've appeared highly suspicious for it to be there right when we received a surprise visit from Earth," she said.

"I know."

"Was her name stamped on her clothes like the other Earth visitors?"

"Yes, her name is Captain Joan Jones."

"What about companions? She was supposed to have had two male companions."

"There was evidence of them. They appeared to have run in opposite directions. They left footprints, which I covered up, of course," he said.

"Good, DeNitor." She then allowed him to grope her body.

He gripped her waist on both sides and simulated a thrusting movement.

"I hate the idea of having free-ranging males about," she said, stopping his erotic play.

"I know you're not a fan of plan B," he said, caressing her arm, "but Densip Pi was the mastermind of all this, and it's just too late to change it now."

"I'm so worried, DeNitor. I wish they had been instructed to check in with you."

"No," he said, taking a step backwards. "It would've implicated us."

"I just want this all over and done with. I wish we could force the Earth woman's recovery to be quicker, and I wish my mother hadn't insisted on waiting. It's sheer agony to wait."

"Well, your mother was right about being patient, Mălīn. You should let things happen naturally, or they'll be onto you."

"You need to go now. My mother will be home soon."

WHEN MAERORA MA arrived home, she peeked at each of her sleeping daughters then headed to her bedroom. Her home was a magnificent work of architecture, combining both modern and age-old design. It was multi-level and located amidst a densely populated metropolis on top of a plateau surrounded by plenty of natural acreage. The bottom level filled the hollow middle of the plateau and consisted of all the practicalities of a home (i.e., storage, electrical sources and terminal panels, servant quarters, etc.). The second level rested on the plateau's surface and was an enormous pentagonal prism constructed almost entirely of large crystal-clear windows. The building could be rotated in four positions to view the Magentan surroundings. The pentagon-shaped floor plan was divided into four sections, a banquet area; a study area, which contained an exclusive Earth museum; a family area that occupied two sections; and private quarters. A vast observation room occupied a large part of the family area, and an air-vehicle landing filled the top of the home as well as a thorough collection of communication equipment and military apparatus. The original architect had effectively applied the best elements of aesthetics with bold uses of elegant geometrical shapes that crowned the top and gave it a slightly imperial look.

Magentan flora and fauna flourished on the land surrounding the home, except for on one large green strip of land that Maerora

Ma called her garden of earthly delights and always had the rotatable building set in the position where her bedroom was near the garden's entrance. During the day, the full spectrum of simulated sunlight flooded the piece of land to facilitate photosynthesis. Consequently, the garden's trees, shrubs, and plants thrived.

Before getting into bed, Maerora Ma headed out to the garden. She strolled over to an unadorned plaque, which bore the name "Morgana." As she gazed at the plaque, sorrow pulled down on her face, and almost instantly rage flashed across it with a fury set on subduing any chance of letting grief arise. A sudden rustle in the bushes nearby startled her and interrupted the incipient war between her conflicting emotions. She quickly darted back inside to her bedroom.

I AWOKE to loud noises—clinking and clanking. "What the hell!" I yelled and consequently startled two burly Magentans who seemed to be differently colored than the other Magentans I had seen so far. They were bigger too. I was unable to tell what color they actually were because everything was drenched in magenta. The noise didn't cease. "What in the hell are you doing?" I asked, and they mumbled something back in an unfamiliar language. It appeared as if they were setting up a giant machine next to me. Of course, I was still shackled and lying flat on my back, so I didn't have the whole picture of what was going on. I was feeling irritable too and uncertain whether or not I would be able to execute my mission to kill Maerora Ma.

"Oop! Oop! Oop! Now, now, settle down, Captain Joan Jones," said Bonson, scurrying over to me. "I am very sorry about the noise. These Oaktobrons are in such a hurry to setup this rapid-healing machine," he said and gestured to the machine technicians to keep quiet. "I am happy to inform you, Captain Joan Jones, this machine is for you and was sent by Maerora Ma herself. Is that not exceptional? You will be up and running around in no time with the help of this machine. It is just like

Maerora Ma to think of everything. I love Maerora Ma."

I pity Maerora Ma. She's hastening her death, I thought. "Why is Maerora Ma so interested in me?" I asked.

"I told you! She's the realm's foremost Earth scholar, and she has never met an Earth woman before," he said, moving to hold his head directly over my face. I smiled at him. His talk of Maerora Ma made it seem like she was a schoolteacher. I wondered if perhaps he might be talking about a different Maerora Ma than the one I was supposed to kill.

"What else does she do?" I asked.

"Who?" he asked.

"Maerora Ma!"

"Come now, certainly you are not that unaware," he said.

"Hey, I only just dropped in recently."

"She is the beloved leader of Magenta and the total ruler of the realm, and she'll be the ruler of your realm too someday."

Well, it seemed we had the same Maerora Ma in mind. "So, tell me more about the Octobers," I requested.

He chuckled and then corrected me in a hushed tone, "They are *Oaktobrons*. Oaktobron is the planet nearest to us." He pulled in closer to me and lowered his voice even more to say, "We have a *love-hate* relationship with them. They constantly compete with us and abhor the fact that a Magentan rules the realm, but, nevertheless, we Magentans cannot resist exploiting their technology. We *love* it," he said, putting on his pair of glasses and tapping one side of them with his index finger.

"Oh, so, what do those glasses do?" I asked.

"Everything, Captain Joan Jones," he said, standing straight and looking in the direction of the Oaktobrons in the room.

"Please call me Joan, Bonson."

He looked down at me and chuckled.

"How many planets are there in this realm?" I asked.

"Many, and Maerora Ma is the total ruler of them all," he said.

"What kind of life forms are there?"

"All sorts, but only humans are intelligent. The rest are just evolutionary stepping stones," he said.

"Humans *and Magentans*, right?" I asked.

"Correct."

"What is your cosmology?" I asked.

"Cosmology?"

"How did the realms originate?"

"I should think you would know that one."

"The Big Bang?" I offered.

"I know not what that is," he said.

"Well, perhaps it's not worth knowing since it falls short of explaining how something came from nothing," I said.

"It's 'nothing comes from nothing,'" he said.

"No, it's everything came from nothing," I said.

"No, King Lear said, 'nothing comes from nothing,'" Bonson insisted.

"I don't know what you're talking about," I said.

"Shakespeare!"

"What does Shakespeare have to do with anything?" I asked.

"I thought you were quoting Shakespeare. Maerora Ma loves Shakespeare and can recite tens of passages. I too can recite quite a few," he boasted.

"Well, that's nice, but we were talking about cosmology. I want to know what you believe. Do you have gods or goddesses?" I asked, remembering the Indian woman from the ceremony.

"Earth is the source of all things," he said and stood straight so that I could no longer look into his eyes.

"Well, if that's what you believe, then your creation myth is one step away from a *big* disappointment," I said.

He turned to converse with the technicians, and it sounded like they were beginning to bicker. As I listened to them, the Oaktobrons walked over to me and started touching me and running their flattened hands up and down my arms. They pressed their fingers into my skin and pinched me all over. It was very creepy.

"Hey! What's going on? Why are the Oaktobrons poking me?" I asked Bonson.

"They just learned that you're from Earth," he said and then awkwardly hesitated to tell me, "Captain Joan Jones, I regret that the machine is not calibrated for your biology."

"Well, it's a good thing you discovered that before you used it on me; otherwise, I might've come out all purple," I said.

He then escorted the two Oaktobrons out of the room, and I started to think about William and Porter. I hoped they were safe. I knew they would kill Maerora Ma if I couldn't because Porter's contingency plans would ensure it, but I didn't want *them* to kill her because *I wanted* to be the hero of this mission. *I wanted* to be the one to kill Maerora Ma, not that anyone on Earth would know exactly how this mission went down, but, still, I wanted to die a hero so that leaving Butterfly would not have been in vain. I hated that I was laid up. Porter would probably blame me for my failure to land without injury. Just what contingency plan did he have in the works? I couldn't risk losing faith, so I engaged in mental practice of breaking necks. Images of one hand on the side of a head and the other clawing into the traps at the base of some anonymous neck filled my mind's eye.

Atop Maerora Ma's home, she and her daughters prepared themselves to load into an air vehicle. The huge dark sphere of the dwarf star was emerging from the horizon. Maerora Ma stared out at the conspicuous Earth garden as she waited for her daughters to climb into the vehicle. The youngest one started in first while Maerora Ma turned to a nearby attendant.

"Could you please have the Earth garden checked for animals? I was in the garden last night, and I think there were animals of some sort there. We don't want the native animals destroying the Earth garden. Could you please have it checked?"

"Yes, Ma'am," answered the attendant.

"Mama, what kind of animals?" Mălīn asked as she passed through the door of the air vehicle with her mother right behind her.

"I don't know, but I think there were two."

"Well, Mama, please don't have them killed."

"I would never do that. Why would you even think such a thing?"

"I just wanted to make certain," Mălīn said.

Maerora Ma then received a call through her glasses. The ever-ready-camera ball floated in front of her. "Yes, Yaylor Pi, good morning, what is it that can't wait for me to arrive at headquarters?"

"Ma'am, good morning, I wanted to report to you that the rapid-healing machine is not calibrated for the Earth woman's biology."

"Well, of course not, that would have been too easy," she said, turning away from Mălīn. "What needs to be done?"

"DNA extraction, analysis, replication, then testing and implementation."

"So, is the purpose defeated then?"

"No, Ma'am, this all can be done in a relatively short amount of time, but the problem is . . . well, do you want the Oaktobrons to have all that knowledge of Earth biology at their disposal?"

"That is a problem. It's amazing how impatience snags itself on every snarl it can find?" she said, turning towards Mălīn who appeared to be intensely interested in the conversation, though she was only able to hear one side of it. Maerora Ma then gestured both her daughters away and told them to go into the other section of the air vehicle.

Katydid hemmed and hawed while Mălīn pulled her along in a dramatic performance featuring reluctance.

Once they left, Maerora Ma resumed her conversation with Yaylor Pi. "Tell the Oaktobrons to proceed with the calibration of the machine but first ensure that their communications are isolated. They're too technologically advanced to have knowledge of the flesh of humans from Earth. They'd use it to their advantage, which would naturally be detrimental to Earth. After the Earth woman is healed, verify that she has completely recovered. I need her to be healthy, Yaylor Pi. She's going to restore my favorable destiny."

"Yes, Ma'am."

"Now, listen, the Oaktobron technicians will then need to be eliminated, *killed*, and it needs to be staged as an accident, *an air-vehicle accident*—"

"Ma'am—"

"Hush, Yaylor Pi, I'm not finished. "It's very important to leave no scent for revelation to sniff out. I want nothing traced back whatsoever."

"Yes, Ma'am."

"Do you have any questions?"

"No, Ma'am."

"But you had something to say. What was it?"

"It was nothing," he said. The two terminated their communication session, and Maerora Ma called her daughters back.

"Katydid, come sit next to me and tell me your favorite nursery rhyme in Earth English," Maerora Ma said.

"Bumpy Dumpy fat on wall/Bumpy Dumpy fad great fall . . . ," the little girl recited while Mălīn gazed into her glasses.

The air vehicle finally landed and once inside the daytime dwelling, Maerora Ma spoke to Katydid's governess. "Please focus on Katydid's Earth-English skills."

"Yes, Ma'am," answered the governess.

Maerora Ma knelt down to kiss Katydid, but the little girl had just caught sight of the intelligent ball and ran over to it, neglecting her mother's affection.

"Mălīn come up to my station with me," ordered Maerora Ma. Mălīn followed her mother to her console. "Let us start speaking in Earth English. It will be good practice for when we meet the Earth woman."

"Ok, Mama," Mălīn agreed in English.

"I'm sorry, Mălīn, that I was ill-tempered yesterday, and I hope I didn't embarrass you in front of DeNitor."

"No, I should've been with you when the MIC alarm sounded."

"Please, Mălīn, never ever go near the MIC."

"*I know*, Mama."

"I could never cope with losing another daughter—"

"Mama, be strong. Don't think bad thoughts."

Maerora Ma acknowledged her daughter's advice with a weak smile. Mălīn then descended to the abode below where Katydid and her governess were engaged in Earth-English drills.

"The rain in Spain falls mainly on the plains," the governess enunciated.

"The fain in rain falls mainly on the pains," Katydid repeated.

Mălīn moved out of earshot into her bedroom to call DeNitor through her glasses. The camera ball floated dutifully in front of her.

"DeNitor, there's a possibility the Earth males are in my mother's garden."

"How do you know?" he asked.

"My mother said she heard movement in the garden last night, and she ordered household staff to check. It could be the Earth males."

"Yeah, it could be. I'll go there, right away."

"But contacting them will put you at risk," she said.

"I know, but if they're in the garden, it would be very easy for them to kill Maerora Ma this very evening. You told me your mother stands at Morgana's grave almost every night, right?"

"Yes, she does, and it makes sense for us to now rely on plan B, especially since we're uncertain whether Captain Joan Jones will recover or not."

"I'll go right now," he said.

"DeNitor, please be careful."

"Of course, Mălīn, don't worry. I've had stealth training."

"Ok, well, be careful anyway."

"Of course, I'll be careful, and when I return I'll sneak into headquarters to see you," he said.

"No, DeNitor, don't come here. My mother's too insecure right now and keeps frantically watching out for me and Katydid."

"Why is she so insecure?" DeNitor asked.

"The MIC alarm disturbed her yesterday. It made her think about Morgana."

"Poor Maerora Ma," he said.

"I know," Mălīn said, "it's sad to think how great my mother once was, but she's ruined now, and the Oaktobrons hate her, and, as difficult as it is to admit it, they are superior to us except for the fact that *we* still rule the realm. Must we talk about this endlessly? Maerora Ma must die."

"I'm not doubting that for a second, Mălīn. I just happen to suffer from . . . well, I don't know perhaps compassion."

"Compassion fosters weakness of mind," she said.

"I'm not weak, Mălīn."

"No, DeNitor, you are not . . . *yet*, but your fondness for my mother's vulnerabilities will weaken you."

"No, Mălīn, not at all. I'm just expressing my *respect* for Maerora Ma," he said.

"You should be *losing respect* for her."

"Oh, Mălīn," he whispered.

"Oh, DeNitor, I know it sounds harsh, but we have to remain focused. The Oaktobrons are on the verge of taking over, and that's why Densip Pi sacrificed his own life. My mother is too weak to stave off their ascendancy. Recover from your sentimentality, DeNitor."

Late in the afternoon, Maerora Ma and her daughters finished their dinner and spent time together chatting and playing simple games with the families of the household staff in the large observation room of their home. No one bothered to wear pan-omni glasses during these shared occasions and all participated happily in the fun.

Four of Katydid's playmates surrounded her as she demonstrated how to play checkers on a life-size checkerboard, which was located in the distant end of the room, away from the main observing planes. Closer to the windows, Mălīn sat across from her mother. The view of the Magentan sky and scenery filled the room with Magentan pleasure, and the dwarf star occupied more than half the sky, never slipping in its majesty of presence.

Maerora Ma quizzed Mălīn's knowledge of Earth. "Mălīn, name the seven continents of Earth."

In English, Mălīn enumerated the names of the continents, "Africa, Europe, Asia . . . ."

"Good. Now, name the five oceans."

"The Arctic Ocean, the Atlantic Ocean, the Indian Ocean . . . ."

"Maerora Ma, quiz *me* about Earth too," a young woman nearby asked.

"All right, name the eight planets from the sun."

"Mercury, Venus, Earth . . . ," the young woman answered.

Maerora Ma applauded and praised the young woman. Several others then proceeded to ask Maerora Ma to quiz them, and she obliged. When a young mother who was seated nearby was having trouble with her fussing baby, Maerora Ma took the baby in her arms to calm it down. In a sing-song voice, she recited nursery rhymes in English, and gazed into its eyes and rocked it gently.

Mălīn intently watched her mother. "Mama, you look tired. You should go to bed. Will you be walking in the garden to-night?" Mălīn asked.

Maerora Ma returned the now sleeping baby back to its mother and sat down in her seat near Mălīn. Mălīn again suggested to her mother that she looked tired, and Maerora Ma caressed her brow as if the suggestion of being tired was enough to convince her she was.

One of the young girls who Maerora Ma had been quizzing earlier heard Mălīn mention the garden and said, "Oh, I saw DeNitor in the garden today. He is such a handsome Magentan. I spy on him every chance I get."

"*DeNitor* was in the garden?" Maerora Ma asked.

"Oh, Mama, I forgot to tell you how worried I was about the animals you mentioned were in the garden, so I asked DeNitor to check for them. I didn't want any harm to come to them," Mălīn said then incessantly explained her newly found concern for animal welfare, and while she droned on, Maerora Ma turned to the spy girl.

"I would like to speak to your mother. Would you please go and return with her for me?" she said to the girl.

Mǎlīn ceased her chattering seeing that her mother was now distracted, and she then anticipated her mother's intention. "Yes, Mama, she was spying . . . the worst offense," Mǎlīn said.

The girl returned with her mother, and Maerora Ma walked them to a private area away from the huge viewing planes and far from all the social activities.

"Your daughter admitted to spying today," Maerora Ma said.

Clearly distraught at what Maerora Ma had said, the mother apologized profusely. "I am ever-so sorry, Ma'am . . . ."

"She's young," said Maerora Ma, "but spying shall not be tolerated. If I let such a seed of a weed grow in the garden of order, what will become of the garden?"

"Ma'am, it will never ever happen again. I simply have never had the reason to punish my girl for such an offense. This is a lesson for us here and now, and it will never escape us. I promise. Please let it be a lesson learned, Ma'am," the girl's mother pleaded.

"Whose lesson is it?" Maerora Ma asked.

"It is *our* lesson," answered the mother gesturing between her and her daughter.

"Don't you realize the complication here? You've put me in a difficult position by failing to instruct your daughter the rights and wrongs of life, and according to her, this was not her first offense. She carried on about how she always spies! I am dumbfounded by the audacity, and I'm angry about being nudged forth into the inevitable role of tyrant. Do you think I have an affinity for speaking to you like this? Do you realize how you, yourself, will now resent me for this? Complications abound! That is why this type of weed cannot be allowed to root itself here. If I let this go, I will have only pulled the shoot system, not the root system. You are the root."

"Oh, Maerora Ma, there is value in retaining us. Our example will warn others—"

"But your resentment will fester, and it will take root and

grow into a tree and then a forest of discontentment where malcontents roam and prey on the innocent."

"No, Ma'am, we adore you . . . always."

"Your adoration is not the point. My concern is how your story will affect the discontented among us. When I eliminate the weed by its root, it does not return . . . not until another pestilent seed is somehow dropped into the fertile soil of harmony. Harmony is always under attack. There's always someone discontented with the idea of abiding by harmony."

"We are good, Ma'am. We are very abiding. We just made this one mistake. Please, Maerora Ma, please give us one more chance."

"What would you do if you were me?" asked Maerora Ma.

"I would most definitely let us learn from our mistake," answered the mother, "because learning this way is very effective. I promise it will be effective."

"Perhaps, but what about this tyrant who stands before you?" Maerora Ma asked.

"No, Ma'am, you are a great leader, not a tyrant."

"No, you're quite wrong. I'm a weak leader, especially because of decisions like the one here and now. Go along and never *ever* spy again," she said, glaring at the girl.

LATER, when all had ended and everyone had gone to bed, Maerora Ma looked out at her garden of earthly delights through a window near her bedroom. All was dark and still, and perhaps she could see her reflection in the window more than she could see the garden itself. She stood there for a long moment, watching, looking, and observing. She then slowly moved away from the window and headed into her bedroom.

I HATE TO CRY, especially out of self-pity, so I fought against it when I saw myself in a mirror as they tilted me upright on a gurney they had strapped me in to prepare me for the healing machine. The fall and the shelling I had endured left me significantly disfigured, downright hideous looking, so much so that I threw up to add more unsightliness to the horror of what I was seeing.

There is an acidity so distinct and so corrosive within the human psyche that no amount of psychological dilution can reduce its strength. My mission sat in my mind like a beaker full of that acid. If I were to come out of this healing machine intact, there would be *nothing* that could stop me from spilling myself all over this Magentan world.

"Here we go, Captain Joan Jones. You are going to feel much better in just a little while," Bonson said, dabbing up my vomit. I sneered at him with severe contempt and almost spat upon his fuchsin face.

"My, my, Captain Joan Jones, you seem reluctant about feeling better," he said. I refused to look at him, and inside my head, I chanted Maerora Ma must die repeatedly. I remained focused on my mission and knew success would come by embracing the Medusa I had become.

Bonson and the Oaktobrons installed me into the machine. The machine was like an isolation tank. No sound and no light surrounded me as I floated supine. It reminded me of being in the realm barrier. The presence of my essence engulfed me, yet it felt so unfamiliar to me. Who . . . *what* was this essence? Was I not a captain in the U.S. military? Was I not a mother? Or was I now only a Gorgon, a creature fit for Hell? That was it. I had died at the MIC, and I was now in Hell, in Hell for abandoning my daughter. What kind of mother does that? Tender, innocent child, vulnerable, dependent . . . . Forgive me, please, forgive me, sweet babe. I deserved to look as hideous on the outside as I was on the inside. I deserved it.

MAERORA MA ordered her daughters to straighten the pillows on the seats in the family observation room. She inspected every nook and cranny of the seemingly boundless room. The Magentan sky illuminated the area with a beautiful iridescent-like magenta light. The luminous lines and cracks of the dwarf star were extra bright, almost as if the star itself were cooperating with Maerora Ma in her endeavor to welcome the Earth woman.

None of the invited guests had arrived yet. Maerora Ma had invited several other Magentan Earth scholars to be present during the official greeting of the Earth woman.

"Mama, can I give this to the Earth woman?" Katydid asked, holding a smooth miniature dome-shaped ornament she had picked up randomly from the room.

"No, baby, the only gift you need to give is your smile, all right, little one?" Maerora Ma said and then noticed that her older daughter seemed distraught about something as she paced back and forth near the windows. "Mălīn, is there something wrong?"

"No, Mama."

"Well, be more helpful to me then," Maerora Ma said.

"Mama, the room looks fine. *Everything* is fine, Mama," she whined. "I do *not* understand why you insist on doing these things yourself when there are planets full of people who should be doing it for you."

"Mălīn, when you inherit my position, you'll never want to be too out of touch with the people you rule."

"Oh, Mama," Mălīn mumbled, shaking her head.

"More important, you'll never want to lose your sense of self-reliance because being at the constant mercy of others will lead to a loss of control," Maerora Ma said.

Mălīn turned away to roll her eyes up into her head.

Maerora Ma continued to exert herself dearly to ensure that the finest Magentan greeting would be presented. Her home was tidied and prepared. Her daughters were primped and beautified, and Maerora Ma had reinvigorated her own pulchritude to a level that rivaled the vibrant Magentan light of day.

I HAD been retrieved from the healing machine and was to be taken to Maerora Ma's home to meet the ruler of the realm herself. A small team of Magentans had fitted me into a one-piece tailored garment, which was magenta of course. It zipped from the front and was sparingly adorned with a few smooth, flat rectangles around the narrow collar and cuffs. The machine had restored me physically to something better than I was before. I felt strong, very strong. I would have loved to have been tested for my neck-breaking skills. Where I could do three necks in thirty-six seconds then, I could have done five now.

For the first time since I arrived, I walked out of the small hospital room they had kept me in. I was unshackled—unleashed. Two armed guards walked in front of me and two behind me. I studied their holsters, their weapons, and their stature. A few meters down the hall, Bonson was waiting for us and donned a nice-looking outfit. He held out his arm for me to loop mine into his.

"I'm so happy you're feeling better," he said with a beaming smile.

I merely nodded at him, feeling ashamed of how I had treated him upon entering the healing machine. We proceeded to walk through a series of corridors, and I continued to assess the virility of the guards. I believed I could take four armed Magentans and one unarmed one. I imagined the assault routine in my head. Snap, kick, grab, push, snap, snap, grab, kick, push, push, kick, snap, snap. Easy. We headed upward in what seemed like an immensely tall hospital building, which had sleek empty halls that amplified the softest of sounds such as the swoosh of our stride, the thump of our feet, and the small gusts of our respirations.

"I am delighted beyond all senses that I have been chosen to present you to Maerora Ma," Bonson said, blasting the monotony of minor sounds. "I've studied Earth English relentlessly for this day."

He pulled me in closer to express his excitement, and a bit of compunction bled in my stomach when I thought about how

I would be ruining his day in just a little while. I wondered why Magentans were obsessed with Earth. If they were so crazy about us, why did they attack us?

We finally reached a door that opened onto the top of the building, and when I walked out into the magenta-tinted outdoors, I saw a humongous planet or moon in the sky, and its splendor literally weakened my knees. Bonson's grip tightened on me as I relied on him to steady me.

"Wow! What planet is that, Bonson? Is that Oaktobron?"

"No, that's not a planet. It's a star," he said.

"Aren't stars supposed to be too bright to look at?" I asked.

"It's a dying star," he said, and then he helped me climb into a transport vessel. All four guards boarded too. The air vehicle started to go into a lock-down sequence, and then it quietly and smoothly launched into the air.

The view was stupendous as we flew over the terrain. There were buildings, trees, bodies of water, hills, outcroppings, grasslands, forests . . . not unlike Earth at all, and it all made me wonder about the Magentans. Just why did they attack us?

Bonson tapped on the window, which rattled me out of my thoughts. He pointed to a large circular area of land that had a single tall building at the center of it. "There it is," he said, "the home of our magnificent leader. I'm certain Maerora Ma and her daughters are eagerly awaiting our landing."

"Maerora Ma has daughters?" I asked.

"Of course," Bonson replied, consistently amazed at my continual unknowingness.

The building didn't look like a home. It was a five-sided tower that seemed entirely made up of glass planes and topped with a tiara of wicked-looking things. As we drew nearer, I noticed a normal-colored patch of land. It was dazzling to my eyes. Green foliage never looked so good. "Now that's the color of Earth," I said, pointing to the patch.

"Yes, that's Maerora Ma's garden of earthly delights," Bonson said.

"Like the painting?" I asked.

"Yes, of course," he answered.

We silently landed on top of a flat area within the building's crown. Six armed guards appeared and stood alert for action. From within the vessel, I checked to see how their weaponry was attached and what sizes and how many, etc. Once outside of the vessel, I didn't want them to see me assessing their sidearms, so my plan was to act like a naive civilian and unassumingly look into their faces with a kind smile.

As I exited the shuttle, a military man named Vysender introduced himself to me, and then there was an exchange of guards. Bonson remained by my side, moving away just slightly to allow Vysender to pat me down. When Vysender stared challengingly into my eyes, I let a gentle smile cloak my ultimate intention. He then ran his hands down my waist and ran them back up to under my breasts. I loathed the invasion yet forced myself to provide him full access. He squatted to engulf my upper thighs in his hands. The top side of his index finger pressed into my labia majora.

Finally, good ol' Bonson looped his arm through mine, and we proceeded into a large cylindrical chamber that lowered us into the building. Four guards remained with us once inside. Vysender, who was armed, led the way. Two guards preceded Bonson and me and two followed us.

I only had to break the neck of Maerora Ma and not worry about my own escape. Execution had to be timed just right to ensure success. Hastiness, if I were to let it, would be my only impediment at this point. I would thoroughly assess my access to Maerora Ma before acting.

The chamber ceased its downward motion, and two retracting doors opened into a larger cylindrical area, which appeared to be a foyer of minimalist decor. The walls looked like they were made of wine-infused alabaster, and four sets of over-sized doors were firmly framed within the walls. Each door was located in opposing directions and was covered with low-relief filigree. When I looked up, I saw an extensive set of windows in the ceiling that extended to the very top of the building. The

Magentan light entered through the windows and struck my optic nerve. Alas, there was just too much nauseating magenta.

Vysender took us to one of the sets of doors and ordered them to be opened.

CHAPTER 4:
THE MAGENTAN EARTH

As THE DOORS OPENED, my eyes landed on the massive dying star that dominated the view through the upper parts of huge windows. The small entourage I was at the center of moved inward beyond the doors. Vysender turned around and ordered the two front guards to stand aside, and then he, himself, moved away to expose a mother and her two daughters.

"Welcome to my home," the mother said, standing behind her smallest daughter. The little girl instantly reminded me of Butterfly. My mission drained from me in that instant, and it felt like a sudden dehydration of the soul.

"This is Maerora Ma, the ruler of Magenta," said the older daughter who had quickly moved forth and bumped her mother forward. Maerora Ma extended her hand to me and seemed slightly baffled by her daughter's behavior. A ripple of reflexes flowed through the guards as I reached to accept her hand. All my conscious awareness surged towards her touch, and alarms blasted throughout my head, alerting me to the fact that my mission target was in the crosshairs! Kill Maerora Ma, but I could not kill Maerora Ma.

"This is my daughter Mălīn and my youngest daughter Katydid," she said. The little one grinned generously at me, and I felt like a fiend because here stands before you, child, the would-be slayer of your mother. I wanted thoughts of my assignment to depart at once, for they made me much too nefarious to be in the same room with this little girl.

"Captain Joan Jones of Earth," Maerora Ma said, "we are pleased that you have come to visit Magenta. Allow me to introduce you to these fine inhabitants of Magenta, many of whom are renowned Earth experts." She gestured for me to follow her down a line of individuals who stood in a straight row in front of the wall of windows.

As I moved towards her, the guards moved with me, and Bonson retreated to the back of the pack, letting little Katydid take his spot, which she insisted on having. When Vysender attempted to grab her away from her close proximity to me, she jerked herself free from him and stood her ground. Mălīn remained at her mother's side, eyeing me intently.

"First and foremost, this is Yaylor Pi. On Earth you would refer to him as my right-hand man," Maerora Ma said. I shook his hand firmly. "You have already met Vysender and Bonson. Vysender is the head of all the military throughout the entire realm, and Bonson is Magenta's foremost medical healer."

Maerora Ma introduced the rest of the notable individuals as I smiled, nodded, and shook hands with each. Mălīn readily allowed access to her mother each time Maerora Ma drew closer to me, and little Katydid smiled widely whenever I looked down at her.

"Captain Joan Jones, your miracle visit delights us," said one of the Earth scholars.

I nodded in an ongoing effort to appear agreeable to this assemblage of individuals, all of whom varied slightly in shade of magenta and size but were distinctly human otherwise. The optimal time to have made my move had already passed. The sight of this mother and her two daughters had neutralized me. What a weapon. I guess women soldiers aren't superior after all, but *surely* my mission wasn't over. No, it had to have been circling around in a holding pattern, waiting for its opportunity to land, I told myself.

"Come, Captain Joan Jones, we will now take you to our Earth museum," Maerora Ma said, touching my arm to direct me to the museum.

Again, her touch sounded the alarms in my head. My target was at hand, and even though I could have easily snapped her neck then and there, I would not . . . *never* in front of children.

And then the most treasonous of all questions crept in. Why must Maerora Ma die? She's a mother for God's sake. But was I not here on behalf of the U.S. military to kill Maerora Ma for ordering the murder of hundreds of innocent people? Were mothers not among the dead? If for every action, there's a reaction, well, then, I'm just a link (albeit a very weak link) in the long chain of causes and effects.

As we made our way to the Earth museum, we tracked back through the Spartan foyer, and Maerora Ma informed us of the evening's banquet to honor my visit. Her voice bounced off the smooth surfaces of the bare alabaster and spiraled upwardly towards the ceiling windows. We then continued through a set of doors towards the Earth museum, and Maerora Ma then revealed that she had curated the exhibits herself.

"I suppose it's a bit silly for us to trot out our Earth museum when it seems we ought to be showing you a Magentan museum. After all, you've travelled far, and I'm certain it's not to see a few ordinary household items from home," she said lightheartedly.

Correct, I wasn't here to see her museum, and so far she had no clue as to why I was here, but I wasn't so sure Maerora Ma's older daughter didn't know. Mălīn continually watched me in a very peculiar way, almost as if she knew me, but, of course, I didn't know her. Surely, I would have remembered a purple person if I had known one.

As we approached the museum, which had a gaping arch-like entrance, I could see a gigantic astronomical model suspended from the ceiling. Upon entering, an Earth scholar reached in through the guards and tugged at my sleeve to tell me, "Maerora Ma is proud of her museum, and *we* are proud of her." One of the guards then immediately reacted by sharply elbowing me away from her, and Maerora Ma squinted a glance at the small ruckus I was in the center of.

The model was a replica of not just the solar system and not just the Milky Way galaxy, nor did it end at the edge of the Universe. It was inclusive of the Universe plus the Magentan world. And at the center of it was Earth.

I studied the model and could see from out of the corner of my eye Maerora Ma watching me intently. "It's magnificent," I said, turning to her. She beamed with joy. "Is Earth at the center of this model because we're in an *Earth* museum, or is there some other significance?" I asked.

"This model depicts the fact that Earth is the source of all things," she said.

I recalled Bonson saying the same, and I remembered even the Densip Pi transcripts contained the claim that Magentans had an Earthly origin.

"Have you been to Firth?" asked little Katydid.

"No, I haven't been to firth, but I was born on Earth," I said and laughed as did the others. I wanted to pick up the little girl and hold her in my arms like I would have done with Butterfly, but the guards would have killed me if I so much as leaned towards her.

I continued to peer at the impressive astronomical model. It had an outer parabolic shell made of clear crystal and a second shell that partitioned the Universe from the Magentan world.

"Your Aristotle was right about celestial spheres, but I believe his scale was off," Maerora Ma said.

One of the Earth scholars piped up and added, "Your Aristotle also said a god from each realm maintains the motion of each sphere and is motivated to move them merely by the force of love within the realm. Maerora Ma is *our god*, and our love for her and her divine lineage keeps all things in order here. Let it be known we love Maerora Ma."

"Indeed! Hear, hear," numerous attendees shouted.

"Let it be known I object to this notion. Everyone here knows better than to bring it up in polite company," Maerora Ma said.

"Ours is a humble goddess," said the Earth scholar, and then a few others started to debate the divinity of Maerora Ma, and as they did, I stole a glance at her profile. She was a regal-looking woman. She had dark-magenta helicals of hair draping down her shoulders, an erect stature, and a straight nose with slightly flaring and curved nostrils. She wore a tailored tunic top, which had double rows of buttons that ran full length and terminated in a collar emblazoned with insignia. I could easily draw a correlation between Maerora Ma and the goddess that the Indian woman spoke about at the mission send-off ceremony. I wondered if Maerora Ma herself had ever visited Earth.

"Mama, do you not want to be alone with Captain Joan Jones? Let the others go to the banquet, and you find out why she's here," Mălīn abruptly asked.

"Mălīn, your bad manners are unbecoming. There will be plenty of time for business after we properly welcome our long-travelled guest," Maerora Ma said.

Apparently irritated by her mother's comment, Mălīn unquietly stormed away with a blatantly disdainful up-and-down scan of me. Everyone fell silent as she exited the crowd.

"Did everybody enjoy my daughter's theatrical rendition of an Oaktobron fit of impatience?" Maerora Ma asked. The group laughed, and I wondered about Mălīn. Was she just jealous of me because I was receiving so much of her mother's attention, or was she in the know about my assignment to assassinate her mother? Densip Pi had refrained from naming any others involved in his mission, stating he feared Magentan retribution for those in the know. Mălīn could have been aware of the plan, but why would she want to be party to the murder of her mother?

Maerora Ma moved ahead, stopped at a centrally located exhibit, and waved the group over. Little Katydid had drifted towards Yaylor Pi, leaving me alone in the middle of an ever-constricting pod of guards. We inched over to the display, which contained a large book that was illuminated by soft lighting. The book was a compilation of the entire works of William Shakespeare. I looked at it closely and noticed it wasn't an antique. It wasn't all that old, relatively speaking. My guess was it had been new maybe twenty years ago. Essentially, it was just a mass-produced coffee-table book. I felt Maerora Ma watching me, seemingly anticipating a favorable reaction. Clearly, Magentans had prized Shakespeare more than Earth people, or at least more than I did.

"To be or not to be," I said almost flippantly because it was the only Shakespeare quote I knew, and I was certain I was on the verge of disappointing all the Shakespeare fans present, especially Maerora Ma.

"'To be, or not to be, *that* is the Question:/Whether 'tis nobler in the mind to suffer/The Slings and Arrows of outrageous Fortune,/Or to take arms against a Sea of troubles,/And by opposing end them: to die, to sleep/No more; and by a sleep, to say we end/The heartache, and the thousand Natural shocks/That flesh is heir to?'" Maerora Ma recited.

"Oh, is that how the full passage goes?" I said.

"Do you not know Shakespeare?" Maerora Ma asked.

"Well, I know *of* him," I said.

"Ah, thank goodness you're not an expert. Now, I won't have to suffer your criticism of my recitation," she said with a smile.

I found the Shakespearian passage to be very relevant. To kill Maerora Ma or not *that* was the question, right? And were the circumstances not outrageous with me the guest of honor at the home of the leader of, well, not just a country or just a planet but *an entire realm*? Outrageous, indeed!

Maerora Ma proceeded to direct us through to a row of half a dozen other showcases, each exhibiting North American items. There was an old Commodore 64, an array of cassette tapes, several record albums, an IBM Selectric typewriter, an old cap gun . . . nothing too impressive, but I didn't want to appear jaded or unappreciative, so I oohed and aahed over all that I saw, and Maerora Ma exhibited more and more contentment with each approving expression I made.

"All the items here are from the United States. What about other countries?" I asked, thinking about the Indian goddess culture.

"The MIC was dropped into Earth's atmosphere at a time when a profusion of specific electromagnetic waves was emanating from North America," Maerora Ma explained as she watched Mălīn saunter back into the group of dignitaries. Mălīn's return distracted her, so Bonson completed her explanation.

"We could estimate the level of advancement Earth had attained by the band of frequency being used, and, thus, we located the MIC at a worthy proximity," he said.

"Nearest to where all the action was taking place," I stated.

"Yes, that was the idea. Mind you, that Magentans have evolved along a similar track as Earth humans. We too had our radio-frequency days," he said.

"Although, truth be told, our technological advances don't overshoot Earth's by far," Maerora Ma said.

"Did you ever visit India?" I asked, looking at Maerora Ma.

"No, we have been unable to reach other areas on Earth. Magentans are not downward compatible," she said.

"'Downward compatible'? You're not androids, are you?" I asked, and everyone giggled.

"We are human," Maerora Ma said in a serious tone.

"Our origins are with Earth," Bonson echoed.

"Well, you most definitely look like humans to me, although you're all a little *lilac* if you know what I mean," I said lightheartedly.

"Adaptation," Maerora Ma said.

"Yes, we have adapted to Magenta," Bonson explained. "A thin layer of our atmosphere consists almost entirely of ionized nitrogen, which results in a magenta-colored cast over all of Magenta."

"Unfortunately, Magentans are unable to stray too far from a regular dose of magenta," Maerora Ma said.

"Which means we can only subsist on Earth for a few days," Bonson said.

"Naturally, this has limited the range of our study of Earth. Consequently, all we know about Earth is through the North American perspective," Maerora Ma said.

"Well, that sounds like the average American," I said.

Maerora Ma showed us a few other minor displays as the guards increasingly cramped me inside their box. No one was keeping them in check while a panicky claustrophobic tension was mounting in me. Compulsively, I jabbed a guard in the ribs with my elbow. Instantaneously, the guard grabbed my elbow and pulled it clear into the middle of my back while another one knocked my legs out from under me by shoving his foot down my calves, causing me to fall flat on my back with my head slamming against the floor. The pain at the point of impact was intense and made me feel sick.

Gasps and exclamations emitted from the group as Mălĭn hastened close proximity, hollering, "Mama, we can't treat our guest of honor like this."

Maerora Ma ordered Bonson to assess my condition, and then she spoke to Vysender in Magentan. Mălĭn listened intently.

Bonson attempted to examine me, but I interrupted his inspection with a speedy return to standing. The guards then immediately resumed their tight box around me. The back of my head acutely hurt as I struggled to maintain a steady posture.

"The guard said you charged him," Bonson told me.

"I'm sorry, Bonson, I'm only human," I said.

"So, you were the aggressor. Is that right?" he asked.

"Yes, Bonson, I pushed him away from me."

Gain in the volume of Vysender and Maerora Ma's voices increased, but it was hopeless for me to decipher Magentan.

"I agree with my mother," said Mălĭn in English. "The guards should relax their stance. Actually, they are not needed at all. Clearly, Captain Joan Jones is a delightful and charming Earth woman who intends no harm or else she would have already assaulted my mother," she said with an unmistaken glare at me.

"I strongly advise against provoking Maerora Ma's deadly guards again. *They will win*," Bonson said to me.

Maerora Ma then allowed Vysender to part the guards, and she proceeded to stand directly in front of me. The displeasure of the situation appeared clearly on her face.

"The circumstances are such that Magentans are wary of Earth humans. Admittedly, there's a certain ambivalence of my own. I hope I'm wrong in sensing your discontentment," she said, sighing heavily. She then looked me narrowly in the eyes.

"You aren't going to harm me, are you, Captain Joan Jones?"

"No," I answered softly . . . not right now, I said in my head, all the while holding my glance straight and steady at her eyes.

She eased back from her nearness and let the guards resume their positions. "Have we had enough of the Earth museum then?" she asked the crowd, but no one answered. "Come, let us visit my garden," she said perfunctorily, waving us all back into the foyer.

"Mama, may Katydid and I check on the banquet preparations while you go to the garden?" asked Mălīn.

"Very well, go ahead," Maerora Ma said and then ordered Yaylor Pi to accompany them.

"Ma'am, shall we rotate the building?" asked an attendant.

"Yes, please do so. I don't think everyone wants to traipse though my personal quarters to get to the garden," she said. "We'll wait here."

Moments later the entire building slowly began to roll, and it felt like a small temblor. Many of the Magentans engaged in random conversations with each other while Maerora Ma spoke to Vysender. Forceful thoughts entered my mind, thoughts that insisted I make a choice to take the action of a fiend or that of a traitor—kill Maerora Ma or not.

The building ceased rolling, and then we were led to the garden by Maerora Ma who had apparently decided to discontinue eye contact with me. Her slipping cordiality had me feeling regret over my jab at the guards. She maintained a conspicuously large physical distance too, which made any chance of completing my mission all the more difficult, and with her daughters now gone, there was no excuse for me to not proceed with my mission orders, but Katydid's smiling face had stained my conscience. I felt as if my ability to execute mission orders was indelibly marred.

The garden appeared through the windows, and the initial sight of it dazzled my eyes. A choir of angels might as well have been present to rejoice in all the blessed colors. The emerging malaise I had started feeling from Maerora Ma's cold shoulder soon faded as the beautiful colors stimulated my eyes. As we walked out into the splendor of the garden, I could smell the familiar essence of Earth. I breathed in deeply and lavished in the pleasure of sight and scent, and when I looked over at Maerora Ma, I noticed her magenta-colored skin contrasted sharply against the full-spectrum of colors. My mind re-registered her as a menacing Magentan alien, the creature I had come all this way to kill. Energy to attack swelled within me, and I expressed it in another nudge against the guards. The four guards reacted with rapid yet quiet restraint. Bonson glanced at me, and I quickly averted my head away from him. Maerora Ma was too far ahead to have even noticed my latest petit fray with the guards.

"Halt!" Vysender ordered. "Do you need to rest? Do you need to drink? Do you need anything at all?" he asked me.

"Yes, I need to be closer to Maerora Ma. Is she speaking? If she is, I cannot hear her."

"We can grant you that, Captain Joan Jones; however, we must restrain your arms to do so," he said.

"No, never mind, I'll enjoy the tour from back here. It's no problem," I said.

"Do be aware, Captain Joan Jones, one more provocation of the guards will result in more severe restraint. I hesitate now not to tie your arms behind your back," Vysender warned.

He too had become incredibly alien-like to me against the backdrop of the Earth garden and Bonson as well. All of them were creatures now, and I couldn't stop natural fight-or-flight instincts from heightening in intensity within me. I strained to hear Maerora Ma.

She was naming the plants, bushes, and trees. "Those are nasturtiums," she said, pointing left, "and that's an apple tree there . . . ." As she continued docenting, I scanned the garden and thought if William and Porter could make it here, they could sustain themselves for a long while.

"Just the other day, a couple of Magentan animals were roaming through here. I do hope they were removed. Earth vegetation is very fragile, and for some reason the Magentan animals are eager to feast on it, though it is rare for them to actually make it in here," Maerora Ma said to the crowd.

A few of the Earth scholars murmured in Magentan as Maerora Ma continued to talk about the garden, and despite the earlier objection to my request to be closer to Maerora Ma, the tight box of guards I was in the middle of had come within fairly close proximity to her. I watched her, and she still refused to look at me. She caressed her brow, and through the magenta I could not entirely tell, but she appeared quite fatigued. Actually, most everyone seemed tired, and few conversations persisted, and when Maerora Ma spoke, she did so falteringly.

"Maerora Ma, Ma'am," Bonson called.

"Bonson . . . speak," Maerora Ma said.

"I suggest we head back inside."

She agreed, and then we turned back, even though we had only covered a quarter of the garden, which seemed to be a few kilometers in its entirety. Maerora Ma set a sluggish pace back, and we paused every so many meters. The guards too exhibited weariness.

"Bonson, why is everyone so tired? Are they ok?" I asked.

"We'll be fine. The symptoms of magenta deprivation can suddenly come on, but we'll be fine after we rest in magenta for a while."

While the Magentans took a standing rest, I observed the beauty of the garden and saw brilliant yellow-colored peonies on the path's edge, and then I scanned more deeply into the shrubbery. A bit of movement had caught my eye. It was well within the dense brush. I squinted to improve my focus. If I could have kneeled down, I could have had a better look at what was rustling in the bush. Nonetheless, the guards, tired as they were, appeared more-than apt to seize me in less than half a second, so I looked no more.

The slow-moving procession continued its crawl back to Maerora Ma's well-windowed palace, and as we walked down the narrow path, all conversation was abandoned and no sounds at all emanated from the garden. Only the soft thud of our foot-steps could be heard, and when a well-worn trail crossed our path, I looked down its way. It was flanked with death lilies and appeared to dead-end just a few meters down. I tried to pause to see better what looked like a tiny shrine or altar or a commemo-rative plaque of some sort, but the guards had rudely shoved me along.

Maerora Ma was assisted into the building, and as I watched her be taken away, I realized I'd probably never be privileged to be in her company again. My whole purpose in life smacked me across the face. All for naught, I said in my head, and then I was brought back inside the magenta-drenched world, down to a windowless old portion of the building and into a small room where the guards shoved me across the floor and slammed the door shut. The room was bare except for a toilet, washbasin, and cot. The walls and floor had no seams, and the source of light was dim. Thoughts of self-hate raged loudly and relentlessly through my mind. I grabbed both sides of my head and let the fury of frustration flow through me. I kicked the cot completely over two or three times. What a blow. What an *idiot*. All that work, the effort, the time, the team who got us here . . . oh, God, what a waste. I reneged! I betrayed my country. I alone failed, and now Butterfly has a loser for a mother. I dropped to the floor and cried.

CHAPTER 5:
GOLDEN

IN HER BED, Maerora Ma slept nested in linen. Her bedroom occupied a wedge of the building where her bed was situated on the ground floor, and nothing obstructed the view of the ceiling, which rose clear to the top of the structure. A large elongated antechamber preceding her bedroom provided a sitting area. It was furnished from ceiling to floor in a Magentan style similar to Earth's western Baroque period. Gigantic original oil paintings covered the four walls and depicted Magentan history in dramatic scenes of battles and triumphs, all of which bore no scarcity of nudity and sexual motifs. Heavy ornate molding accented the room while two sofas and two French chairs encircled a large low table.

Once past the antechamber, the decor was sparser but no less grand. Two of the internal walls contained three colossal floor-to-ceiling pilasters while the same low-relief filigree that was in the home's foyer weaved its way upward upon the wine-saturated alabaster. A well-framed open doorway led to a dressing room and a bathroom. The external-facing wall was comprised entirely of tint-adjustable windows, which currently had been darkened against the light of day.

Yaylor Pi walked through a set of guards, through the antechamber, and into Maerora Ma's bedroom. He stood at her bed and watched her sleep. He then sat beside her and was careful not to wake her as he continued to study her, and then slowly he leaned towards her to kiss her.

Without opening her eyes, she pushed his face away. "Don't take advantage. I'm not well," she said in a weak voice.

"You'll be fine in a little while," he said, placing his hand on her forehead.

"Let me rest *alone* please."

"I can't," he said. "I'm upset."

"You can lie beside me if you wish," she said, "but don't disturb me."

He refrained from responding and just sat on the edge of the bed.

"Dammit, *what's wrong*?" she asked impatiently, squinting to see him.

"I've done your sinister service, and it's left me with a strained sense of self-respect."

"Well, it comes with the territory," she said.

He then reached to roll down the linen that covered her and then began to unfasten her chemise.

"I shall be angry with you if don't stop," she said, awakening her eyes enough to deliver a frightening glare.

"After what I've done for you today?" He then proceeded to expose her breasts.

"All right, if you need to talk, we can talk right now then," she said, closing her garment and tucking herself tightly under the cover.

"No, Maerora, let me *have you now*," he begged, "*please.*"

"No, I'm not prepared."

"I'll pull out," he said, removing the cover again. This time he took it down clear below her thighs.

"No!" she said, reaching for the cover, but he had then straddled her and held her arms down.

In English, he said: "'O fairest beauty, do not fear nor fly!/ For I will touch thee but with reverent hands;/I kiss these fingers for eternal peace,/And lay them gently on thy tender side.'" He then resumed speaking in Magentan, "It's never mattered to you, I know, but I remain ever-so faithful to this," he said, ogling her.

"That's so ludicrous. Your reproductive singularity is irrelevant. What matters are mothers."

"Ah, but, what you fail to appreciate is that someday Katydid will celebrate her true uniqueness in being the only offspring of the rare and exclusive Yaylor Pi," he said.

Maerora Ma snickered and then Yaylor Pi joined in and laughed. He released her arms and unstraddled her. She then quickly drew her cover back up to under her chin.

"What's *really* bothering you, Yaylor?" she asked.

"As if killing Oaktobrons is not troublesome," he stated.

"After one hundred and one? Surely, it has become second nature," she said.

"Throw in all the banishment of spies and the crushing of discontented souls, and, yes, you're right. It has become second nature but *second* only to your *first* inclination, Ma'am."

"Like I said, Yaylor Pi, it comes with the territory, especially this territory where we all live assured that our masses are well-maintained. *You did* stage it as an accident, right?

"Yes, an air-vehicle accident just as you requested," he said.

"All right, then, good. Please let me rest now."

He remained in place and didn't move, so she reached to touch him. However, he squirmed in reaction to her touch.

"What's the matter with you!" she said, retracting her arm and scowling at him.

"It's time, isn't it?" he said.

"What time?" she asked.

"For the changing of the guards . . . when the gold is gone, and you banish me like you did Densip Pi," he said.

"You know you'll never give me reason to banish you. You love Katydid far too much for that," she said.

"And Densip Pi? Did he not love his daughters?"

"He loved Mălīn," she said and then closed her eyes as if to fall asleep, so he kissed her lips, and then he moved down to kiss her neck and then her breasts and paused to rest his head on her belly. She maneuvered her body to push the cover down and her chemise up for him, and he then resumed kissing her downwardly until he stood to remove his clothing. He quickly returned to her and checked her for her readiness.

"You're so wet," he said.

"Who needs gold, then?" she said.

With a familiar confidence he pushed himself in, causing her to forcefully expel her breath.

"Ahh," he sounded with each rhythmic thrust.

"Mmm," she uttered sporadically.

Then quickly, he grabbed his penis from within her as it rained opaque dollops all over her thighs and onto her garment and bedding. She then let him lie beside her with his head on her shoulder. She reached to fix the fallen locks of hair on his forehead.

"Do you feel better?" she asked.

"No, Ma'am, I don't."

"Dammit, Yaylor, stop fixating on that old myth. It's foolish to rely on the glistening gold of a Magentan woman's touch. So much affects it: age, emotional stress—"

"Diminished love," he said, adding to her list.

She remained silent for a moment and then quietly said, "I'm afraid the flesh of my heart is now basalt. Don't you know how much I miss Morgana—"

"I know, I know," he said. "There's no need to bring up Morgana."

"Oh, Yaylor, I can't sleep at night. I close my eyes and there she is, and the only thing I can do to make her go away is to berate myself for what I've done . . . for ordering the deaths of the doctors who couldn't bring her back to life and for ordering that dreadful attack on Earth. Don't you know how badly I've destroyed my grandmother's dream? How can I ever return Magenta to its source if our source hates us? Do you think I rest easy ever for one second of any day? I've been hollowed out by the agony of regret and remorse and loss and grief and all the psychologically destabilizing things you can think of. Of course I'm not going to bleed gold for you! Dammit!"

"Well, all that comes with the territory, doesn't it?" he said.

"Humph," she snorted. "Don't bring another disturbance for me to bear on my shoulders. Be strong," she said.

"I can't," he whispered.

"Why?" she asked in a harshening tone.

"Because, whether one is from Earth or Oaktobron or where

ever, one needs to be loved deeply by a companion," he said.

"And what we just did doesn't count?" she asked, but he didn't answer. "Humph, love . . . do you even know *why* you crave it so much? You don't know what it's like to care for a newborn infant who is completely helpless and utterly dependent on its mother. It's needy. It feeds from her breasts. It urinates and defecates all over itself, and she cleans it up. It might die in its sleep, so she never fully rests. No, she merely slumbers to ensure she can hear it breathing at all times. And it screams. Oh, how it screams if it doesn't see or hear its mother regardless of how many others try to calm it down. What an incredibly high level of care a mother has for her newborn, and she goes on completely undaunted by the huge imposition it is, and *that* is love. It's the *love* of our mothers that makes us yearn for it throughout the whole of our lives, but don't ever forget, Yaylor Pi, that nature has saturated a new mother's brain with chemicals to help her cope with administering all that *love*."

He arose and then entered the bathroom and returned with a damp cloth to dab up his spewn ejaculate from the bed and from Maerora Ma herself. "You used to be so embarrassed by all the gold running up your arm when I'd ask you to touch me," he said.

"We have a lot of *used-to-be* memories," she said.

"Yes, but I never thought the gold would be a used-to-be," he said, putting on his pants. "Ma'am, if I may, I would like to take leave of the banquet tonight."

"Where will you go instead?" she asked.

"To see my mother," he said, and they both chuckled.

"Oh, Yaylor, you're so narrowly focused on yourself that you can't see the promise of the future now that the Earth woman is here."

"No, *you* can't see the future quite the way it's going to be," he said.

"Ah, I see. You're some great fortuneteller now, is that right? Well, 'If you can look into the seeds of time,/And say which grain will grow and which will not,/Speak then to me, who neither beg nor fear/Your favours nor your hate,'" Maerora Ma said in English.

"Well, that's just it, isn't it? Your Shakespeare's spot on today," he said, heading to the door. Maerora Ma shook her head in bewilderment and watched him leave.

"Hurry, DeNitor, come this way," Mălīn said.

"Gee, Mălīn, where in the world is your bedroom anyway?" DeNitor asked.

She stopped at a door and stared into her glasses to open it. The two then entered her bedroom, and startled one of the household-staff members who was cleaning.

"Oh, I forgot you might be cleaning my room," said Mălīn, recognizing the woman as the mother of the spy girl. "Are you finished?"

"No, I was just starting," said the woman.

"Well, don't worry about it. Take a break. It doesn't need to be cleaned today," Mălīn said.

"Thank you," she said and then exited the room.

"Oh, how pathetically weak my mother is," Mălīn said.

DeNitor removed his shoes, tossed himself onto Mălīn's bed, and gestured to her to join him.

"My mother should have instantly banished that woman and her daughter for spying, but instead they're still creeping around," she said, joining DeNitor on the bed.

"Wow, Maerora Ma lets spies run around here?" he asked.

"Yes, that was the mother of the girl who saw you in the garden," she said and then immediately gulped in regret at what she had just revealed.

"What!" DeNitor exclaimed. "I was seen in the garden?" He quickly flung himself off the bed. "You didn't tell me I was seen in the garden."

"DeNitor, I forgot," she said.

"I'll be connected to the Earth males and then to Maerora Ma's death. I'll be executed," he cried, covering his mouth and running to the bathroom.

Mălīn chased after him. "No, we'll fix it."

He sobbed while embracing the toilet bowl.

"Listen to me, DeNitor. You can go right out to the garden and get rid of the Earth males during the banquet tonight, and we'll forget about plan B," she said, kneeling beside him.

"No, it won't work," he said.

"Yes, it will."

"What do I do with the corpses?"

"Bury them."

"I'm Magentan. I'd last two seconds in that garden, let alone dig two deep graves," he said.

Mălīn sat down on the floor and rocked her body for a solution. "This is what I'll do," she said. "I'll report to my mother that the spy girl was spying again, and I know my mother won't give them a second chance. She's still Maerora Ma deep down inside. She'll have them banished right away without discussion, and that will eliminate the problem."

"Except for Maerora Ma, who knows I was in the garden," he said.

"She'll be dead, DeNitor."

"Ok, ok, I believe you're right about Maerora Ma. She'll instantly banish the spy girl and her mother if you tell her the girl was spying again. She won't question you," he said, standing up from the floor.

"I'll go to her right now," Mălīn said, getting up from the floor. She then exited her bedroom and hurryied over to her mother's room. She stopped abruptly at the two guards in front of her mother's bedroom door and stood for a moment to catch her breath, and then she called her mother through her glasses.

"Mama, may I enter your bedroom?" she asked. "There's two guards preventing me from entering."

"Mălīn, I'm in a hurry. I'll visit with you when I return,"

Maerora Ma said.

"Gosh, Mama, I was told you had been very ill in the garden today. I just want to see how're doing," Mălīn said. "Don't you have time for your daughter?"

"Come in but not for long, all right?" Maerora Ma said.

Mălīn darted in through the antechamber and straight through to the bedroom where her mother was buttoning the last button of her tailored tunic top. "Mama, please forgive me."

"What for?" Maeora Ma asked, receiving her daughter's hug.

"I snuck DeNitor into my bedroom," Mălīn revealed.

"Dammit, Mălīn, your firstborn daughter is to be from a male of my choosing."

"I know," Mălīn said.

"We'll discuss it later. I don't have time right now."

"All right, Mama, but that wretched spy girl . . . ," Mălīn said, tapering her sentence.

"What about her?" Maerora Ma asked.

"I caught her peeking at us," she said. "Gosh, Mama, if you'd only banished her and her mother the first time."

"All right, Mălīn, I'll take care of it," Maerora Ma said. "Now, go along. I'm in a hurry."

"Can you please order Yaylor Pi to take care of it right now?" Mălīn asked, grasping at her mother's arms.

"No, Yaylor Pi's not feeling well. I'll have Vysender do it when I get back, which I don't like doing. A leader should never take her head of the military for granted. That's an inherently precarious relationship."

"Mama, can you please order him to do it now?" Mălīn asked, still holding her mother's arms.

"I will do it later, Mălīn. Now, let go of me," Maerora Ma said, heading towards the door. Mălīn followed her. "Wait," Maerora Ma said, stopping and turning towards Mălīn. "Do me a favor and distract the guards while I slip away."

"Mama, where are you going?"

"Don't worry about it. Just do as I ask."

WHEN A GENTLE TAP and knock on the door woke me up, I found I was lying on the floor next to the tossed cot.

"Captain Joan Jones, I'm going to enter the room, all right?"

I had no time to respond as the door squeaked open on old hinges.

"Oh!" I said, shocked to see it was Maerora Ma herself. I quickly stood up from the floor as she entered.

She took care in quietly closing the door, and then she turned to face me. "Oh!" she said, looking at the cot. "Are you all right?"

"No, are *you* all right? You were very weak a little while ago," I said, reeling inside from her larger-than-life presence in this little dungeon we were standing in.

"I'm better now," she said, pausing and squinting at the cot. Her clothing, though tailored, was unadorned. "I haven't much time. I've had to sneak away, and it won't be long before I'm discovered missing. I apologize for this old dark room you're in and the way the guards have treated you. Unfortunately, the *notion* of my safety and protection has become a monstrous tyranny of sorts. Vysender and the guards are irreversibly programmed to protect me, and only brute force reigns supreme in their minds. It was my intention to meet and greet you in the most hospitable of ways. I do sincerely apologize . . . ."

And while she spoke, the idea of second chances beckoned me to restore the valor of Butterfly's mother.

"I don't have much time before the guards come kicking down the door, but rest assured we will treat you properly at the banquet tonight," she said, turning towards the door and reaching for its handle.

My glance landed on her neck, and then a cool automaton-like feeling possessed me. My mission duty had finally returned by manifesting into a powerful lunge towards Maerora Ma. My hands were splayed and rising when simultaneously the door flew violently open, bashing Maerora Ma's hand and sending her stumbling backwards. My forward motion morphed into startlement.

VYSENDER AND MAERORA MA agreed to meet to redefine security, and as Maerora Ma headed to the small library within the study area of her home where Vysender was waiting, she spoke to a household attendant through her glasses. Her two door guards followed her, and a camera ball sailed along in front of her as she spoke.

"That looks beautiful," Maerora Ma said. "Thank you for selecting the ones that I told you were peonies. Now, what about the note? Can you please show it to me? Ah, yes, that is perfect. Well done, thank you."

Retracting doors slid open as Maerora Ma approached the entry of the room, which had three of four walls lined with shelves of books, all of which were Magentan antiques. The fourth wall, which contained the entrance, consisted of the same low-relief filigree set in wine-infused alabaster that was in the foyer. The two guards had remained outside the door, and when Vysender saw Maerora Ma, he arose from the conference table.

"Maerora Ma," he said, "can I get you anything before we start?"

"No, I'm fine," she said, setting herself at the head of the table, which forced Vysender to move to a seat nearer to her.

"Ma'am, do we have Yaylor Pi with us?" he asked, looking around for a floating camera ball.

"No, he's taken leave for the day. I'll brief him later," Maerora Ma said, setting her glasses on the table.

"Acknowledged, Ma'am," he said. "How's your hand?" he asked.

"Well, it's not broken," she said curtly.

"Unfortunate timing . . . but I do have my objective, which I know you understand."

"I do," she said.

"Well, now, I propose that we allow Captain Joan Jones more freedom just as you have requested."

"Good," Maerora Ma said.

"Well, now, naturally, I still have my objective to achieve, and so I propose that two guards accompany you at all times, just as we have done this afternoon. They will be posted at the door of any room you may be in at any time, and—"

"All right, I'll accommodate this proposal of yours for a short while until *you're* convinced Captain Joan Jones is trustworthy. I'm, myself, of course, am already convinced," she said.

"Yes, but there's more to it, Ma'am," he said. "We will also assign two guards to Captain Joan Jones, herself. She'll be able to come and go as she pleases, but the guards will accompany her."

"All right," she said, "but what if I want to be alone with her?"

"The two sets of guards will accumulate, making it four guards total who will remain outside the door of any room in which you choose to keep private company, Ma'am, and please understand that this is a major compromise on my part," he said.

Maerora Ma looked away to ponder the deal.

"Uh, Ma'am, there's more."

"Good grief, Vysender."

"Ma'am, we will be very much out of control when you're keeping private company with Captain Joan Jones; therefore, we must protect your heir," he said.

"Mălīn?"

"Yes, Ma'am."

Maerora Ma chuckled heartily. "You hadn't better assign DeNitor as her guard."

Vysender laughed. "No, Ma'am, I won't do that, but, um, there is an intricacy here that perhaps you haven't yet realized."

"And what is that, Vysender?" Maerora Ma asked.

"We must keep you separate from your heir at all times."

"No."

"Maerora Ma, I realize it is heretical to ask a Magentan mother to be separated from her daughter, but you happen to be the ruler of the realm, and we cannot risk losing you. Nevertheless, we have agreed to take that risk, and in doing so, we must compensate for the possible loss," he explained.

"Agreed," she said.

A FRESH BOUQUET of flowers, presumably from the Earth garden, had been delivered to my new, well-accommodated living quarters. The new room provided sweepingly expansive views of the Magentan surroundings through its many enormous windows, and even though the sky had darkened with the evening, I could still see the outdoors well. I looked as far as I could possibly see, and there appeared to be cities in the distance, discernible only by their numerous tall skyscrapers. The acreage nearer to the building was full of trees and shrubbery. The huge dying star was not observable. It must have dipped below the horizon or was on the other side of the building. Nor could I see the Earth garden from my vantage point.

I breathed in the aroma of the flowers, most of which were yellow peonies like those that I had seen earlier in the garden. Maerora Ma had sent the flowers, which were accompanied by a hand-written note that repeated her earlier apology and promise about how the evening's banquet would be a much more pleasant experience. I wondered if she had written the note herself, considering her hand might have been injured.

A serious rumination then bulged hugely in my mind. It was the Shakespearean question: to kill Maerora Ma or not to kill Maerora Ma. I had to kill her. To have come all this way and not to kill her was an outrageous waste of effort, but I couldn't be the one to kill Katydid's mother. I tried, but coincidently the door swung open. Humph, maybe Maerora Ma is divine after all and was protected by some supernatural force. If only I had properly executed my mission orders right off the bat, Maerora

Ma would have then been dead, and I wouldn't be here mulling over why I shouldn't, wouldn't, or couldn't.

A knock on the door disrupted my thoughts. Two female Magentans had brought some clothing and insisted on helping me get ready for the banquet. Their English wasn't perfect like Bonson's and Maerora Ma's, but they were kind and fun. One plucked a peony and pinned it to her hair and then strutted around the room swinging her hips exaggeratedly. We all laughed together, and they seemed genuinely thrilled to pamper and beautify me. I begged them to call me Joan, but they just giggled meekly and continued to call me by my title and full name. The outfit they had brought me was made up of plush fabric. The top zipped from the front and was covered in ornate embroidery and had slightly billowing sleeves and was a light shade of magenta while the pants were dark magenta and felt like velvet. When the two women were finished, they each insisted on receiving a huge bear hug from me.

A LITTLE WHILE LATER, I was opening the door again, and this time Maerora Ma and Katydid had come calling. Four guards were present behind them. Katydid rushed straight to me, wrapping her little arms tightly around the middle of my legs. Her affection was precious, and I wanted to reciprocate with all my heart. She then held her hands in the air, signaling me to pick her up.

"May I?" I asked.

Maerora Ma nodded.

I lifted the little girl and adored her as if she were my own. The joy of holding her rekindled my grief over Butterfly, which released a tear from the corner of one of my eyes. Katydid placed her hand on my cheek.

"Mama, she frying," she said.

"Crying," Maerora Ma corrected her. Maerora Ma was wearing a multi-layer robe of silk and velvet, which bore a dozen or so finely embroidered symbols, both seemingly civic and martial in nature.

I told Katydid she was adorable and that she would like Earth because there were many little girls to play with there. She looked at her mother and giggled when I spoke. Eventually, she reached for her mother, and Maerora Ma retrieved her from me. She smiled widely while in her mother's arms and affectionately leaned her head against her mother, reminding me of similar endearing moments I had had with Butterfly. It was always those small gestures of affection that overwhelmed me with joy.

"Did you receive the flowers?" Maerora Ma asked, stretching to peek into my room.

"Yes, they're very nice," I said. "Is your hand ok?"

"It's fine. Fortunately, I retracted it from the door quickly enough. Thank you, by the way, for trying to come to my rescue. I noticed you had moved quickly towards me to help me before the guards grabbed you away," she said.

Katydid then started fidgeting, and Maerora Ma asked her to tell me who she chose to tuck her into bed, but Katydid shyly declined to answer and buried her face in her mother's hair instead.

"Come on, Katydid, tell her," Maerora Ma coaxed but to no avail. "Well, would you believe she chose you, Captain Joan Jones?"

"Good choice," I said, smiling at the little girl.

Maerora Ma set her down and gestured to her to walk on her own. "Show Captain Joan Jones where you sleep." We all then started to follow the little girl.

"Ma'am, Mălīn is within close proximity to our destination. We must take the time to request that she change her location," said one of the guards, halting further forward movement.

"Very well, then, have her move," she said to the guard and then turned to me to say, "The guards and I have an agreement, one that causes me some distress. They will limit their protection of me and restrain you less; however, they will, in turn, exert more safety and protection around Mălīn, and the two of us—Mălīn and I—shall remain separated while you are in my presence. Mălīn, of course, is the heir to . . . well, she will assume my role here on Magenta and throughout the realm if I should become incapacitated."

"I'm sorry for the imposition," I said.

"No, don't be sorry, Captain Joan Jones. I would agree to be separated from my daughter for no one except you. You're a very important visitor. You should know that Magentan mothers do not part from their daughters so readily. The very suggestion of it is sacrilege, and I'm telling you this not for you to feel it as an *imposition* but rather for you to understand the situation," she said.

The guards then signaled that we were free to proceed to Katydid's bedroom, and as we walked, I thought about the implication of Mălīn as heir to an unbelievable span of power and control. It certainly provided a convincing motive to want to eliminate the incumbent, even if it was your mother. I had to wonder whether William, Porter, and I were on the honorable side of this plan to assassinate Maerora Ma. Densip Pi had sacrificed his life to warn Earth about Maerora Ma. He said she was set on destroying Earth, but she hadn't exhibited any ill will whatsoever towards Earth so far. Actually, she seemed to be very much the opposite, what with her Earth museum and her garden of earthly delights and her Shakespeare.

AT THE BANQUET, I was seated between Bonson and Maerora Ma at one of many rows of tables, none of which were different from each other, not raised nor lowered nor decorated any more or any less. Sitting across from me were several of the Earth scholars. The four guards lined up against a wall behind Maerora Ma and me. Hundreds of Magentans filled the tall room. Numerous balconies were scattered upwardly many stories high and were all populated with energetic Magentans, some of which appeared to be draped and dangling over the edges. Large windows made up the external wall, and with the dark cast of night, there was not much that could be seen out of them. The voices of all the Magentans echoed up, down, and around.

All the commotion seemed to naturally calm and center me. I contemplated whether Mălīn was in on the plot to kill her mother, and I thought if she were, then there might be others. I decided to watch and observe for hints of motives in any one who may want to kill Maerora Ma. Plus, I had to flesh out the idea that Densip Pi may have provided false intelligence.

A speaker appeared at a podium and began to address the crowd in Magentan. Maerora Ma placed her hand on top of mine and apologized to me and explained that many of the Magentans here tonight did not speak Earth English and were being instructed to enable or update their language translators in their glasses. Maerora Ma then headed over to the podium, and when the crowd recognized her, they clapped and cheered heartily. The regalia she wore glowed and flowed and reflected her innate stateliness.

"I am speaking to you in Earth English tonight for the benefit of our guest who has come here to our realm—Magenta in particular—all the way from Earth, risking life and limb by an unregistered mission through the MIC."

All the Earth scholars around me clapped and saluted me.

"'The mother of invention is a very well-endowed woman, and she has been suckling technology forever at her perpetually full breasts.' Those were the words my grandmother, Eldora Ma, opened with during the great convention of engineers at which she formally presented the concept of the MIC, which was a very long time ago. Of course, we all know that *necessity* is the mother of invention, and it was a *necessity* to link Magenta together with Earth, and that is what Eldora Ma set out to do. Long before I was born, the MIC was well on its way to being completed, and when Eldora Ma sadly died before its completion, my beloved mother, Amora Ma, triumphantly completed it and quickly launched the first Magentan mission to Earth." Maerora Ma paused for applause. "After eighteen celebrated Magentan missions, I stand here tonight full of goose bumps and shivering to say that Eldora Ma's dream— the mission of Magenta and the charter of the realm—is now within arm's reach of fulfillment."

The multitude of Magentans in the hall verged on a pandemonium of celebratory vigor as tears flowed down Maerora Ma's cheeks. I scanned the crowd assertively, looking for that single one who was not clapping, but none could be seen. While Maerora Ma was struggling to hold her composure, Bonson grabbed my hand and squeezed it tightly and rubbed the side of my arm, comforting gestures that I'm sure he intended more for Maerora Ma than for me.

"Earth," Maerora Ma said and then paused to wait for the tumult to subside. "Earth," she said, is the source of all things, and the source has now come to us, and her name is Captain Joan Jones, and she shall liaise between Magenta and Earth and will be forever known as The Great Liaison."

More demonstrated celebration carried on in an awe-delivering rumble, and as the passion of the audience increased, Maerora Ma tapped on the side of the podium to signal for calmness.

"When I was an infant, my mother arranged for a special distillment of aufillo, which was intended for the night I was to conceive my firstborn daughter. Everyone here, I know, remembers the story of how the batch—enough for over a thousand Magentans—was lost, and you know too that it was finally discovered just a few years ago, and I had then set it aside for my own first-daughter's eve to conceive *her* first daughter. And with the passing of that chance, I now wish to share it with everyone here tonight to celebrate the beginning of the assimilation of the realms and more importantly, to consummate our new marriage of cooperation with Earth's representative, Captain Joan Jones. Please enjoy," she concluded and walked away from the podium while the hall thundered with excitement and energy and unrestrained revelry.

The rowdy crowd knocked me off that center I had found comfort in earlier, and my mind was trying to reel in all what Maerora Ma had said. She certainly had made huge sweeping assumptions about my intentions, but nothing she said was aggressive or hostile, although I didn't know what the 'assimilation of the realms' entailed. I wondered why Densip Pi's testimony was not consistent with what I had already experienced, and I desperately felt that William and Porter needed to know about this new information. I was also amazed that she had referred to me as a liaison just as the Indian woman did at the mission ceremony and it was too coincidental to ignore. Somehow, Maerora Ma or her mother or her grandmother had to have been presented to the people in India, and subsequently one of them was deified.

"May I leave you in the company of the others here, Captain Joan Jones?" Bonson asked, "Maerora Ma hasn't returned, and it's my duty to be concerned."

"Of course, Bonson, don't worry about me."

As he left, I looked around among all the Magentans for which one may be hostile towards Maerora Ma. Rhythmic music then strummed my awareness, and I looked around for its source. The tables were being removed, and many in the hall were standing and mingling ever closer to their fellow Magentans. As more Magentans squeezed in tighter together, we ended up constantly brushing up against each other, and since not a one was speaking English, analyzing the music became my focus. The monotony of it enticed my brain into matching its pattern of frequency. It was slow and made me feel as if I were going around in a huge circle.

I continued to weave through the mass of Magentans and had no true bearing other than just forward movement. The guards that had stood behind me earlier were apparently gone, and I was glad to have been able to wade freely through the joyful maroon humanoids.

The music most definitely had hypnotized me, and all the variations of the color magenta formed into a vague and indefinite pattern that was completely monotonous to me until the most beautiful glimmering gold emerged. Two long flute-like glasses focused crisply in my sight, and behind them was the eminent and arguably transcendental Maerora Ma, who had dispensed with her ceremonial gown and returned to another tailored Mao suit, one that accentuated her figure.

She extended one of the glasses towards me in offering, but I refused it. My eyes, however, would not stop ogling the opulent-amber oasis that ostentatiously sparkled in this mono-colored desert of magenta.

"Do people drink with their eyes on Earth?" she asked and laughed.

"The gold is . . . ." I was unable to finish my sentence.

She again offered me the glass.

"No, I'd rather not," I said and felt like an old fuddy-duddy teetotaler refusing a cocktail.

A Magentan woman then stumbled backward between Maerora Ma and me. Maerora Ma smiled at her encouragingly and saluted her with one of the glasses. The woman squinted a wink back at Maerora Ma and disappeared quickly into the crowd. Their exchange seemed almost flirtatious.

When Maerora Ma resumed her moment with me, she pressed in uncomfortably close. "Why won't you have the au-fillo?" she asked.

"I don't want to lose control," I replied and backed away slightly to recover my own space.

"You will not lose anything. You will gain, not lose. Will you just merely *hold* one of these glasses to free me from having to hold two?" She offered the glass yet again, and I accepted it but did not drink from it

My arm was then inadvertently bumped from behind by a frolicking Magentan, which caused some of my aufillo to spill. Maerora Ma grimaced at the spilt gold.

"Please, Captain Joan Jones, this aufillo has endured a couple of missed opportunities. Let not this momentous event be yet another. Please deliver me from a growing displeasure and have a taste."

"All right," I said, realizing I was on the losing end of this argument. I brought the glass to my mouth and let the gold liquid touch my lips. "Mmm, it tastes like honey," I said and enjoyed it

so incredibly much that all urges to resist another sip were unde-
tectable. The fear of losing control had no more influence on me
than a neutrino passing through paper. I sipped more and more
and more until it was gone.

She called over a nearby server who brought two more tall
flutes of glistening gold. We both placed our empty glasses on
the tray, and she then lifted the full glasses and handed one to
me. "To Captain Joan Jones," she saluted.

"You can call me Joan," I said, and she softly giggled.

Another Magentan then unintentionally bumped into her
and upon noticing her announced Maerora Ma's presence to all
in the immediate vicinity, causing a little swarm of Magentans
to form. They hugged their leader, kissed her cheeks, held her
hands in theirs, and profusely sang her praises. I watched her
gracefully and graciously receive the love. All the sentiment
that flowed forth seemed genuine and even contagious, as I too
felt compelled to partake in the love fest but refrained from any
demonstration.

The swarm of admirers gently gravitated towards the center
of the hall where the music wasn't necessarily louder but could
be felt pleasantly vibrating strongly through the body. An arousing feeling in me then began to stir. The crowd was becoming
denser in the center. One could definitely not flail one's arms.

Maerora Ma reached for my hand from beside me, exert-
ing a certainty in not letting me go. Everyone moved in a slow
gyration to the music. I too swayed with the wave and quickly
gulped down my second glass of aufillo then handed the empty
vessel carelessly to the Magentan next to me who passed it on to
the next then to the next until who knows where it ended up.

"Is this not sensational?" a Magentan whispered in my ear.

"Yes, it's sensational," I answered without turning my head.
Internal urges to resist were being ameliorated by pulsing waves
of tranquility. The center of the room calmly whirled into a slow
rotating vortex. A spiraling galaxy of Magentans was accreting
with more who were drawn by the allure of undulations. The
duration of time jostled about in my mind. It was slow then

fast then slow again. I floated within the ever-growing sea of Magentans, feeling the motion of the ocean and the increasing size of the sea and was starting to approach a deep, deep ecstasy. Giving in to a trance, my mind and body merged with the twirling mass of Magentans. I could barely distinguish my hand from Maerora Ma's. All bodies were pressed up against each other, and the music was grabbing me from within while I was being touched from without. The glory of unity was softening me; the elation of oscillation was loosening me; and the anticipation of the cresting flow was concentrating my thoughts into golden imagery where I seemed to have hit the mother lode, and all I could then see, hear, and feel was gold.

THE WARMTH of the light of day heated my backside. Turning over and opening my eyes seemed unimaginable, for I felt too relaxed to move and feared the opening of my eyes would evaporate the euphoria in which I lay, so I listened to sounds instead and heard birds chirping and a consistent buzz of cicadas stridulating. Golden swirling imagery still dazzled my mind's eye. I replayed the delight of last night in my head until I recognized that someone was breathing next to me. I looked and saw Maerora Ma lying beside me asleep under a light cover. We both still had on our clothing from the evening. She rested on her side with her back to me. We shared a thin soft pad in the middle of a meadow on the side of a hill. A small air vehicle was parked nearby. I studied her. Her presence was mythical. A maternal aura seemed to emanate from her. Even in her sleep, she was regal. I studied me. I wanted to twirl the thick loops of her hair with my fingers and run my hand softly down her arm to feel the temperature of her skin and to know how soft it might be, and I wanted to chase the source of pleasure stirring in me.

She rolled over to face me, and I turned away slightly to lessen the potential intensity. A small part of the disc of the dying star emerged from the horizon straight ahead.

"Tell me about Earth, Captain Joan Jones," she said.

"What can I tell you that you don't already know?" I said, staring directly ahead. She responded by laughing softly.

"All right, then, describe what it was like when you crossed through the realm barrier."

"It was white."

"Hmm, white . . . ," she said lowly. "Passing through the realm barrier used to result in instant insanity. My mother, herself, was able to figure out the cause and offered the solution as well."

"What was the solution?" I asked.

"To enhance self-awareness."

"Where are the guards?" I asked and scanned the scenery in search for them.

"They're in the air vehicle."

"How'd we get here?"

"I arranged it. This meadow is my most favorite place to be, and I wanted you to be here with me," she said, looking into my eyes as if she were behind a two-way mirror.

"What happened last night? All that gold . . . ?" I asked.

"We celebrated you," she said.

I felt myself blush with the thought of such a sensual celebration then didn't want to explore the topic any longer. "In your speech last night, you mentioned the 'assimilation of the realms.' What does that mean?"

She then rolled onto her back and laid her arm over her face to cover her eyes. "It means the two realms should cherish the knowledge of each other and should join to explore the third realm."

"So, 'assimilation' doesn't mean the domination or annihilation of one realm over the other, does it?" I asked.

"Maybe a little domination perhaps . . . annihilation no," she said, still covering her eyes.

"What is a 'little domination'?" I asked.

"Just an aligning of values. Too many dissenters dilute the potency of progress," she said.

There was so much information to understand, but there was so much delight still lingering in my veins, and it had the viscosity of honey, which seemed to slowdown my ability to think, so I halted my interrogation and instead observed the surroundings.

Adorable little animals popped in and out of the meadow. One roadrunner-like bird quickly crossed the open space as if its legs were attached to wheel hubs, and then a large butterfly, the size of a Frisbee, skimmed the dense glade and was followed by three more, all flapping sporadically and swooping erratically.

"Incredible butterflies," I said.

"Do you like butterflies?" Maerora Ma asked, sitting up.

"I love butterflies," I answered, thinking how amazed Butterfly would be by these giant wonders. The patterns on their wings were similar to those on the wings of butterflies from Earth, but they naturally lacked a variety of color since Magenta had only magenta.

"I enjoy them tremendously too," she said.

"I have a daughter . . . ," I offered and then paused with a gulping reminder of how much I missed my Butterfly.

"Do you? How wonderful. She must love butterflies too then," Maerora Ma said.

"Her *name* is Butterfly."

"'Butterfly'" she said, "is a lovely name."

"When I saw your Katydid, I immediately thought about Butterfly. They're close in age," I told her.

"Ah, I thought I sensed your joy when you met my daughters, but I wasn't certain because you seemed so tense," she said. "Daughters are precious . . . that I know." She then turned her head away and stared out at the lively field of magenta.

Fleeting memories of Butterfly swept through my mind, and I fought like mad to suppress them. "Look . . . more butterflies over there." I pointed.

"Tell me more about Butterfly," she said.

"She's rambunctious."

"Just like Katydid," she said, smiling and leaning in towards me. "You're so far away from home . . . from your daughter."

I just shrugged and quietly hoped she would stop asking me about Butterfly.

"I'm sorry. I shouldn't have reminded you . . . ," she said patting me on the wrist. Sparkles of gold twinkled brilliantly just under her skin where it contacted me. She watched me observe the glittering flashes and then withdrew her hand. "It's just a chemical reaction."

"Is it from the gold drink we had last night?" I asked.

"Maybe a little bit," she said.

"Or perhaps you *are* divine like the Earth scholars claimed you were," I said.

"No, no, that notion is just folklore," she protested.

"Have you ever been to Earth?" I asked.

"No, there's not enough magenta on Earth. You saw what happened to me in the garden. I would die in no time on Earth."

"Did you know there's a small population of people on Earth who worship a goddess?"

"Humans have many gods and goddesses," she said.

"Yes, but this goddess seems to be a lot like you."

"How so?" she asked.

"She's the same color as you are."

"Earth has many colors," she said.

"I know, but there's something uncanny about it."

"Well, it's possible that someone on Earth saw a female Magentan during one of our many missions," she said.

"There used to be so many claims of crazy UFO sightings and alien abductions," I laughed, "but they were all in North America. Or maybe they had them in India too. I don't know, but India is where the goddess culture is, so how could a female Magentan be seen there?"

"Well, first of all, we never abducted anyone, and we only ever retrieved a few items, and we saw to it that we didn't take anything too valuable for fear it may cause suffering. We managed to capture *all* of the data on your network of computers, though, but, of course, we haven't been back for a while, so we don't have any new data," she said, studying my eyes as if they were on exhibit.

I searched the meadow again for more butterflies while she continued to stare at my eyes.

"I can check our mission records for something that may tie in with what you're saying about the goddess culture," she said, putting on her glasses.

As she studied her glasses, I reclined and started to recount the imagery of golden ecstasy from the night before. My body must have still been full of that honey-flavored aphrodisiac as I could not resist re-living the moment of the touch that exploded in gold. The thought of it yielded an arousing shockwave-like feeling that shook my body. Embarrassed within myself, I turned away from Maerora Ma, but like an addict I re-played the productive image several times over, repeatedly experiencing the pleasure waves it produced.

As Maerora Ma continued to research data in her glasses, I started to slip into a slumber and felt as if I were surfing on golden waves. I was half in the meadow and half in an amber ocean of endorphins when the unmistakenly real touch of a hand crossed over my arm, slowly down to my belly, and gradually up to my breasts. I felt Maerora Ma's body up against my backside. The sensation of her warmth absorbed the fading pleasure waves. I could barely think of the consequences of what was happening. The idea of resisting her sizzled and evaporated on the surface of my soul. I let her press, hold, and embrace my body. The ruler of Magenta then guided me from my side to my back, and I kept my eyes closed despite desperately wanting to watch this goddess explore me. She simultaneously kissed my lips and unzipped the front of my outfit. She exposed my breasts and set her palm over one of my hard nipples. Stimulating passion streamed through my body, and I involuntarily responded with a quiet expression of pleasure. She nuzzled into my neck and kissed me below my ear, and then she leveraged herself over me to undo my pants. She then placed her warm hand on my belly and caressed me softly and slowly and tantalized me by tentatively approaching and then retreating from my pelvic region. The point of no return fast approached, and I arched to let a forceful flood of pleasure through. All negativity seemed to have become dislodged from my mind, and then she firmly pressed my vulva to wring out every last bit of gratification. I could feel myself pulsing against her palm while a peaceful and blissful sensation lingered in me, but when the pleasure sub-sided, the feeling of shame from impropriety welled up from the depths of my conscience, and she seemed to have sensed it since she turned away to let me recover. I quickly pulled up my pants and closed my top.

"I don't know why this had to happen or what the point of it is, and *I know* the aufillo is an aphrodisiac," I said irritably. "And what about the guards? Were they watching?"

"Don't worry, Joan, we merely had a moment of intimacy," she said.

"On Earth we reserve that sort of intimacy for the one we love," I said and then thought how William and Porter would have hanged me on the spot for such a treasonous act.

"Well, Joan, you're not on Earth," she said.

"You're calling me Joan now."

"That's right. We drop titles during moments of intimacy. Of course, here on Magenta we really only have two titles—'ma' and 'pi,' which indicate mother or father of a potential future ruling daughter."

"But my title is neither of those," I said.

"Yes, but it's still a title."

"I recall meeting a pi earlier. Who was that?" I asked.

"Yaylor Pi. He's Katydid's father," she answered.

"I thought he was your 'right-hand man,'" I said.

"He is," she said, reflectively.

"What about Mălīn?"

"What about her?"

"Is Yaylor Pi her father too?" I asked, fishing for a link to Densip Pi.

"No," she said. "And I was unable to find anything in our

records of all nineteen missions that would connect the Indian goddess culture to us," she said. "I'm sorry if that disappoints you."

"Nineteen missions? In your speech, you mentioned there were only eighteen."

"There are eighteen *celebrated* missions and one that is not," she said. "Ask me not about the nineteenth mission."

"It's ok. I know about it," I said.

"Do you?" she asked.

"Well, it's the reason I'm here—"

"Please, let us talk later," she said, tapping my wrist. "Come along with me. We'll bathe in the water just around the grove of trees there, and then I'll take you somewhere truly special." She stood, and I accepted the hand she offered me. Gold twinkles illuminated her skin where it contacted mine.

"DeNitor Pi, DeNitor Pi," Mălin said in a sing-song voice.

"Oh, Mălin, what are you saying?" DeNitor asked, lying next to her in her bed.

"After last night, you're going to be the father of a daughter. I'm certain of it," she answered.

"Well, let us make more daughters right now," he said, rolling on top of her. Golden specks shimmered under Mălin's skin where they touched. She gazed at the gold adoringly, saying, "Look, DeNitor! Do you see how much I love you?"

"I knew someday your mother would go away long enough so we could enjoy each other," he rejoiced.

"I can't wait for her to go away forever," she said.

"Soon, Mălin, soon. All we need is for your mother to step out into her garden."

"Too bad that cowardly Earth woman couldn't complete her mission," she said.

"Well, that's why we're fortunate that plan B is still intact."

"Oh, DeNitor, I feel so bad every time I think about how upset you were," Mălin said, holding DeNitor's torso tightly.

"It's all right now that the spy girl and her mother are gone. We just need to get Maerora Ma into that damn garden," he said.

"Do you think the Earth males are ready?" she asked.

"Well, I'm certainly not going back there to find out and risk being seen by someone else," he said.

"I know," she said. "Have you thought about what we're going to do with them afterwards?"

"They'll be hunted and killed," he said.

"Do you think we could hide them in a secluded prison?"

"No, Mălīn, it's far too risky."

"But it would give us the opportunity to study them," she said.

"No, Mălīn, we're supposed to sever that tie. Earth doesn't matter. The MIC is to be destroyed. The first realm is useless to us. Densip Pi was very certain that we were to abandon the pursuit of Earth and instead break through to the outer realm before the Oaktobrons do. Don't you see that wanting to study the Earth males is in alignment with Maerora Ma's vision? You're going to be different than your mother, Mălīn, and you know it too, so don't even suggest otherwise," he said.

"DeNitor, don't talk to me that way. I don't like it," she said.

"Dammit! You'd better appreciate that Densip Pi died for this, and I'm risking my life too," he said. "Things aren't going to be the same. We're going to work together like a team. We're going to be equal, all right?"

"All right," she whispered.

"Has your mother checked in with you at all?" he asked.

"No."

"How much longer should I stay?"

"I don't know," she said in a sullen tone.

"Don't be upset," he said, holding her tightly.

"I'm not."

"Yes you are," he said, "but don't worry. Everything is going to be all right. You know I'm so glad you're not going to Oaktobron with your mother. There's some heavy-duty rioting going on there."

"What are you talking about?" she asked.

"All of Oaktobron is furious about the *accidental* deaths of two Oaktobrons who had come to Magenta by way of personal invitation from Maerora Ma."

"I know nothing about this," she said.

"Everyone knows about it except Magentans," he said. "Oaktobrons have something called a free press, and I have special access to it since I serve as an auxiliary to Maerora Ma's personal guards."

"Tell me more," she said.

"Two Oaktobron technicians accompanied a shipment of a rapid-healing machine from Oaktobron to Magenta, and days later they were found dead in an air-vehicle mishap."

"Well, air-vehicle mishaps aren't exactly uncommon. Why would Oaktobrons be suspicious of that? I'm curious about the rapid-healing machine, though. Where did it go?" she asked.

"I don't know, but it was ordered by Yaylor Pi, and the Oaktobrons concluded it was at the express request of Maerora Ma," DeNitor explained.

"Hmm, they must have acquired it to heal Captain Joan Jones. Tell me, DeNitor, did you get a chance to see her with your own eyes when she fell out of the MIC?"

"Yes, she was completely mangled and full of holes all over the place. The woman was dead when I saw her," he said.

"And you haven't seen her since, have you?" she asked.

"No."

"Well, she's no longer mangled. In fact, she is perfectly proportionate, physically fit, and rather attractive to boot," she said. "Clearly, DeNitor, the rapid-healing machine was for her."

"I feel like an idiot for not figuring that out," he said.

"I know, it now seems amazing how quickly she recovered, but I just didn't think about it. After all, I didn't get to see her before she recovered. Anyway, obviously, the two Oaktobron technicians discovered something, something so threatening to my mother that she ordered their deaths," she said.

"It's really bad there, Mălīn. I would be surprised if Yaylor Pi doesn't cancel the trip. He protects your mother so much."

"We need to make sure he doesn't cancel it. Maybe we now have a plan C," she said.

"Yeah, the likelihood of an Oaktobron attempting to assassinate Maerora Ma will be high," he said. Mălīn's mood lifted as she watched her skin turn gold where she touched DeNitor. She then spread herself for him once again.

"Are you still playing that game in your glasses?" asked the mother of the spy girl, but the girl didn't answer. "You know you're going to have to resume some social normalcy eventually. Maerora Ma has forgiven you, and did you know Mălīn let me skip cleaning her room today? If they were still angry, they'd be working me real hard."

The girl still didn't answer.

"Would you like for me to play the game with you?"

"Ok," said the spy girl.

Her mother then hunted around for her pan-omni glasses. "I can't find my glasses. Can you find them with yours?"

The girl contemplated instructions into her own glasses and reported that the missing set of glasses was in Mălīn's bedroom.

"Uh-oh, I must have accidently left them in there when she hurried me out. I'll see if I can retrieve them now," said the mother.

"Uh, Mother, wait," said the girl, patching through to her mother's glasses. Mălīn is in her room with someone."

"Stop listening at once," her mother ordered, but the girl could not resist.

"Whoa!" she uttered as her mother attempted to snatch the glasses off her face, but the girl maneuvered away. "She's calling him DeNitor *Pi*. They must have had sex," she said.

"Stop!" the mother yelled, chasing the girl around the room.

"Mother, no, they're talking about something very important."

"Please, stop. Whatever they're saying does not concern us," the mother said.

"Oh, but, Mother . . . ."

"Stop!"

"No, this is important. Oh, gosh," said the spy girl.

"Stop!" the mother screamed.

"No, they're talking about us . . . I think."

"Maerora Ma will have us killed," said the mother, inching her way towards her daughter.

"No, *Maerora Ma is going to be killed*," said the girl.

"What?! No! Don't listen anymore."

"Something's in the garden," the girl said, and then her mother snatched the glasses from her face, threw them to the floor, and stomped on them until all that was left was a spot of glistening-glass and plastic beads.

CHAPTER 6:
MORGANA

"THE NAME of the town below is Morgana," Maerora Ma said.

The view from the air vehicle revealed a seaside town, which had modest homes and buildings moderately scattered throughout a mostly flat span of land enclosed by rolling hills that were covered with fields of grass. Groves of wide-canopy trees thrived in the crevices between the hills, and the huge dying star was lingering over the curvy horizon.

"My sister lives near the harbor," Maerora Ma said. "She'll be surprised to see us. My mother brought us here often when we were children, and I used to bring my own daughters here with Yaylor Pi, who would take us sailing on the bay."

Our air vehicle had landed on an empty patch of tarmac, which was located on a peripheral part of town. Maerora Ma and I, along with four guards, had deplaned and started walking towards the main-street part of town.

Morgana was not a modern place, and despite all the magenta, it reminded me of an old gold-mining town I had seen back home in northern California. The road we walked on was dusty, and weeds had spurted through the many cracks in the pavement. The temperature was warm, and the air was slightly humid. Maerora Ma had lifted her hair a number of times to cool the back of her neck as she led the way. Though we bathed in the water at the meadow, we still wore our clothes from the night before. Maerora Ma was in her Mao suit, and I was in dark-magenta slacks and an embroidered blouse.

Birds flew about, and small four-legged animals dotted the scenery. Maerora Ma pointed to and named a number of the plants and animals that made an appearance during our trek.

She also explained the geography and weather patterns of the region.

As we walked, my mind processed the presumption that Densip Pi was Mălīn's father since Yaylor Pi was Katydid's father, and he must have duped the U.S. military to try to put Mălīn in power. William and Porter needed to be informed of this new intelligence because their emergence was inevitable, and they would kill Maerora Ma at first opportunity. I had to prevent that. I shuddered at the thought of their impending discovery. Maerora Ma will never forgive me.

"You're always so pensive, Captain Joan Jones," Maerora Ma said, moving to affectionately pat me on the back. Her touch sent a shockwave through me, and I figured the aufillo was still in my system, facilitating fleshly pleasure. A few times, she grabbed my arm to gain my attention to have me observe a wild animal. Gold then streamed through her skin when she touched me.

"What causes your skin to turn gold?" I asked as we strolled along many meters in front of the guards.

"I told you it's a chemical reaction," she said.

"Does it happen to others?"

"Only Magentan women turn gold."

"But do you turn gold for other people?" I asked.

"Other than you? Let's just say there are very few," she said.

"What does it feel like?" I asked.

"Sometimes like feathers delicately landing on my skin and other times like whirls of warmth. By the way, gold is the only color we can see other than magenta."

"Really? I hadn't realized you couldn't see colors," I said.

"Ah, but we can discern the many millions of variations of magenta. Your eyes, for instance, appear as a shade of magenta that I don't think I've ever even seen before. Many times I've had to force myself to stop staring for too long at your eyes for fear of having bad manners. They're extraordinary and truly unusual," she said.

"My eyes are blue," I said.

"Well, that's what you call it. 'A rose by any other name . . . .'"

As we arrived at the center of the town, a number of Magentans quickly accumulated around us to demonstrate their adoration for Maerora Ma. Everyone spoke in Magentan, and Maerora Ma apologized to me for the fact that no one spoke Earth English.

An elderly male offered a glass of fluid to me from a tray. Apprehensive about accepting it, I looked at Maerora Ma. She nodded and gestured for me to drink the fluid. Two females then carried over huge fans made of peacock-like fathers. The fans had long wooden handles, and the women began to wave them slowly over us to cool us. A group of three musicians started to sing and play old hand-made musical instruments. Their song reminded me of something from medieval times or the Renaissance period.

I scanned the growing group of townspeople and assessed how happy and healthy they all were. They seemed to be artisan types—creative and quirky. A part of me drifted away in a daydream that had the theme of how nice it would be to live out the rest of my life in Morgana. If I lived here, I would walk to the shoreline every day and learn Magentan and make friends with all the cheerful inhabitants of this town, and maybe even Butterfly could be brought here to visit or stay.

The appearance of an angry face at the edge of the crowd startled me out of my dream. An Oaktobron had attached himself to the throng of happy Magentans. Hostility emanated from him like ionizing radiation, causing the happiness in my head to melt away.

"There's trouble there," I said to the guards and nodded towards the ornery-looking Oaktobron. They responded by forming a loose box around Maerora Ma.

"Ease up," Maerora Ma said to the guards.

"Ma'am, there's an unfriendly face in the crowd. We're just putting ourselves at an advantage."

"This town is pure," she said. "No one here is a threat."

"There's an Oaktobron present, and he has a less-than pleasant look on his face."

Maerora Ma spotted the Oaktobron and then approved the guards' box. "Let us make our way to my sister's home now," she said.

As we moved on, many of the residents followed, including the Oaktobron, and when another ire-bearing Oaktobron tagged along, the guards pulled in tighter, and Maerora Ma readily allowed it.

"Do you think it's a good idea to lead the Oaktobrons to our destination?" I asked.

"Don't worry, my guards are deadly and can easily handle two troubled Oaktobrons," Maerora Ma said.

We then stopped in front of an ordinary-looking single-story home that faced numerous piers and docks, and Maerora Ma ordered one of her guards to enter it.

All told, about twenty townspeople had followed us and settled in front of the small waterfront home, and while we waited for the scout guard to indicate all was clear, I looked out at the landscape for hidden Oaktobrons. There seemed to be no one out on the docks nor up or down the street. The scout guard then reappeared in the doorway and waved us in.

"My sister is a very bitter person. Please don't be alarmed when she begins to exhibit her animosity towards me," Maerora Ma advised me as we stood in the entryway.

Two of the guards remained on the outside of the home while the other two accompanied us inside. The entryway opened to a dining room, which had a kitchen attached to it. Maerora Ma sat at the head of the table, and I took the seat to her right. I looked around at the home's decor. It was cluttered with ornamental objects, which hadn't been dusted recently.

Maerora Ma's sister then entered the room, and it was as if a block of ice had been rolled in. When their eyes connected, a winter's worth of freezing coated the room, and the moment became too brittle to even breathe.

Maerora Ma finally asserted herself and said, "Here's my peace offering. She's from Earth, and she has been through the realm barrier. Her name is Captain Joan Jones. The hope of linking Magenta with Earth is now recovered. So, let us achieve some civility between us for whatever it's worth." But her words merely precipitated into hard particles of ice that seemed to fall to the floor with a clink, chink, and ping.

Neither sister would avert her eyes. They kept them aimed and both were certain not to lose the stare down.

I studied Maerora Ma's sister. She looked like Maerora Ma but paler, and her nose was altogether different, thicker, flatter, and asymmetrical. She was wearing unflattering old coveralls that maybe an artist or plumber might wear, and I couldn't tell which sister was older.

Maerora Ma's sister finally broke out of the visual freeze and walked into the kitchen. She filled a glass with fluid from a fancy-looking bottle and then returned and set it in front of me. It wasn't gold, so I knew it wasn't aufillo, but I sure as hell wasn't going to drink it. She then poured a glass for herself and neglected to serve any to Maerora Ma.

"Drink some of this truth serum, Captain Joan Jones, and let me tell you a few things on which I'd like your feedback," she said, seating herself across from me.

"Noma, she doesn't need to hear your opinions. She's here to tell you about her experience through the realm barrier." Maerora Ma then turned to me to say, "My sister took after my mother and studied the realm barrier. She's an expert. She'll enjoy hearing what you have to say about it."

"My sister has failed to learn that I have no more interest in the MIC, or Earth for that matter," Noma said, speaking directly to me.

"Well, evidently, you've picked up an interest in miniscule debris instead then," Maerora Ma said, rubbing dust between her fingers and looking around the room in disgust.

"My interest lies in familial allegiances these days because someone needs to compensate for your callousness," Noma said.

"Very well then, Noma, we will leave if you have no meaningful value to experience from Captain Joan Jones' visit," Maerora Ma said, rising from the table.

"Oh, don't be so hasty. I'll listen to the recount of her realm-barrier trip. Go ahead," she said, looking at me.

"It was white—" I started to say and then was abruptly interrupted.

"Why haven't you been back to Morgana? You should've at least offered Morgana's grandmother your condolences." Noma shouted and slammed her open hand on the table. "Morgana wasn't *only your* loss."

"This is not what I came here for, Noma," Maerora Ma said, rising from the table again.

"All right, then leave. Only, I ask for one small favor," Noma said.

"What do you want?" Maerora Ma asked harshly.

"Please, come and observe my 3D DNA-sculpture collection. It's the most incredibly vivid new art you'll ever see," she said in a softening tone.

We followed her down a short hallway to the first door on the left. She stopped at the door and took a moment to look closely at Maerora Ma as if she were memorizing her face. When she opened the door, we entered the room. It was full of Magentans. They weren't moving, but they were real, and one of them was Densip Pi.

"What are these?" I asked while closely examining Densip Pi.

"Sculptures of our deceased family members constructed from DNA," Noma answered.

"What's *his* name?" I asked, pointing to Densip Pi.

"That's Densip Pi, and this is his daughter, Morgana," she said.

"Let's go," Maerora Ma said, grabbing and jerking my arm.

Noma watched gold shine and glow on Maerora Ma's skin where it touched mine. "Oh! My! Oh, wow, Captain Joan Jones, it appears you've managed to melt the hardened heart of the ruler of Magenta."

"Let us leave at once," Maerora Ma said.

"So, my sister *can* feel love again, and we thought the organs of her love had calcified," Noma said.

Maerora Ma looked at me, and I was careful not to react to

Noma's comments. I remained stoic and expressionless.

"Maerora Ma," Noma called sweetly, "just quickly take a gander at your daughter."

"Absolutely not!" Maerora said, marching to the door.

Noma then pushed her sister and caused her to lose her balance. In an instant, Noma swiftly moved to catch Maerora Ma and twirled her around towards the sculpture called Morgana.

I immediately dashed to detach Maerora Ma from Noma, but Maerora Ma had then seen what she tried to avoid seeing, and it caused her to lose her fight. I tossed Noma back a few feet and gestured to Maerora Ma to leave the room, but Maerora Ma was transfixed by the girl statue.

"There, there, sweet sister, let it out now. It'll be all right," Noma said, returning to embrace her sister.

I didn't know whether to intervene or leave the room, but Maerora Ma was frozen and vulnerable, and I felt compelled to protect her, so I remained present while her sister tried to coax a catharsis.

"Maerora Ma," I said, "we can leave now if you need to."

"Captain Joan Jones, now that you're a member of the family by rite of golden love, it's important for you to know that my sister has never truly grieved the death of her firstborn daughter. She prefers feeling anger over sorrow. It's so much easier to be angry than it is to feel wrenched and torn and scathed and scored deeply by the torment of loss."

"Well, people have to do what they have to do at their own pace," I said.

"Ah! I see why she likes you. You enable her blockage, but, fool, you don't know how reckless and retributive she's been," Noma said. "You wouldn't know that she ordered the deaths of six doctors who failed to revive Morgana after—"

"All right! That's enough now," Maerora Ma said, struggling to break from out of her sister's arms. "No mother *ever* recovers from the loss of her daughter, and since you're not a mother, you wouldn't know."

Noma's eyes then filled with tears, and she lost *her* fight. She let Maerora Ma go and turned away from us. "You always think you're the only one who has suffered, Maerora Ma," she said to the wall. "You, in your oversized glass palace with a thousand windows to see out of, but you only look in at yourself. Well, others have suffered too, Maerora Ma. Others have suffered too," Noma said.

"C'mon, Captain Joan Jones, let's go," Maerora Ma said.

Noma then turned around to watch us leave. Thick tears like motor oil rolled down her cheeks. "Go ahead, Maerora Ma, run away before you see someone else suffer. Don't get weighted down by the witnessing of others' losses, especially my loss. You do know that I lost something terribly dear to me too, don't you?"

"And what did you lose, Noma? What in the world did you lose?" Maerora Ma yelled.

"I lost you."

"Well, I'm sorry for your loss," Maerora Ma said. "Let's go, Captain Joan Jones."

I followed Maerora Ma out of the room and didn't look back at Noma.

"Ma'am," said one of the guards as we re-entered the dining room, "we've secured our departure. There are no Oaktobrons left in the area. We're ready to leave when you are."

I looked out of the kitchen window and saw a few elderly Magentans still straggling about, presumably waiting to shake hands with their beloved leader. I then searched for Oaktobrons in the distance, and there were none to be seen.

"Sister," Noma hollered down the hallway. "Let me share a parting word with you," she said, entering the dining room. "Your Earth woman is strong and quick on her feet and unusually obedient."

"So, should she be feeble and recalcitrant?" Maerora Ma said.

"No, but I'm sure she is well aware of the nineteenth mission. I mean, who on Earth wouldn't be? I have a feeling about her."

"Noma, don't be rude. We're leaving now," Maerora Ma said.

"The desire for revenge never really dies. It just merely goes dormant," Noma said.

"Yes, I'm certain you're familiar with that," Maerora Ma said.

We exited the house, and my mind was whirling in computation with all the new information, and I was especially concerned about the seed Noma had planted and hoped to God Maerora Ma would not nurture it. I felt dreadfully sad that Maerora Ma had lost her first daughter. I couldn't imagine experiencing the worst thing in the world, and that surely would be the worst thing.

Maerora Ma seemed most definitely unsettled, but, nonetheless, she put on a cheerful face for the few Magentan stragglers who were waiting for her in the front yard, and after she finished shaking their hands and receiving their affection, we started walking back to the airship. When we turned around the first corner, six fierce Oaktobrons hurled themselves at us. Their bulky bodies were plunging towards us, and as the guards lunged and subdued one each, two were left flying at Maerora Ma and me.

I drew my leg up and pushed one square in the middle of the chest to delay his attack and then immediately grabbed the other to orient him so I could break his neck, but he had twisted my arm behind my back, rendering me useless for an instant, and when I saw that the one I had delayed had recovered and was headed for Maerora Ma, a powerful surge of energy enabled me to free myself from the Oaktobron anchoring me. I landed my hands on the side of the attacking Oaktobron's head and base of his neck and wrenched him with all my might, but he reacted with a violent twist and turned his body, which caused me to lose optimal hand placement.

Maerora Ma was now totally clinched by the other free Oaktobron, and again I experienced a powerful rush of energy that allowed me to jump up and on to the Oaktobron that was holding Maerora Ma. I placed my hands where they needed to be, and since they had just been instantly calibrated for the Oaktobron's thick skin and brawny neck, I was able to force a cervical break so severe the Oaktobron arched and convulsed in a grotesquely revolting manner. The second Oaktobron then attempted escape and was subsequently held down by the few Magentans who had witnessed the ruckus.

The four guards had stunned each of their Oaktobrons with weapons and were still in the process of restraining them with electronic devices while local Magentans tended to Maerora Ma.

"Let us return to Noma's home," Maerora Ma ordered. She then spoke in Magentan and appeared to give orders to those tending to her. They then scurried off to carry out their orders.

We all trekked back to Noma's home, and once inside, Maerora Ma discovered that her communication glasses had been destroyed in the attack, so she ordered one of the guards to contact Vysender and then ordered a second guard to contact Yaylor Pi and ordered a third guard to kill the restrained Oaktobrons while the fourth guard continued to standby.

"But, Ma'am, do you not want the opportunity to interrogate them?" asked the third guard.

"No, they never speak," she said.

The guard then exited the house to execute his orders.

"Trouble seems to follow you around, Maerora Ma," Noma said, emerging from the hallway like a praying mantis clinging to the ceiling of a child's room.

"Yes, that's why I'm especially grateful for safe havens such as this," Maerora Ma retorted.

As I watched Maerora Ma bicker with her sister, a terrible pain in my shoulder began to pervade my upper arm. I remembered the moment when one of the Oaktobrons twisted my arm. The excessive dopamine in my body had masked the pain, but with a rapid return to normal levels, an unbearable soreness then surged. It was so bad that I started breathing deeply for relief.

"Captain Joan Jones, are you all right?" Maerora Ma asked.

"I'm in pain," I said.

"Noma, do you have anything for her," Maerora Ma asked.

"Just my truth serum," Noma said, smirking.

"Don't worry, Captain Joan Jones, the town's doctor will be here shortly," Maerora Ma said.

"Ma'am, Yaylor Pi is incommunicado," reported a guard.

"How can that be?" Maerora Ma mumbled.

A couple of Magentans entered the house and headed towards Maerora Ma. "Do you speak Earth English?" Maerora Ma asked the doctor.

"Little," the doctor answered.

"Please tend to this Earth woman," Maerora Ma said, gesturing towards me.

"Ma'am, I am little-full doctor, not big-full doctor," she said.

Maerora Ma then spoke to her in Magentan, and when she had finished, she turned to her sister and asked, "Since when have Oaktobrons been coming to town?"

"I don't know. I've never invited any into *my* house," Noma said.

"Ma'am, Vysender is sending a retrieval crew for us immediately," a guard reported.

Maerora Ma watched the doctor place my arm in a sling. "Is her arm broken?" she asked.

"This part," the doctor said pointing to her shoulder and explaining in English, "has unjoined joiners."

"I think you mean ligaments and tendons," Maerora Ma said.

"In Magentan, I can explain but not so well in Earth English," she said. "I gave her this chemical."

Maerora Ma examined the empty vile that was handed to her. "She's human. Can her biology handle this?" Maerora Ma asked.

"Magentans are human, and she is human," the doctor said. Maerora Ma returned the empty vile and stared at me watchfully until a guard started talking.

"I've never seen anyone kill with bare hands before," the guard said.

"What did you say?" Noma asked.

"She," the guard pointed to me, "killed an Oaktobron without a weapon."

Noma then looked at her sister.

"She saved my life," Maerora Ma said.

"So, it's interesting that you can kill without weapons," Noma said, looking at me. "That's an unusual skill."

THE CONTINGENT of twenty troops that Vysender sent marched us out of Morgana. We then loaded ourselves into a large military airship, which had parked on the small patch of tarmac next to the air vehicle that Maerora Ma and I had arrived in earlier. The ship extended well over the tarmac and dwarfed the little air vehicle. The pilot of the ship greeted Maerora Ma, and Maerora Ma asked her to take us to the ship's secured-communications room. The room was located directly behind the helm and had one wall that was made up entirely of electronic equipment. In the center of the room was a conference table. The rest of the room contained seating designed for VIPs, and the other three walls contained cabinets, shelves, and drawers.

Maerora Ma opened a cabinet, pulled out a pair of glasses, which were marked with her name, and slid them onto her face. "Send the ship's doctor here, please," Maerora Ma ordered the pilot.

"Ma'am, we have no doctor," the pilot said.

"What?"

"I'm sorry, Ma'am."

"All right, call a soldier in to monitor this Earth human. She's been injured," Maerora Ma said.

"Please, don't worry. I'll be fine," I said, feeling no pain.

"Do as I ask," Maerora Ma told the pilot, "then get us to headquarters immediately."

"Mǎlīn, I'm being called into headquarters," DeNitor said.

"What for?" she asked.

"I don't know, but it's at the highest level an emergency alert can be, which means our leader is in peril," he said

"My mother?" Mǎlīn asked.

"Yes."

"Oh, DeNitor," she said, dropping to the floor. "I wasn't prepared for this." He lifted her up and hugged her.

"My heart's pounding badly, DeNitor," she said. She stood and watched her hands begin to shake.

"You're having a panic attack. Here, lie down," he said, reaching to pull the bed covers. "I have to go, you know. Other personnel are very likely on their way to account for you. I'll do what I can to stay in touch, but it may be difficult."

"DeNitor, do you think she's dead?" Mălīn asked.

"I don't know. I've never seen this level of alert before."

"What if she's only maimed? What will we do?" she asked.

"Well, I suppose we've been quite horrible about contingency planning, haven't we? Look, Mălīn, I'd better get out of here, ok?" he said then kissed her and left.

Moments later, several military soldiers knocked on Mălīn's door, calling her name. Mălīn jumped up out of the bed and opened the door.

"Mălīn, we're here to ensure your safety. There's been an incident of attack, and you are at risk along with Katydid. Katydid is already secured. Come, follow us."

"Please can you tell me more details," Mălīn asked as she hurried along with the swift-moving set of troops.

"Ma'am, I've told you all I know."

"Is my mother ok?" she asked.

"We don't have any more details." The troops brought Mălīn to a room at the bottom of the house. Katydid was in the room and ran to Mălīn as soon as she saw her enter. Katydid cried, and Mălīn placed her hand on the little girl's shoulder.

"How long do we have to be here?" Mălīn asked.

"Until this structure is completely secured," the soldier answered.

"That will take hours," Mălīn mumbled. "Are you securing the surrounding grounds too?" she asked.

"Of course."

"I left my glasses in my room. It's important that I communicate with my mother. I must have my glasses right away."

"Security first, and then we'll retrieve your glasses."

"No! I must have them now!" Mălīn screamed. "I'll have my mother banish you so fast if you don't get those glasses for me now."

"Mălīn, security supersedes all else. You'll have to wait."

"Ok, now, listen to me, please. I have two Magentan animals in the Earth garden. Please communicate with the surveilling crew that they are my personal pets, and they mustn't be approached, or else they'll be frightened. Can you at least do that for me, please?" Mălīn asked.

"Will do."

THE AIRSHIP was swiftly en route to its destination, which was headquarters, and I wasn't certain how far away it was or how long it would take us to get there. A young, dozy Magentan soldier was seated across from me. He stared at me for a while until he started nodding off. I closed my eyes to rest and listened to Maerora Ma officiate through her glasses as she sat at the conference table in the middle of the room.

"Vysender, please order a realm-wide report of Oaktobron incidences. I'd ask Yaylor Pi, but it seems he's incommunicado at the moment," Maerora Ma said. "I'm also receiving no answer when I call Mălīn. I'm assuming she has become separated from her pan-omni glasses."

Maerora Ma's demeanor was calm, and her steady voice was making me feel sleepy.

"Once I arrive at headquarters, we'll work on a plan to determine whether or not Roble had prior knowledge of this attack. It could be he's just failed to control his discontented Oaktobrons. Either way we need to know . . . ."

As I listened to Maerora Ma speak, her voice was coming through increasingly muffled. She might have been covering her mouth, trying to keep her voice low so I could sleep.

"Vysender, you need to be evasive with him. I want him to believe I'm incapacitated, but you must behave as if you are rigorously covering up that I am. This will prolong his communication with us and give us a chance to read him," she said.

"It's cold in here," I told the tending Magentan soldier, who slowly awoke with the sound of my voice.

"Did you say something?" he asked.

"It's cold. Do you think there are blankets in the cabinets over there?"

"It's not cold in here, but if you want a blanket, I'll get one for you," he said and then clumsily rummaged through the cabinets for a blanket.

"What're looking for?" Maerora Ma asked.

"A blanket."

"Those are always kept in the hallway supply closets of military ships, *soldier*!" Maerora Ma said irritably. Her voice sounded far away. I thought about looking to see if she had relocated herself from where she was at the conference table, but my mind had started to replay scenes of old, and I was captivated by them. I watched the moment I gave birth to Butterfly, and the time when I graduated from college, and my first day at boot camp, and then more recent scenes appeared in my vision. I saw Maerora Ma touching me in the meadow and Noma surprised to see her sister turn gold when she touched me. I heard Maerora Ma say, "It's not cold. She's going into shock," and then her voice became louder, and I could hear her calling my name, and I fought like mad to open and focus my eyes and . . . .

"Captain Joan Jones, can you hear me?" Maerora Ma shouted. "Stay with me, Captain Joan Jones. C'mon . . . ." Maerora Ma shook Captain Joan Jones, but there was no response, so she called Bonson through her glasses at the highest-level of priority.

"Yes, Ma'am," Bonson answered.

"Captain Joan Jones is unconscious. She received a dose of painkiller a little while ago, and I think she's had a reaction.

What can I do?"

"Get to the nearest hospital *immediately*."

Maerora Ma raced to the airship's helm and ordered the pilot to land at the closest hospital.

"We're too big to land, Ma'am. We can only land at headquarters, a base, or atop your home," she said.

"Have an air ambulance intercept us. Captain Joan Jones mustn't die."

CHAPTER 7:
MATRI

AFTER CAPTAIN JOAN JONES had been transported from the military airship, Bonson and his team stabilized her condition, but she remained unconscious. Bonson tended to her in the same hospital she had been in before and in the same room where the large rapid-healing machine was still in place.

"Maerora Ma, we've done everything we did before and more, but she hasn't regained consciousness. Perhaps with more rest, she'll pull through," Bonson said, staring into a camera ball.

"No, we're not going to leave this to chance. We're going to do something about it. The rapid-healing machine is still there, isn't it?" Maerora Ma asked while seated at her headquarters console.

"It's still here, but I don't know how to use it myself, and I don't know what the ramifications would be if we were to use it on an unconscious patient," he said.

"Figure it out," she ordered.

"Ma'am, if only my Oaktobron were as good as my Earth English," he said.

"Dammit! You should be prepared for misfortune's contingencies, not reacting to them like some hopeless ignoramus throwing his helpless hands in the air." She terminated the call and then turned to Vysender. "And what're you going to do about the threat of malcontented Oaktobrons running around loose, Vysender?"

"Are you suggesting rounding them all up?" Vysender asked.

"I'm asking *you*," she said.

"One incident does not total anarchy make, Ma'am," he said.

"Is that what you think?"

"Well, yes, Maerora Ma," he said.

"Do you know what I think?"

"Not exactly, no," he said.

"I think the military leader of the realm needs to ready up his strategies and tactics and most of all his armed-forces management."

"Maerora Ma, we can't rush into war over this," Vysender said.

"Who said anything about war? I just want to be able to step onto a full-service military airship and know there's a doctor aboard just in case I'm ever physically attacked again," she said, glaring at him.

"Mama! Mama!" Maerora Ma's two daughters then appeared, rushing to hug their mother.

"What happened, Mama? Did Captain Joan Jones try to kill you?" Mălīn asked.

Maerora Ma heartily embraced her two daughters and then turned to Vysender. "We'll resume our meeting exactly five hours from now." She lifted Katydid and kissed her twice on each cheek. "I apologize for the harsh words, Vysender. Thank you for having my daughters safely brought to me." She then descended with her daughters to the dwelling below.

"Mama, please tell me everything that happened," Mălīn demanded.

"Mălīn, I'm tired. It's so late. I'll tell you after I've rested," Maerora Ma said as she started to undress for bed.

"Hah! You have bruises! Did Captain Joan Jones do that?" Mălīn asked.

"Why do you keep accusing Captain Joan Jones of attacking me? She saved my life, Mălīn," Maerora Ma said and then turned to Katydid. "Katydid, do you want to sleep with Mama tonight?"

Though the little girl appeared sleepy, she expressed glee at the idea of sleeping in her mother's bed.

"Mălīn, you can sleep in my bed too if you wish. I missed you while I was away."

Maerora Ma stared adoringly at Katydid, and as she watched her small daughter sleep, her brain pumped the day's events through her mind's eye. She turned on her side away from her daughter then soon tossed back to face her again, and having failed to fall asleep, she grabbed her glasses and walked out to the dwelling's large balcony.

The dying star hovered over headquarters and could be seen through every window. She reclined into a lounge chair and checked Captain Joan Jones' vital statistics through her glasses. There had been no change in her status. Maerora Ma then called Yaylor Pi but received a notification that his pan-omni glasses were not registered as on.

"Mama, what're you doing?" Mălīn asked in a groggy, whiny voice.

"Oh, gosh, Mălīn, you startled me."

"Mama, do you remember when I asked you to banish the spy girl and her mother?"

"Yes."

"Well, did you do it?" Mălīn asked, standing over her mother.

"Mălīn, don't bother me with that right now," Maerora Ma said.

"Oh-no, you didn't do it."

"Don't worry about it. If DeNitor is the one you want to have your firstborn daughter with, then I'm fine with it. You don't have to hide it anymore."

"Mama, that's not the problem. The problem is that spies are not to be tolerated, especially spies who live in our very own home," Mălīn said, emphasizing her remark with a single stomp of her foot.

"I'll take care of it when I see fit. Don't you know I have more important concerns at the moment?"

"I know you do," Mălīn said, surrendering her topic and

pulling up a lounge chair beside her mother. "Please tell me who hurt you."

"We were ambushed by Oaktobrons in Morgana," Maerora Ma said.

"Whoa."

"There were six of them. They attacked us all at once."

"At least you had guards with you," Mălīn said.

"Yes, but it was Captain Joan Jones who actually saved my life. She took on two Oaktobrons and killed the very one that was attacking me. She did it with her bare hands . . . broke his neck, just like that," Maerora Ma demonstrated.

"Wow, where *is* Captain Joan Jones?" Mălīn asked.

"In the hospital. She's comatose."

"Is she going to live?"

"I don't know."

"I can't believe there were Oaktobrons in Morgana. Why'd they attack you, Mama?"

"I don't know."

"Well, Mama, I might know, but don't get mad at how I know."

"What're you talking about?" Maerora Ma asked.

"DeNitor told me about the free press the Oaktobrons have, and he said there was news of Oaktobrons demonstrating outrage over the death of two technicians who had visited Magenta—"

"What?"

"Mama, why don't you know this?" Mălīn asked.

"I haven't received my daily reports since Yaylor Pi's been away, plus I've been occupied with Captain Joan Jones." Maerora Ma then accessed the Oaktobron free press through her glasses, and as she pored over all the information, Mălīn watched her mother frown and grimace.

"Mama, can you tell me how the Oaktobron technicians *really* died?"

"They died in an air-vehicle accident."

"But was it fixed like they claim?" Mălīn asked.

"It was an accident," Maerora Ma said, removing her glasses

and flinging them away so that they'd be out of her own reach. "I'm going back to bed now. I have to meet Vysender in a couple of hours."

"Wait, Mama, I want to talk with you more."

"Mălīn, I need to have at least *some* sleep."

"I know you do, but I want to hear more about your trip to Morgana," Mălīn said.

"It was awful. You wouldn't believe the perverse thing Noma has done."

"Tell me, Mama. Tell me."

"She has a room full of life-like sculptures of all our family members who have died. It's so horrible. I can't continue to think about it," Maerora Ma said.

"Really?"

"Yes, and I was mortified that Captain Joan Jones had to see it. I'll tell you that Noma is as crazy as a cracker," Maerora Ma said, and they both laughed.

"How many sculptures were there?"

"Plenty."

"Was there one of my father?"

"Yes."

"Was there one there of my sister?"

"Yes."

"What did it look like, Mama?"

"It looked like Morgana . . . like she was there in the room . . . ." Tears started to roll down Maerora Ma's cheeks. "I looked into her eyes . . . ." Maerora Ma then began to weep significantly.

"Oh, Mama, be strong. Be strong and don't think about it."

"Mălīn, don't say that anymore." Maerora Ma said, congested from crying.

"Say what?"

"'Be strong.' It's flippant and dismissive. Don't you know it takes more strength to *feel* your feelings rather than to just suppress them and deny them until they come out all evil and abnormal?" Maerora Ma said. "Mălīn, you're an adult now.

You should be exhibiting more maturity."

"Ok, go ahead and cry, yell, scream! I'll sit here and take it like a mature old woman," Mălĭn said.

"You're as petulant as an Oaktobron," Maerora Ma said.

"Well, I can't help it. I'm a product of my environment."

"I'm sorry, Mălĭn. I don't want to bicker with you," Maerora Ma said, holding her hand out to her daughter, but Mălĭn remained still. "I've been harsh—"

"Mama, I don't care. I don't want to talk about it," Mălĭn interrupted.

"All right, but let me just say that I know Morgana was your loss too—"

"Augh!" Mălĭn sounded.

"Mălĭn, listen to me. I feel ashamed of myself for all the terrible acts I committed when Morgana was killed—"

"Please, Mama, it doesn't matter at this point," Mălĭn said.

"No, Mălĭn, it will always matter, but listen to me. I just want to tell you that I was too paralyzed by my grief, and as a result, I neglected you. Poor baby, you lost Morgana too, and I failed to help you through it. I know you've been brave, and inside your soul you've been able to deburr all the rough edges of grief and loss, and on the outside you're a good girl, and it shows, and you're a good daughter, and I love you so very much," Maerora Ma said, moving to kiss Mălĭn on the forehead.

"I'm not so good, Mama," Mălĭn said.

"You're one hundred thousand times better than I am, Mălĭn."

"No, Mama, you should know . . . ."

"Know what, daughter?"

"An awful image plays in my head," Mălĭn said.

"Tell me," Maerora Ma said, holding Mălĭn's hand.

"I can never get rid of it to this day," Mălĭn said, retrieving her hand from her mother. "It makes me cringe each time I see it. It's you, Mama, and I hate it." Mălĭn covered her eyes with her hands.

"Tell me more," Maerora Ma said.

"The day Morgana died, they had to sedate you many times, and each time when you awoke and realized what had happened, you bayed like a wild animal. It was a horrible sound," Mălin said.

"I'm sorry, Mălin. You and the baby should have been sent to Noma's home to be taken care of."

"At first, it was just a frightening sight and sound in my head, and I had hoped it would go away, but then it transformed into a despised thing, and it made me hate you. It *makes* me hate you."

"Oh, daughter," Maerora Ma said.

"And I've hated myself for hating you, and all the hate has had its way with me," Mălin said.

"It's ok to hate me. You can hate me. I'd rather you hate me anyway. I just wouldn't want you to be indifferent towards me because indifference is the true opposite of love. Hate isn't."

"Oh, Mama, don't you know how evil and dangerous hate is?" Mălin said.

"I know it well. You're not unaware of all that I have done."

"I know, but you acted out of rage and despair in an instant too swift for thought to have stopped you, but those who hate calculate and have plenty of time to convince themselves to be good," Mălin said.

"Mălin, you're my daughter, and I love you," Maerora Ma said. "Don't get carried away with this notion of hate." Maerora Ma placed Mălin's hand between her own hands and leaned into her. "If you squirm when I touch you, it's not because you're a bad daughter. It's because I hurt you. If you feel hate towards me, it's not because you're evil. It's because I hurt you, and I'm sorry for hurting you."

The two sat in silence for a moment and stared at the dying star.

"Mălin, I realize that you've been living in the dark shadows of Morgana's death, and even when she was alive, I gave her extra-special attention that was probably detrimental to you in some way. She was my direct heir after all, but let us move on now. You're my heir, and I must prepare you to lead. I have a project for you. Do you want to accept it?"

"Yes."

"Good. I'm giving you carte blanche to deliver to me the facts about Yaylor Pi's whereabouts."

"What do you mean his whereabouts?" Mălīn asked.

"I haven't seen or heard from Yaylor Pi, nor has anyone else, since before the banquet we held for Captain Joan Jones."

"Well, where do you think he is?" Mălīn asked.

"I don't know. It's for you to find out. You need only to answer to me, and you must keep this project private between you and me only, which means DeNitor must not be involved in any way. Don't ask him questions. Don't change your behavior around him. Don't reveal anything to him. I will unobstruct any obstacle you may come across."

"Good morning, Ma'am," Vysender said as Maerora Ma ambled up from the dwelling below, looking haggard from exhaustion. "Did you rest well, Ma'am?"

"Do you aspire to be a comedian, Vysender?" Maerora Ma said, setting herself at her console across from Vysender. "Why didn't you inform me of the riots on Oaktobron?"

"I'm unaware of any news out of Oaktobron. Yaylor Pi's reports have not been forthcoming. Is he expected to return soon?" Vysender asked.

"I don't know," she said.

"Well, what's happened to him?"

"*I don't know*," she said impatiently.

"Well, we'll need to make arrangements for his daily tasks to be completed," Vysender said.

"I want DeNitor to assume some of his duties. Start him on report management right away. I already have Mălīn involved in assisting me, so please expect her increasing presence. She'll need high-level access to everything, and please broadcast these personnel changes to all headquarters staff."

"Yes, Ma'am, by the way, I have the report of realm-wide

Oaktobron incidences plus another report for you. It's the one we generated upon securing your home after we were alerted of the attack in Morgana. There's nothing concerning in it whatsoever, and I only included it to ease your mind for when you return home."

"Thank you, Vysender."

"About medical staff aboard the airship . . . ." Vysender said and then paused to breathe deeply.

"What is it?"

"You should be aware that Magenta has many fine medical healers. There's no shortage of them at all. However, most of them are reluctant to work at the higher echelons of the military for fear they may put themselves at peril if they should disappoint you," Vysender said.

"Humph, I see. It's my fault there were no doctors aboard, eh?"

"Well, Ma'am—"

"Vysender, just competently—or as competently as you can—lead the armed forces, and I will overlook the bungled medical-staff situation. Now, let's discuss Roble. The six Oaktobrons who attacked us in Morgana were probably avenging the deaths of the technicians, which means Roble is just an utter failure at controlling his discontented malcontents."

"So, you don't think he had prior knowledge of the attack?" Vysender asked.

"I don't know."

"Well, we ought to find out. I have a team available at a moment's notice to communicate with Roble."

"Let us proceed then," she said.

"DeNitor, we need to make a sea change," Mălīn said, speaking to a camera ball from within her bedroom in the headquarters dwelling.

"What do you mean?" DeNitor asked.

"Well, first of all, my mother has approved of you as father to my firstborn daughter. We don't have to sneak anymore."

"That's wonderful. When can we consummate?" he asked.

"Oh, DeNitor, anytime, but listen to me. We have to get rid of the Earth males and Captain Joan Jones."

"What?"

"I beg of you not to give me trouble on this," she said, and then she heard a banging sound through her glasses. "What're you doing?"

"I'm trying to fix my glasses. I don't think you're coming through clearly," he said, "because I hear the sound of betrayal, and it doesn't sound right."

"Please tell me how to reverse a volcano," she said.

"The only thing that can stop a volcano is total annihilation of the mountain," he said.

"I just want to halt the momentum of our hate," she said.

"I don't hate anybody."

"That's right; you don't, so why would you want to kill my mother?"

"Oh, Mălīn . . . ," he uttered.

"You don't know why, do you?" she asked.

"Mălīn," he snarled, "What about your father? What did he die for?"

"Just explain to me why we're doing this," she said.

"Do you have amnesia or what? We're going to stop the Oaktobrons from taking over, and we're going to explore the third realm, and we're going to rule Magenta and preside over the realm too—you and me together."

"No, DeNitor," she said.

"What has gotten into you?" he asked.

"I don't know . . . maybe love or maybe logic, but I can't kill my mother, and I won't kill her either because it's wrong to kill her for all the reasons we wanted to."

"I won't let you get away with this, and you won't be able to get out from under it," he said.

"Not unless I annihilate the mountain."

"You'll need an army for that," he said.

"DeNitor, I may very well be pregnant with your child. I don't know if I am, but I certainly took in a lot of your semen. So, if holding on to the heinous plan to kill my mother is what you want to do, then your child will never know you."

"Is that the best you can do, Mălīn?"

"Humph," she snorted. "You're right. It's pathetic to believe a volcano would cease its fatal flow for a baby. I'll be back with that army," she said.

IN THE SECURE-COMMUNICATIONS ROOM around the corner from Maerora Ma's station at headquarters, a panel of psychological experts sat in a circle along with Vysender and Maerora Ma. Data images from Vysender's pan-omni glasses were patched through to all present in the room. The experts were instructed to analyze Roble, the leader of Oaktobron, and to provide an immediate summary of his truthfulness.

"Is everyone ready?" Maerora Ma asked and all affirmed. "Good, please begin, Vysender."

Vysender contemplated instructions into his glasses. The official Oaktobron emblem of the office of the leader appeared and then was followed by a click and a tap and Quercus' face.

"It is Vysender I see," Quercus said.

"Yes, you're correct. I am requesting formal communication with Roble," Vysender said.

"Roble speaks only to supreme leaders, which in your case, as far as we know, is Maerora Ma. Nevertheless, if Maerora Ma is unavailable, you may speak to me, and I will happily convey your message."

Vysender paused and waited for instructions from Maerora Ma. She sent him a text-based instruction to proceed to talk to Quercus.

"Very well, Quercus, please inform Roble that the Magentan armed forces have terminated the lives of six visiting Oaktobrons, and we request instructions for their return to

Oaktobron. Furthermore, in the interest of preventing a re-occurrence, we wish to discuss with Roble the cause that led to the event of these necessary terminations."

"Roble will most definitely be involved in this matter; however, he will only speak to your supreme leader. Do you not have one available?"

"There is only one. You seem to believe otherwise," Vysender said.

Quercus shrugged.

"What are you instructions for the bodies?"

"We will arrange for a transport vessel to retrieve them," Quercus said.

"No, we prefer to ship the bodies out of Magenta and will agree to bring them clear into Oaktobron or deliver them to any one of numerous stations between Magenta and Oaktobron. Your choice, Quercus."

"Bring them along during Maerora Ma's upcoming visit, which is just a few days away now."

"In light of circumstances, we are considering the cancellation of Maerora Ma's trip."

"Interesting . . . . Would you care to shed some of that light?" Quercus asked.

"Uh, let's see, as I understand it, you function as the technology leader of Oaktobron, and I believe there will be some shortcomings in that office with regards to the nature of our needs. It is best if I speak to Roble."

"Maerora Ma herself may contact Roble at any time. At the moment, it is within my realm of responsibilities to confirm Maerora Ma's anticipated presence at our technology summit celebration. Will she attend or not?"

"Until we can resolve the issues that led to the termination of the six aforementioned Oaktobrons, consider Maerora Ma's trip to Oaktobron as undecided."

"Maerora Ma has always openly accepted my calls. I will contact her myself," Quercus said.

"You know very well that Yaylor Pi filters all of Maerora Ma's communications. You'll only reach *him* when you call *her*."

Quercus paused, and his eyes shifted away. He then said, "Roble will speak to Yaylor Pi."

"Well, I do hope they will enjoy a light-hearted conversation because Yaylor Pi will naturally defer to me all discussion about the six Oaktobrons."

"This is nothing more than a battle of wits," Quercus said.

"Yes, and communication should never be this difficult," Vysender said.

"Maerora Ma herself ought to call back," Quercus said, terminating the conversation.

The psychological experts in the room glanced at each other as if searching for the right answer in the eyes of their peers. Maerora Ma stood up and prompted them for their summaries. One spoke in favor of the theory that Roble had prior knowledge of the attack and explained her conclusion by describing the cagey behavior of Quercus. Not a single fellow expert disagreed. Maerora Ma and Vysender then thanked them for their input, and they all exited the room.

"They don't know," Maerora Ma said.

"Perhaps, you're right, but I'm quite certain *I* know," Vysender said.

"What do you know?" she asked.

"The air-vehicle accident was not so accidental."

"Vysender, if the Oaktobrons intend on attacking me every time one of them gets into an accident—"

"It wasn't an accident."

Maerora Ma aimed a severe glare at Vysender. "Dust the cobwebs off the realm's fleets."

"Any unified military wiggling around at this point will be perceived as Draconian by the Oaktobrons," he warned.

"We mustn't be lax. Besides, if the realm's forces are in any shape ours are in, then my suggestion is a long-overdue necessity."

Vysender remained unmoved with his eyes fixed on Maerora Ma's eyes.

"Do it!"

He clenched his jaw and turned away from her.

Maerora Ma then moved towards the door. "I'm tired. I need to rest. Return here in a couple of hours." She then walked down to her residential dwelling where Katydid was receiving geography lessons from her governess.

"Mama!" Katydid said, running to hug her mother. Maerora Ma patted her on the head.

"You look so tired, Mama," Mălīn said, emerging from her bedroom.

"Come, along. We're going to go visit Captain Joan Jones," Maerora Ma said.

"Is she conscious now?" Mălīn asked.

"No, not yet."

"Well, why visit then? You should get some rest instead," Mălīn said.

"I don't want to go." Katydid said, siding with her big sister.

"We care about Captain Joan Jones, don't we?" Maerora Ma asked.

Mălīn shrugged, and then the three exited the dwelling and made their way to the air-vehicle landing, which protruded from the side of the headquarters structure. A constant flow of air traffic departed and landed. A light breeze freshened the air, and the light of day brightly illuminated the airdrome. Two guards accompanied Maerora Ma and her daughters as they climbed into the air vehicle.

"Mama, can you ask the guards to go into the other section so we can talk about my special project?" Mălīn asked, but Maerora Ma had already fallen asleep. Mălīn then smiled sheepishly at the guards and asked, "You haven't seen Yaylor Pi around have you?"

"No, the last time we saw Yaylor Pi was when we were standing guard in front of Maerora Ma's room just after we brought her in from the Earth garden. She was suffering from magenta deprivation, and Yaylor Pi had gone in to check on her. He stayed for well over an hour and then left. Is he missing, Ma'am?"

"I wouldn't say he's missing, but, you know, it's a private matter, so, you know," she shrugged in gesture.

The rest of the ride took place in silence until Mălīn asked her mother to wake up, but Maerora Ma continued to sleep, and when the air vehicle landed, Katydid pulled her mother's arm in an effort to awaken her, and Mălīn tapped and rocked her a few times until she finally awoke.

The two daughters held their mother's hand all the way to the hospital room, and once they entered, Maerora Ma dropped their hands and hurried towards Captain Joan Jones. She reached to feel her forehead, and flecks of gold then raced up and down Maerora Ma's arms.

Mălīn gasped quietly when she observed the gold.

"How is she, Bonson?" Maerora Ma asked.

"The same, Ma'am."

"What about the machine?"

"We need the user manual or an expert operator. Plus, we cannot use the machine until the patient regains consciousness," Bonson said.

"Somehow I need to obtain an Oaktobron technician in the flesh," Maerora Ma said, gazing beyond Bonson. "Will you be able to bring her out of her coma?"

"It's dangerous, Ma'am, to prematurely bring her out of coma. After all, a coma is the gallant effort of the body to heal itself. It shuts down non-vital functions to re-focus the energy on healing. If we take her out too soon, she will not have benefited—"

"The machine will compensate for it," Maerora Ma interrupted.

"But there are inherent risks in reviving her prematurely, one of which is permanent brain damage."

"Won't the machine compensate for it?" Maerora Ma asked.

"I suppose," Bonson said, shrugging his shoulders. He then removed his glasses and looked at Maerora Ma. "Are you feeling all right?"

"I'm fine," she said. "Please, let me be alone with Captain

Joan Jones for a few minutes."

Bonson, Mălīn, and Katydid then left the room.

"Joan," she whispered, caressing Captain Joan Jones' cheek with the topside of her fingers. Gold streamed clear up to her shoulder, and she watched it glimmer and shine. "All this gold is love trying to make its way to my heart. It will fade if you fade, so please don't fade. Besides, you're the only one who can rescue my destiny. You're The Great Liaison, and together we're going to fulfill my grandmother's dream. Magentans will be reunited with their source, and *we* will have delivered it, Joan—you and me."

When Maerora Ma exited the room, the two guards on the outside of the door followed her down the hall to the sitting room of a nearby medical station where Bonson, Mălīn, and Katydid were waiting and staring into their pan-omni glasses.

"Bonson," Maerora Ma called.

"Yes, Ma'am."

"I have very important business to conduct . . . I haven't slept very much, and I need to be acutely alert for something I have to do. Can you administer a stimulant?"

"Oh, no, Mama, don't do that," Mălīn piped up, but no one responded to her.

Bonson nodded and gestured to Maerora Ma to follow him into a private room. Once in the room, he explained that he had to administer the stimulant intravenously, so Maerora Ma removed her top, and set herself on the room's bed. Bonson then inserted a tube into the vein of her arm.

"What would happen if we used this on Captain Joan Jones?" Maerora Ma asked.

"It is what we will use if we must, but it won't heal her torn ligaments or repair any brain damage that may result, but it can very well bring her out of the comatose state. And as for you, Maerora Ma, you will most definitely need to rest after the desired effect wears off, and since I'm the one administering it, you'll be under my direction. This is serious, Ma'am," he said, holding back on the release of the chemical.

"Go ahead, Bonson," she said, and he released the stimulant

into her bloodstream. "Please don't tell Vysender about this."

"I won't," he said.

MAERORA MA AND HER DAUGHTERS were once again on the air vehicle headed back to headquarters. Maerora Ma started reviewing the Oaktobron-incident report in her glasses while her two daughters entertained themselves with apps in their own glasses. Mălīn, however, kept a watchful eye on her mother.

"Mălīn, why do you keep watching me? It's bothersome," Maerora Ma said.

"I'm worried about the stimulant, Mama."

"I trust Bonson with my life. There's no need to worry."

"I saw the gold," Mălīn said.

"Gold happens. The fullest cloaks and the heaviest veils can't conceal it."

"I know, but what about you and me, Mama?"

"Mălīn, you're the heir to Magenta and the second realm and most likely the first realm. I assure you there is no time for the worry of jealousy. It's wasted energy."

"But you just became mine, and now I have to share you."

"This is not the confident sentiment of a leader, Mălīn."

Maerora Ma resumed reading her reports, and Mălīn looked out the window to see headquarters approaching.

"Mălīn?"

"Yes?"

"You'll feel better once we're home again."

"I like it at headquarters," Mălīn said.

"I have a report from Vysender that provides every last detail of how our home was cleared and secured after the attack in Morgana."

"What do you mean?"

"When the Oaktobrons attacked me, it was protocol for our home to be cleared and secured. You were there. They did an amazingly thorough job. I have the report. I'll send it to you. They even scanned the Earth garden," Maerora Ma said. "And now I know about the two pets you've been keeping."

"Pets?" Mălīn asked.

"Mălīn, there's no need to carry on with the cover up. Taking care of two pets in the garden is fine. You can show them to me when we go home, ok?" Maerora Ma said, smiling at her daughter.

MAERORA MA WAS STILL operating well within the time range of the stimulant when she tucked Katydid into bed after arriving at headquarters.

"Mama, why no Yaylor Pi?" Katydid asked.

"Didn't I tell you he was away on a trip?" Maerora Ma said. Katydid shook her head. "Why won't he answer my calls?"

"I don't know, baby. I don't have the answers to everything. Just kiss me goodnight and go to sleep." She then ascended to her headquarters station where Vysender was waiting and sitting across from her console.

"Did you review the report?" Vysender asked.

"Yes, evidently, the Oaktobrons have made inroads into Birchron and Pinovra. That's dismaying. We've been too Magenta centric," Maerora Ma said, setting herself at her console. "My mother used to warn me about Magentan contentment. She, herself, heartily travelled throughout the realm to prevent it."

"I know, Ma'am. It's why my predecessor was more well-travelled than I am," Vysender said.

"Magentans don't travel well," she said. "Do we have a patrolling fleet out and around Magenta?"

"No, Ma'am, it would be perceived as an insecure posture," Vysender said.

"I want my planet protected. Don't forget the Oaktobrons have new technology capable of ripping open the realm-barrier. I have no doubt they've adapted it to weaponry."

"With all due respect, Maerora Ma—"

"Dammit! Vysender, don't be a pacifist!"

"I'm not a pacifist. I'm trying to be a *smartifist*," he said, and the two then laughed.

"Please, place a stealth fleet around Magenta," she said.

"All right, Ma'am."

"We will call Roble again, but we'll continue to be evasive about my health. If he thinks I'm incapacitated, he may make a faulty move because of it. We need the planets of the realm to witness his aggression before we can garner their unquestionable support."

"Agreed," Vysender said.

"By the way, we need to renegotiate the guards."

"All is fine as is. Let's keep it that way," he said.

"Absolutely not! Captain Joan Jones saved my life. I don't need to be protected from her."

"Of course, I understand, but you need the extra protection against Oaktobrons now," he said.

"Only outside of headquarters and my home. I otherwise don't want them around."

"Acknowledged, Ma'am," he said.

"It's late, Vysender. I want you to go home and rest." Maerora Ma then received a call from Bonson and waved Vysender off. "What is it, Bonson? Has Captain Joan Jones regained consciousness?"

"No, Ma'am. I'm just checking in on my patient, the one named Maerora Ma," Bonson said.

"I'm fine . . . feeling great."

"Well, you won't be feeling great in just a little while. Please go to bed at the first sign of fatigue. The stimulant's effects drop quickly," Bonson warned.

"Yes, of course. Now, what about the machine?"

"Maerora Ma, I tried to make it clear that it is impossible for us to figure out how to operate the machine without a manual or without an expert. Can you provide us with one?"

"I'd have to sell my soul."

"Well, then, we'll have to leave Captain Joan Jones in the lurch."

"Oh, Bonson, can't you conjure a miracle?"

Bonson remained silent.

"Bonson?"

"Ma'am, you're in a far better position to do that than I am."

A WHILE LATER, Maerora Ma was still seated at her console and seemed to be in deep meditation with her eyes closed. When she opened her eyes, she appeared as if a newly invigorated will of determination had possessed her. She arose and strode over to the secure-communications room around the corner from her station. She entered the room and then applied a special high-security lock on the door. She sat at the desk in front of the official emblem of the office of the presider of the second realm and paused. She then took in a few deep breaths and called Roble. A few moments passed before Roble appeared.

"What in the world!" gasped Roble.

"Roble?"

"Do you know what time it is?" he asked.

"Well, if you'd have only cooperated with Vysender, I wouldn't have had to call you myself," Maerora Ma said.

"You're abusing the communication line," he said.

Like most Oaktobrons, Roble was burly, and as the leader of Oaktobron, there was no doubt in anyone's mind that he was highly motivated to appear as the superlative he-man. His muscles were huge masses of sweeping elliptical curves that only vanity itself could have manufactured. The eyes of others were often forced to roam his body out of sheer wonder; nevertheless, aesthetic perfection would never be his to claim because his teeth were exceptionally long, and despite the full beard he bore, the conspicuous columns in his mouth were inevitably noticed and always disrupted the beholder's ideal of perfection.

"Roble, we're experiencing a shortage of a precious resource here on Magenta, one that if completely depleted, will result in war."

"I'm unaware of any resource crisis on Magenta. What resource are you talking about?"

"We're growing short of *tolerance*, Roble, tolerance for Oaktobron insolence and dare I say *insubordination*."

"I had nothing to do with those Oaktobrons who attacked you. They were rebels."

"You are not absolved whatsoever of failure to control your dissidents," she said.

"The situation is precarious."

"Is that your argument?" she asked.

"There's no argument. It is what it is."

"For every action . . . Roble," she said.

"Go ahead, then, flick our foreheads."

"Your recalcitrance is consuming the tiny bit of tolerance I have left for your existence," she said.

"My existence is the fulcrum on which peace finds its delicate balance."

"Yes, and it is my dwindling tolerance that prevents a disproportionate force to tumble it down. Roble, how many more quips must we hurl out before we can reach the tender spot of negotiation?"

"Negotiation? What in the world do you want from me anyway?"

"I want . . . ." She paused and subtly grimaced.

"Come out with it!" Roble said.

"I want . . . I need . . . ."

"Oh, come on!"

"All right, Roble, I want you to control your malcontents, and I'm serious. This recent incident was far too treacherous for me to overlook. To declare impunity would be the equivalent of calling for more."

"Well, it's too bad you had to engage in the theatrics of repositioning your fleets. My response must be anything but acquiescent," he said.

"I demand a public apology."

"Oh, Maerora Ma, you shouldn't fuss too much. After all, I have eight dead Oaktobrons whereas you have one insulted queen," he said.

"*Assaulted*, Roble, the word is *assaulted*," Maerora Ma growled. Roble merely shrugged his huge shoulders.

"I'm feeling very exhausted right now, and I can barely put up with your lack of diplomatic aptitude, so let me tell you what I'm going to do." She paused and strained to breathe deeply. "I'm going to scour clean the entire realm of Oaktobrons and then stop off at your planet to wipe off the scum from my cleaning utensils. But first, Roble, I'm going to go take a nap, a simple and luxurious nap, and after I'm feeling nice and refreshed, I'm going to check for messages. You will then have had your chance to end Oaktobron defiance. Over and out."

Maerora Ma terminated the communication and shut her eyes. She then rested her head on the desk and immediately fell asleep.

Mălīn lay awake in her bed and lifted her head each time she heard a creek or squeak or other faint sound. She reached for her pan-omni glasses and checked her mother's location for the twelfth time, but her mother's locator had been turned off a couple of hours ago. Maerora Ma's last known location was at her station console. The count of Mălīn's repeated unanswered calls accumulated, and the rate of her fidgets increased to the point that she finally got up, dressed, and left the dwelling.

She wandered around her mother's station, touching each surface as if trying to divine a clue as to where her mother was. She leaned over an edge to look out into the greater area of the huge open hall. There were fewer Magentans on site at night, which diminished the continuous hum of the building's collective sounds. She sat in her mother's chair and spun around in it slowly. She looked up and out at the Magentan sky through the viewing planes. The dying star was below the horizon and not on display through the windows.

Mălīn then approached the private room across from her mother's console. The retracting door opened for her, and she peered in, but the room was vacant. She then walked around the corner to the next room, which was the secured-communications room. The door did not retract, so she contemplated instructions into her glasses to open it but to no avail. She then called her mother through her glasses, but it was one more unanswered call to add to the list.

She knocked on the door lightly and then increasingly harder, and then she slammed her fist against it. "Dammit!" she said aloud but nothing changed. She then leaned her back against the door and appeared to ponder until a faint expression of relief appeared on her face as she called the janitorial department.

"May I speak to the supervisor?"

"Yes, I-I'm the one in charge on th-this shift," answered a young male Magentan who had a speech defect.

"I need to enter the secured-communications room," she said.

"If your gla-glasses fail to let you in, I don't have th-the authority to let you in my-myself. I am sorry," he said.

"Did you not receive the memorandum about my new high-level clearance?"

"Yes, I di-did."

"All right then, can't you see that since my access is still being propagated through the system, I'm unable to open the secured-communications room and therefore need for you to let me in?"

"Hmm, I don't th-think so," he said.

"Well, I order you to come up here and discuss it with me," she said, and he agreed. As she waited for him, Mălīn spoke aloud towards the closed door. "Mama, I know you're in there. I hope you're ok."

The supervising janitor then arrived, and Mălīn gestured for him to open the door, but the janitor protested.

"I will have my mother award you with whatever you request if you open this door for me right now," Mălīn said.

"Mae-Maerora Ma will ban-banish me for accepting your bri-bribe."

"Dammit! I'm her daughter! Trust me!" Mălīn yelled.

"No, please un-understand—"

"*I* will have you banished if you don't open the door."

"Ta-take it easy," the janitor said.

"All right, I will. Now, listen to me. This is how it is: you can open the door and *maybe* make a mistake, or you can refuse to open the door and *for certain* it will have been a mistake. I've removed the bribe and my threat of banishment, but there's still a risk, and it's the risk of inaction. I cannot reveal anything more because this is highly confidential business."

"Ok, all right, I will o-open the door," he said.

"Now, listen. You mustn't tell anyone that you let me in, and I don't want you entering the room. Just turn away and go. I trust you," Mălīn said.

The janitor turned his back to the door and opened it with his pan-omni glasses and then walked away without turning back.

"Mama!" Mălīn ran to her mother. "Mama, wake up," she said, jerking her mother's body.

"Mălīn," Maerora Ma said, sounding groggy.

"Are you ok?" Mălīn asked.

"I'm all right," Maerora Ma said, laboring to breathe deeply. "Bonson warned me . . . I'd feel very tired," she said and then struggled for more air.

"Mama, why can't you breathe?"

"It's normal. Don't worry. Just help me up," Maerora Ma said.

Mălīn shouldered her mother out of the room.

"Let me rest a minute against the wall," Maerora Ma ordered, and the two then leaned against the wall.

"See, Mama, you shouldn't have taken a stimulant," Mălīn said.

"I needed to be alert for . . . ," Maerora Ma said.

"For what?"

"Business," Maerora Ma said.

Once the two made it back to the dwelling, Maerora Ma crawled into her bed. "Mălīn . . . ."

"What, Mama?"

"I won't be able to wake up easily for a while."

"I know," Mălīn said, standing over her mother.

"Vysender will panic if I'm unavailable to him, and . . . ." Maerora Ma paused to breathe and then appeared to have fallen asleep.

"Mama, what do you want me to do?" Mălīn shook her mother awake.

"What're you doing?" Maerora Ma asked.

"You were telling me something about Vysender."

"I don't want him to know about my condition. Stall anyone who wants to talk to me."

"Ok, all right, Mama," Mălīn answered and then set herself on the bed beside her mother, looking like a cygnet in the reverse role of protecting its mother.

A WHILE LATER, Mălīn received a call from DeNitor. "What in the world do you want?" she asked.

"I'm trying to contact your mother," DeNitor said.

"What for?"

"She's got me compiling reports for her, and I need to know if what I sent is what she was expecting."

"She's sleeping," Mălīn said.

"Well, Vysender's been trying to get a hold of her too."

"Fine, I'll call him," she said.

"Mălīn?"

"What?"

"We need to resolve our issues," DeNitor said.

"I'm way too busy figuring out how to demolish mountains at the moment," she said.

"You're going to have a lot problems on your hand, and two of them are in your mother's garden."

"They're just as much your problem as they are mine, DeNitor."

"Yeah, well, you're such a liar about everything, Mălīn. I read your home security report, and that woman and her spy-girl daughter are still alive and well. I'm going to figure out how to bring you down," he said and then turned off his pan-omni glasses.

Mălĭn grimaced and then cuddled into her mother. Maerora Ma's pan-omni glasses were continually ringing and clicking and buzzing, so Mălĭn set them to forward to her own glasses and instantly received a call from Vysender.

"My mother's not feeling very well and will call you later. Is there anything in particular you want me to tell her?"

"No, we just have a war to avert," he said.

"She'll be up soon," Mălĭn said and then received a call from Bonson.

"She's fine, Bonson. She's sleeping."

"Well, when she awakes, tell her I have good news for her."

"Tell me."

"Captain Joan Jones has emerged from her coma."

"How is she?"

"She's presenting with a normal recovery."

"Should I wake my mother and tell her?" Mălĭn asked.

"No, let Maerora Ma sleep."

She ended the call then turned to her mother. "Mama," she whispered, "Captain Joan Jones is awake."

Maerora Ma remained still, so still that Mălĭn checked to make sure she was breathing, and she was. Mălĭn then answered another call, but this one had a different indicator and was preceded by an Oaktobron emblem and required activation of a camera ball, so Mălĭn moved away from her mother and let the camera reveal her in front of a wall.

"What is this? Is a child answering?"

"I'm young, but I am not a child. I'm Mălĭn, Maerora Ma's daughter.

"Oh, how the mighty have fallen . . . to let a child play with the only communication line between warring nations," Roble muttered.

"Are we at war?"

"Did someone drop a hat? If so, then we are at war," the bearded, burly leader of Oaktobron said.

"Do you have a message for my mother?"

"I prefer to speak to Maerora Ma myself. Is she not available *again*?"

"She's busy."

"Is your mother not well, child?" he asked.

"She's fine."

"Well, here's my message then. Please deliver it to her in the imperative. The message is scour!"

"'Scour'?" Mălīn asked, and Roble just laughed ferociously and then terminated the call. "Oh, Mama, I wish you'd wake up," Mălīn said, petting her mother softly.

CHAPTER 8:
UNHARBORED

NOMA OPENED her front door after hearing someone knock on it. The fresh seaside air softly blew the stray strands of hair of the woman who stood before Noma.

"Noma, there's a dead body at the end of the pier right there," she said pointing out towards the water. "It's floating in the water, and I know who it is?"

"Who?"

"Yaylor Pi."

MURKY IMAGES shuffled through my mind while a dull sensation of pain loafed in my shoulder. I knew I was still on Magenta because when I opened my eyes, everything was some shade of magenta. I somehow believed I might have awoken from this nightmare in the comfort of my own home where Butterfly might be playing and all the colors in the spectrum of visible light would be displaying.

"Hello, Captain Joan Jones," Bonson said. "Are you able to speak now? You've been awake for a while. I know it takes time for all your memories to fill in, but if you can speak, please do so."

"I can speak," I answered and stared past Bonson at the rapid-healing machine.

"How do you feel? Do you feel any pain? Do you remember me?"

"A little pain in my shoulder," I answered.

"What's my name?"

"You are Bonson," I said

"Oh, joy!" He smiled and hugged and kissed me.

"What happened?" I asked.

"Do you remember when the Oaktobrons attacked you and Maerora Ma?"

"Vaguely," I answered.

"You were in a town called Morgana, and six Oaktobrons attacked you. You saved Maerora Ma's life, and then the local doctor gave you some painkiller. I didn't! I wouldn't have given you that painkiller, but anyway it caused you to go into a coma," he said and then paused and stared into his glasses. "I'm sorry to say you're shoulder is injured . . . severely torn ligaments."

"Can't you heal me like you did before?"

"We're trying," he said.

"Where's Maerora Ma?"

"She's at headquarters. You know, she sat right by your side. She came here to visit with her two daughters. She touched you so tenderly, like a mother. If she were divine, you'd have been healed miraculously then and there. Who knows, maybe her touch did bring you back," he said and then peered into his glasses. "Tell me, Captain Joan Jones, have you ever heard of the Midas touch?"

"It's a Greek myth about a king who touched things and made them turn to gold," I said.

"Yes, that's right. Well, you ought to know something about Magentan women that's sort of like Midas," he said.

"What do you mean?"

"Magentan women turn gold at the touch of a mate with whom they are deeply in love. It's a most beautiful phenomenon, and it was a true treasure to the eyes to have seen it right here," he said, smiling at me.

"MAMA, do you want to wake up now? Mălīn asked softly, gently nudging her mother. Maerora Ma stirred a little. "You've been sleeping for many hours. It's late in the day now. Don't you think you should get up?"

"Get me something to drink," Maerora Ma requested in a gravelly voice. Mălīn exited the bedroom and quickly returned with a glass of fluid.

"Mama, there's a lot going on," Mălīn said. "I'm not certain, but I think we're at war with the Oaktobrons. You'd better get with Vysender. I told him you were sick."

"I am. Leave the room. I'll be out in minute."

A WHILE LATER, Maerora Ma emerged from her bedroom. "Where's Katydid?" she asked.

"I told her governess to take her to play with her friends," Mălīn said. "Mama, Captain Joan Jones is out of her coma."

"Oh, what a relief. Is she ok?"

"I think so," Mălīn answered. "But, Mama, what about the war?"

"All right, I'll call Vysender right now. Where are my glasses?"

"In your room," Mălīn answered. Maerora Ma retrieved her glasses and immediately called Bonson. Mălīn stood in the doorway, watching her mother.

"Bonson, how is she?" Maerora Ma asked.

"She's doing very well," he said.

"Thank you, Bonson. Thank you so much. We're on our way."

"Mama, I talked to Roble," Mălīn said.

"Oh-no, you shouldn't have talked to him. What did you say?"

"I didn't say much, but he wanted me to tell you to scour," Mălīn said. "What does that mean?"

"Nothing," Maerora Ma said. "You mustn't tell Vysender you spoke to him. Can you please retrieve Katydid? We need to go see Captain Joan Jones"

"Mama, what about Vysender?"

"I'll call him on the way to the hospital. Hurry up and get Katydid."

As MAERORA MA STEPPED into the air vehicle, she received a call from Vysender. "Where are you headed off to?" he asked.

"Vysender, you don't need to track my movements. I'm going to the hospital—"

"Are you that sick?"

"No, if you'd let me finish . . . I'm going to see Captain Joan Jones."

"Well, with all due respect, Ma'am, let me remind you that we have a war to avert."

"What has been Roble's response to our fleet movements?" she asked.

"We've observed multiple, simultaneous communications going out to all planets from Oaktobron," he said.

"Oh-no," she uttered.

"Their infiltration seems more extensive than we had anticipated," he said.

"What are planet leaders relaying to you?"

"If what they are telling me is not mere lip service, then I believe they're aligned with us."

"Good," Maerora Ma said. "Give me a couple of hours."

Vysender then sighed impatiently, and Maerora Ma assured him she'd be back soon. When the conversation ended, Maerora Ma turned to Mălīn. "Mălīn, please get me something to drink."

"All right, Mama, but you should know that Katydid stomped and screamed and acted like a wild animal when I asked her to come with us, and it was very embarrassing. I know you're busy with far more important issues, but I can't deal with that," she said, pointing at Katydid. Mălīn then exited the section.

"Come here, Katydid. Come sit on my lap," Maerora Ma said. The little girl happily set herself atop her mother's lap, and Maerora Ma kissed her on top of the head and wrapped her arms around her. "Be a good girl, Katydid. Can you be a good girl for me?"

Mălīn then returned with a glass of fluid and handed it to her mother.

"Thank you, Mălīn. Tell me your progress on Yaylor Pi."

"His last—"

"Mama? Mama?" Katydid interrupted and pinched her mother's arm.

"Ouch! Katydid!" Maerora Ma said, glaring at the little girl admonishingly.

"Yaylor Pi, Mama. I want to talk to him too" Katydid said.

"I'm not talking *to* Yaylor Pi. I'm talking *about* him. Now, why don't you go to the other section for me while I talk to Mălīn."

"No!"

"See how she is, Mama?" Mălīn said.

"Why won't you do as I ask, Katydid?"

"I want to talk to Yaylor Pi," she said.

"I know, baby, but Yaylor Pi is away, and I need to talk to Mălīn about business, so please go to the other section for me."

"Mălīn has to go too then," Katydid said.

"No, Katydid, Mălīn is an adult, and she's helping me. Please do as I ask, and go to the other section."

Katydid pouted and then stomped her way into the second section.

"Go ahead, Mălīn, tell me your progress."

"His last pan-omni communication was with a headquarters worker who provides report data, so I asked the worker about her discussion with him, and she told me he asked for the most current data regarding Oaktobron-citizen contentment," Mălīn said.

"That sounds routine. He was planning our trip to Oaktobron. Anything else?" Maerora Ma asked.

"He was last seen exiting your room a few hours before the banquet."

"Well, Mălīn, that's not much information. Is that all you have? Where did he go after he left my room?"

"He's off the radar at that point," Mălīn said. "What did he say to you before he left your room?"

"I don't know," Maerora Ma answered.

"Can't you remember, Mama?"

"All right, Mălīn, he was upset with me."

"Why?"

"I don't know."

"Mama, please try to remember. It might help me."

"He was disturbed because I didn't turn gold for him," Maerora Ma said.

"Oh . . . well, how upset was he?"

"Maybe more than I realized at the time."

"Did he cry?"

"No."

"How come you didn't turn gold," Mălīn asked.

"Love doesn't last forever, Mălīn."

"Did he say where he was going?"

"No, he asked if he could be excused from having to attend the banquet."

"Do you think Oaktobrons abducted him?"

"It's highly possible," Maerora Ma said, reaching for Mălīn's hand. "You know, Mălīn, maybe it's too dangerous for you to continue this project."

"No, no, Mama, nothing's going to happen to me. I'm conducting my investigation from within headquarters."

"You haven't told DeNitor anything, have you?" Maerora Ma asked.

"No, not at all."

THE DOOR OF MY ROOM retracted, and Maerora Ma rushed in with her two daughters.

"Joan," Maerora Ma called.

"Mama!" Mălīn said in an admonishing tone.

"*Captain* Joan Jones, I'm so happy you're awake." Maerora Ma picked up my hand, and golden fireworks flashed all over at the point of contact.

Katydid tugged at her mother, and Mălīn then lifted her onto my bed but held her back from climbing onto me. An unexpected

feeling of joy—the joy of inclusion and of family and of love—
flooded my conscience, and I smiled with one of those smiles that
seem to be attached to the tissue of the heart and the tear ducts of
the eyes.

"Mama, she frying," Katydid said.

"Crying," Mălīn corrected.

"Are you fully recovered? Do you have all your memories?" Maerora Ma asked, holding the side of my face in her
hand. She was in her Mao-like suit, but this one was darker
than the one she had worn before, and the insignia on her
collar were larger and appeared to have a more martial theme.

"Yes, I think so," I said.

"Can you walk? What about your shoulder? Does it hurt?"

"Yes, it hurts a little," I said.

"Bonson, what's next? Can she return home?" Maerora asked.

"Her shoulder is showing permanent and irreparable damage," Bonson said.

"What do you mean, Bonson?" I asked.

"You will have limited range, limited strength, and limited
use," he said.

"No," I said.

"Relax, Captain Joan Jones, you will not suffer this. We'll
have you back in the machine soon," Maerora Ma said, grasping
my forearm and holding it tightly.

"Were you able to obtain the user manual, Ma'am?" Bonson
asked.

"I *will*," Maerora Ma said and then asked the others to leave
the room.

Once they left, she stood over me and smiled. She surveyed
the equipment and accessories surrounding my bed, and then
poured liquid into a glass and handed it to me. "Here, drink
more fluids if you can."

I sipped from the glass and then set it down.

"Joan," she said, "I'm so glad it was you . . . that *you* were the
one to come to Magenta." She picked up my hand and kissed it,
and gold glowed brightly under her skin. "I'm so indebted to

you for saving my life in Morgana." She sat quietly, holding my hand and watching the gold.

"Why did the Oaktobrons attack us?" I asked.

"I don't know. Their leader has always felt entitled to presiding over the realm and resents me tremendously for being the one who does so."

"There's always someone vying for power no matter who is seated on the throne. It seems it comes with the territory, doesn't it?"

"Yes, it comes with the territory," she said reflectively. "I'm sorry your shoulder was injured." She stood and stretched over me to check the tautness of my sling, and I studied the symbols on her collar.

When she sat down again, I offered her my hand to hold, and gold sparkled brightly.

"I wish they hadn't attacked us in Morgana. It's such a distraction for me when all I truly want to do is work with you to unite the realms," she said. "And naturally I can't let it go unavenged. It was just too brazenly treacherous. If I were to let it pass, it would be the same as promoting it as a tutorial on how to get away with attacking the ruler of the realm."

I didn't disagree with her despite that I thought maybe that line of thinking would result in endless retaliation and seemingly juvenile tit-for-tat responses, but wasn't that the world we lived in anyway? Well, on Earth it is. At what point would turning the other cheek ever be right? I then wondered what she had thought when she ordered the attack on Earth. What sort of logic had she applied then? Consequently, a bad feeling released itself in me, and I withdrew from holding her hand.

"Are you ok, Joan?" she asked.

"I'm fine . . . just feeling tired I guess," I said.

"I should let you rest then. I'll return soon. Please remain positive. I won't let you suffer any permanent damage as long as it is in my power to do so because you're indispensible. You're The Great Liaison."

She then sustained her gaze on my eyes. Perhaps she wanted

to study again the unique shade of magenta she saw in them, or perhaps it was something else. I didn't want to dislike her in anyway. The reality of her position and power was actually very reassuring to me, and I had faith in her. I knew I wouldn't suffer this shoulder injury for long. I wanted to dream about the future, a future with Butterfly in it. Maerora Ma was invincible, and there wasn't anything insurmountable for her. Oh, how the appeal of being the liaison between Earth and Magenta stirred optimistically in me. Liaising would be a far better career than killing.

Vysender and Maerora Ma pored over feedback and intelligence provided to them by headquarters staff. The intelligence data included all recent news throughout the realm. Mălīn separately sleuthed for clues about Yaylor Pi's whereabouts. The three were each parked at Maerora Ma's station and stared intently into their pan-omni glasses. The evening had turned to night since Maerora Ma and her daughters had returned from the hospital. Maerora Ma had put Katydid to bed a while earlier.

"The official outgoing message from Oaktobron is to 'assertively protect Oaktobrons because a call for a mass abduction of Oaktobrons has been made,'" Vysender said.

Maerora Ma subtly grimaced.

"It looks as if they're stirring it up, for there's been no call to round up Oaktobrons from us," Vysender concluded.

Mălīn studied her mother's response.

"Vysender, have your team draw up a series of recommendations. Include all options, and present them to me within twenty-four hours."

"Ma'am, I advise we allow more time for a thorough consideration of options."

"No, Vysender, time fosters the opposition's advantage."

"Ma'am," he protested.

"Vysender, you know better than I about the effectiveness of swiftness. Delay is disaster."

"All right," he said, exhaling excessively.

"Also, Vysender, I hereby order a realm-wide injunction against any further communication with high-level Oaktobrons. All direct communication must be intercepted and discontinued on the spot. Restrict access to all communications rooms here at headquarters and throughout Magenta so that access is limited to me and only me," Maerora Ma ordered.

Vysender nodded and semi-bowed in acknowledgement and then appeared to carry out the order. Mălīn gazed at her mother as if to assess her intentions.

DeNitor then entered the station, and all three heads swiftly turned to him.

Maerora Ma stood to greet and hug him. "DeNitor, I've been wanting to welcome you into the family. I'm so sorry that I've been too busy to have had the decency to welcome you."

Mălīn glared at DeNitor, and it did not go unnoticed by Maerora Ma.

"What brings you here at this hour, DeNitor?" Maerora Ma asked. "Oh, forgive my silly question. You've come to see Mălīn no doubt."

"No, actually, I wanted to talk to you, Ma'am," DeNitor said.

"About what?" Maerora Ma asked.

"About Mălīn and me," he said.

"DeNitor!" Mălīn shouted.

"What's going on?" Maerora Ma asked.

"Can you please order your daughter to touch my arm?"

"No, DeNitor, I don't resolve lovers' quarrels. I only advise that you refrain from embarrassing your partner especially in front of her mother and your superior officer," Maerora Ma said.

"We're beyond quarreling, Ma'am, and we are not partners. I've come to demonstrate that Mălīn does not love me and there-fore should not deliver a child that comes not from love."

"Mălīn, are you pregnant?" Maerora Ma asked.

"I don't know if I am," Mălīn answered.

Maerora Ma then paused to size up DeNitor. "Well, DeNitor, in your effort to make a child with my daughter, she was, no doubt, in love with you. In any case, she is free to continue with the pregnancy or abort it as she sees fit."

"Oh, Mama, I'm sorry about this. I didn't know this soldier was such a horrible little boy," Mălīn said. "I don't think it's good for him to walk about freely bearing so much hate in his head for me."

"Vysender, deal with your solider please," Maerora Ma ordered.

"I have something to disclose," DeNitor said.

"Shut your mouth, DeNitor," Mălīn shouted like a child.

"Vysender!" Maerora Ma barked and then exited the station. Mălīn followed her mother down to the residential dwelling.

"Did you tell him about Yaylor Pi?" Maerora Ma asked.

"Uh . . . a little bit, yes, Mama. Please don't be mad."

"Oh, Mălīn, I so desperately needed to trust you," Maerora Ma said.

"You can, Mama, please," Mălīn said with tears welling up in her eyes. "It's not what you think. Please trust me. I want to be your right-hand man."

"Mălīn, I'm disheartened."

"No, don't be," Mălīn pleaded and then started to sob.

"Come here," Maerora Ma said, reaching to hug her daughter. "You have so much to learn," she said patting her daughter. "Tomorrow, we'll pick up Captain Joan Jones from the hospital and then go home and relax for a while, ok?"

AFTER LESS THAN AN HOUR of restlessness in bed, Mălīn called DeNitor through her glasses. "Why are you trying to commit suicide?" Mălīn asked

DeNitor responded by laughing maniacally.

"Where did Vysender put you?"

"Why? Are you going to come let me out of my cage?"

"I might," she said, and then she traced his location with her pan-omni glasses. "You're still in headquarters. Good. I'm coming down to see you," she said. She then turned off the tracking feature in her glasses and stealthily made her way out of her bedroom, through the dwelling, past Maerora Ma's station, and down to the basement of the headquarters building. She paused before passing the janitorial station then tried to walk by unnoticed, but the late-shift janitorial supervisor saw her and called to her.

"Mălīn!"

"Hello," she said.

"Di-did everything turnout all right for you after I let you into the se-secured room?"

"Yes, yes, thank you. You're a good Magentan for having made the right decision."

"You know, I was th-thinking—"

"I'm sorry. I'm in a bit of a hurry at the moment," Mălīn said.

"Yes, but, you know, I really should have ta-taken you up on your offer at the time," he said.

"Well, you're a good Magentan for not accepting a bribe and for having the strength to shrug off blackmail, so it's best you remain a good Magentan," she said and then quickly passed him by and entered a small hallway that led to the reception station of the detention center.

An attending guard immediately noticed Mălīn and smiled at her as she entered.

"Can you please arrange for me to speak privately with DeNitor?" she asked.

"Certainly, pretty lady," the guard said, putting on his glasses.

Mălīn observed the archaic-looking surroundings. She had never seen or even been near a confinement center, and as she stood in the semi-dingy reception area, she became acutely aware of the contrast between her imperial-leaning self and the indelicate backdrop of her present location.

"Yeah, that DeNitor," said the guard, shaking his head. "We all knew you two were sneaking in the loving, but we didn't expect him to get locked up. How'd he manage that?" the nosy guard asked.

"Just a lovers' quarrel," Mălīn said.

"I guess he was fool-hearted enough to anger the fine daughter of the ruler of Magenta." The guard then stood up and gestured to Mălīn to follow him. He led her down a hallway that was lined with twenty or so cells. The cells were cove-like pockets enclosed in thick glass that had become murky looking and unclear from scratches and mars left by locked-up firebrands and malcontents and other angry troublemakers. DeNitor wasn't in any one of the pockets. All the cells were empty. Fillets and rounds appeared on every edge, rim, corner, and frame, which made everything in the detention center appear smooth despite that the walls and other objects present were grubby and un-clean. Mălīn squirmed and was careful to avoid brushing up against anything.

"Where is he?" she asked.

"Oh, I felt bad for the poor chump, so I let him join us in the guards' break room."

"Well, that's not advisable," Mălīn mumbled. "I'll need to speak to him in private," Mălīn said.

"Yeah-yeah, y'all can meet in the room at the end there," he gestured down the hall.

"No one will eavesdrop on us, right?"

"Nope."

"Will, he be separated from me?" Mălīn asked.

"Nope. Y'all will be in the conjugal-visit room."

"Well, he's awfully angry at me."

"The only other option is the visitation room, but we'll all can hear everything you say."

"No, I'd rather have privacy. Please, can you just handcuff him?" she asked.

The door of the end room was the type that hung on hinges, and the guard opened it with a metal key and allowed Mălīn to enter. A lumpy large bed dominated the small room. A toilet with a mere portable partition occupied a corner, and an impres-sionistic mural spanned all four walls. The mural depicted a peaceful-looking countryside scene.

"I'll bring DeNitor in just a moment," the guard said, closing the door.

Mălīn stood in the far corner of the room, staring at the mural. The door then opened, and DeNitor entered, and then the door closed. Their eyes locked together in a dual-ended cold and glaring stare until Mălīn spoke.

"Couldn't you have been smarter about this?" Mălīn said.

"You want smarter? Go read one of your mother's Shakespeare plays," DeNitor quipped.

"Look, dumb boy," Mălīn said, "I've managed to smooth this over once more, and I have a plan to get us both out of this. So, all you have to do is keep your big mouth shut."

"Like I'm going to trust *you*," DeNitor said.

"Do you want to live, or do you want to die?" Mălīn asked.

"If I die, I want you dead too."

"Shut up, DeNitor. I'm offering you the only chance you have to live."

"That's arguable. There might be other chances that you just don't know about," he said.

Mălīn remained silent and once again observed the many scenes of the mural.

"Touch me, Mălīn," DeNitor ordered.

Mălīn stepped closer to him and touched his arm.

"No gold," he said and spit on her.

"What'd you expect?" she said, pulling the bed cover to wipe off the wad of saliva that landed on her forearm.

"You used to turn gold, and then you changed," he said.

"I changed because you treated me horribly. Love doesn't survive in hostile environments."

"No, Mălīn, don't blame me. You changed your mind about killing Maerora Ma, and you know damn well it wasn't because I treated you badly. If anyone was neglectful, it was you. You were the one who didn't tell me about the spy girl and her mother and later lied about their existence. You, dammit!" He growled, clenched his jaw, and glared. "And it was *you* who whimsically changed her mind about the plan after your very own father sacrificed his life to put it into action." DeNitor kicked the end of the bed repeatedly.

"Oh, DeNitor," Mălīn whispered.

"I hate you, Mălīn."

"DeNitor, please work with me."

"I don't trust you."

"Well, don't be a fool about it. You, indeed, have negotiating leverage, but what you did tonight was foolhardy to say the least," she said.

"Not necessarily," he said.

"Yes, it was, DeNitor."

"No it wasn't. I wanted to see you dance and squirm, and, oh, what a pleasant sight it was."

"DeNitor, why can't you be a good Magentan?" Mălīn asked.

DeNitor laughed contemptuously.

"Tell me what I can do to bargain with you," she said.

"I'm a dead man no matter what I do . . . if not now, later."

"There has to be a way for us both to survive this."

"Unshackle me."

"No, I'm afraid of you."

"I like that," he said. "And now that I've placed my first bargaining chip on the table, you need to decide to take it or leave it."

"No, DeNitor, I'm frightened."

"Well, then, you were a fool to have decided to abort our plan to kill your mother without the means to withstand the consequences, and I shall now continue to enjoy the entertainment called dance of the fool," he laughed, and then he immediately turned serious. "Unshackle me."

"I can't," Mălīn said and then contemplated instructions into her pan-omni glasses, requesting the guard to retrieve her from the room.

"There will be no chance for trust if you leave now. How will I know you won't have me killed? I'll be forced to divulge our treasonous little secret sooner than later. Yes, when I see you're mother again, I'll say, 'Oh, Maerora Ma, did you know your daughter was plotting to kill you? Why, yes, it is true. Captain

Joan Jones is in on it too, and do you know there are two Earth males in your garden ready to strike like deadly cobras as soon as you step foot into it? Oh, such earthly delights,'" he mocked.

The door opened, and the guard entered, reaching his hand out to Mălīn.

"Well, it doesn't look like much conjugaling went on in here," he laughed. "Still quarrelling, eh? Come on, pretty lady."

Mălīn and the guard exited the room. The guard tenderly escorted her to the lobby.

"He's an angry bugger," the guard said, "don't know what you see in him or what he has over you."

Mălīn slowly walked away from the detention center in deep contemplation. When she passed the janitorial station, the janitor with the speech defect once again called her.

"Ma-Mălīn, do you have time for me now?"

"Not really. What is it you want?" she asked.

"It's noth-nothing. You're right about being a g-good Magentan. I shall remain a good Ma-Magentan," he said.

"Why aren't you in the military? Is it because of your speech impediment?" she asked.

The janitor nodded.

"But you are otherwise made up of the stuff a military man is made of, is that right?"

"I th-think so," he answered.

"You could kill a man if ordered to do so then, is that right?"

He nodded.

"Do you own a weapon?"

"I do."

"Well, headquarters never had a finer janitor, then," Mălīn said.

"Thank you, Ma-Mălīn."

"You don't carry your weapon on you though, do you?"

"There's no n-need for it here. Headquarters is well pro-protected," he said.

"Sometimes I worry about my mother's safety. There could be discontented individuals among us here at headquarters. You never know, you know," she said.

He nodded.

"I should like to propose to my mother that you carry secretly. Would you like to meet with Maerora Ma?" Mǎlīn asked, and the janitor shrugged. "Would you be able to bring your weapon in tomorrow evening?"

"Well, it w-wouldn't be a secret if I br-brought a weapon in. There are detectors throughout the b-building."

"Bring it anyway, and call me when you arrive. I'll arrange for it to be cloaked."

"And then we w-will meet with Maerora Ma?" he asked.

"Yes, of course," she said. "I'll see you tomorrow evening." She then continued to make her way up through the headquarters structure until she reached the protruding airdrome on the side of the building. She contemplated instructions into her pan-omni glasses to achieve transport to the hospital. Despite the late hour, the headquarters air-vehicle facility was moderately busy with transport of headquarters staff to and fro, along with cargo shipments, and random military training exercises. The sky was dark, but the facility was well lit. When Mǎlīn loaded herself into an exclusive air vehicle, which was reserved for Maerora Ma, she became frustrated when it failed to launch. She deboarded and wandered around for someone to help her. Two guards then approached.

"Mǎlīn, this air vehicle won't launch without appropriate personnel," said one of the guards.

"And who would that be?" Mǎlīn asked.

"Us," he said.

Mǎlīn smiled and gestured them in. She sat in the seat designated for Maerora Ma, reclined, and then fell asleep. When the air vehicle landed atop the hospital, she headed towards Captain Joan Jones' room, and the two guards accompanied her.

"Do you have to follow me?" she asked the guards.

"Our instruction to protect you outside of headquarters is a direct order from Maerora Ma. We're not about to fail those orders."

When they reached the door of Captain Joan Jones' room,

one of the guards suggested that they check in with the attending nurse at the station around the corner.

"Mălīn, Captain Joan Jones is sleeping. You may startle her if you barge right in."

"How about if I just knock on the door lightly and give her a chance to wake up, and then I will enter? I have an important message to deliver, so please don't interfere," Mălīn said, as she rapped on the door but failed to let anytime pass between knocking and opening. Consequently, Captain Joan Jones awoke abruptly from her bed.

I WAS AWOKEN by someone at my door, and then I saw an outline of a person heading towards me, so I quickly jumped from my bed. "What's going on?" I shouted and then grabbed my shoulder to soothe the sharp pain from my sudden movement.

"Shhh," the outline sounded.

A hospital attendant then dashed in and turned on the lights. "Captain Joan Jones, are you all right?" the attendant asked. "Oh, it's you," she said, seeing Mălīn in the room.

"Pain," I told the attendant who then performed a cursory assessment of my shoulder and assisted me back into bed.

"I want you to keep it immobilized, Captain Joan Jones. The pain will then subside," said the attendant. "Your vitals shot through the roof, and I couldn't understand why, but I guess Mălīn startled you."

"I'm sorry," Mălīn said, "I just wanted to talk to Captain Joan Jones alone for a minute. I'm really sorry about your shoulder, Captain Joan Jones. I hope it will be all right." Mălīn then looked at the attendant. "Can you please let me have moment alone with Captain Joan Jones, please?"

The attendant then left the room.

"Look, Captain Joan Jones, I'm going to be very direct with you. I know why you came to Magenta," Mălīn said.

"Do you?" I asked and gulped, partly from the shock of what I was hearing and partly because my shoulder was killing me.

"Yes, my father is Densip Pi. Does that ring a bell?" she said.

"I don't know—" I said, slightly panting.

"You're here to kill my mother."

"What are you talking about?"

"Look, you and I need to become good friends fast because I've made an assumption that you aren't going to kill my mother. I don't know why you didn't follow through with what you came here to do, but I'm glad you didn't," she said.

The truth shall prevail, I thought to myself and then felt sudden relief from the guilt of aborting my mission. The truth was Densip Pi had steered us wrong about Maerora Ma, and Mălīn had now ushered in the incipient end of this nightmarish charade I had been perpetuating.

"You're right, Mălīn. Densip Pi came to us and provided us with intelligence on Maerora Ma. He then advised us to send a woman who could kill without weaponry and that she would be granted close proximity to Maerora Ma, and he was right. I've already had one hundred and one opportunities to kill Maerora Ma, but I, alone, could not bring myself to kill your mother."

"Thank you, Captain Joan Jones, for trusting me with your honesty and for having the wisdom to stand down," Mălīn said, expelling air in a sigh of relief, the same relief I had just experienced.

"I'm so glad too that I didn't kill her," I said.

"What made you change your mind?" she asked.

"Just intuition."

"But do you know that your two male colleagues are on the loose in my mother's garden? You do know that, right?"

"No, I've been desperately wanting to know what happened to them. Are they ok?" I asked.

"As far as I know, they're fine, but they're going to kill my mother, and we—you and I—must stop them, and we've got to act fast because my mother is going home tomorrow, and she intends on bringing you home with her. She'll be out in that garden in no time. They'll kill her."

"I can talk to them," I said.

"There's another problem too, though. Someone else is in on this. His name is DeNitor, and he's gone rogue, or perhaps it's more correct to say he has failed to go rogue. He needs to be stopped. Basically, we have a situation of kill or be killed."

"What do you mean?" I asked.

"DeNitor keeps threatening to divulge our plot to kill Maerora Ma, and if he does, we'll all be put to death—you, me, him, and the Earth males. But not only that, Captain Joan Jones, I don't ever ever ever want my mother to know I was in on the plan to kill her. I was so foolishly mistaken to have been part of the plan, and if she ever finds out, it will devastate her. It would be the second worst thing to ever happen to her."

"What was the first?" I asked.

"Her firstborn daughter was killed."

"Morgana?" I asked quietly.

"Did my mother tell you about Morgana?"

"Well, I know she died, but I don't know how she died."

"Oh, you'd better at least know that. An Earth male killed Morgana."

"What?" I said.

"You don't know that at all?"

"No."

"But you do know that my mother ordered a retaliation mission because of it, right?"

"Densip Pi merely reported that Maerora Ma was set on destroying Earth. How many Magentans were killed altogether?" I asked.

"Just Morgana," she answered. "You and I don't have time to untangle everything right now because DeNitor will most definitely disclose the assassination plot sooner than later, so I suggest you take care of the Earth males while I take care of DeNitor," Mălin said.

"Wait a minute," I said. "By 'take care' you don't mean kill, do you?"

"Of course! We can't trust any of the males. Our lives are at stake here."

"I came to Magenta to die, Mălīn, and I'm very advanced in my preparation to die," I said. "I won't turn on my crewmates. I'll die first."

"All right, ok, but listen to me. *For now*, all I ask of you is to keep my mother out of that garden at all costs. Can you at least do that?"

"Ok, I can do that," I said.

"You know, my mother loves you. Do you know about Magentan gold? Have you seen it on her skin when she touches you?"

"I know."

"I suppose you find it difficult to love a Magentan woman. I can already tell you don't love her, or else you would jump at the chance to protect her."

"I saved her life in Morgana, Mălīn. Did you know that?" I asked.

"I'm sorry, Captain Joan Jones. My mother told me you saved her life. I was wrong in what I just said. I won't question your motives anymore because we need to trust each other. Our lives depend on it now," she said.

MAERORA MA SAT ACROSS from Katydid as breakfast was served. She asked Katydid to speak about her favorite games and if she could invent a game what would she call it.

"I'd call it find Yaylor Pi."

"Oh, baby," Maerora Ma said, reaching across the table and gently squeezing her hand. Maerora Ma then checked Mălīn's location in her pan-omni glasses and discovered her tracker was off. "Do me a favor, baby. Run over and knock on Mălīn's door. Tell her she's missing breakfast."

Katydid scurried off and returned immediately. "She said go away," the little girl reported.

Maerora Ma then walked over to Mălīn's room and knocked

on the door. "Mălīn, it's Mama."

"Yes, Mama?"

Maerora Ma then opened the door with her glasses and walked to Mălīn's bed. "You missed breakfast. What's wrong?" Maerora Ma asked, placing her hand on Mălīn's forehead.

"I'm tired," Mălīn said without turning towards her mother.

"I know you're upset about DeNitor," Maerora Ma said then set herself beside her daughter and patted her arm. "He's not a very good man. We'll find a better mate for you. Now, tell me why you turned off your tracker?"

"I was in the bathroom. I don't like anyone to know I'm in the bathroom."

"Oh, Mălīn, you're so silly sometimes. You weren't sick, were you? If you're pregnant, you may feel sick in the morning."

"No, I wasn't sick. I'm just tired, and I want to stay here at headquarters to work on my assignment. I don't want to go home," Mălīn said.

"Aren't you concerned about your pets in the garden? They've gone unattended for so long. I thought you cared about them."

"They're fine, Mama. They love to eat the Earth foliage, remember?" she said, turning around to grin at her mother.

"They'd better not ruin my garden, Mălīn," Maerora Ma warned and then received a call from Noma through her glasses. Maerora Ma mouthed in silence to Mălīn that Noma was calling, and then she walked out of Mălīn's bedroom and let the floating camera ball hover in front of her. "Hello, Noma."

"Maerora Ma, you need to come to Morgana right away," Noma said.

"Why?"

"I'd rather tell you in person."

"Tell me what, Noma?"

"Please don't play silly games with me, sister. Come to Morgana right away," Noma ordered and then terminated the call.

"What does she want, Mama?" asked Mălīn.

"Oh, I don't know what dramatic role she's playing now,"

Maerora Ma said, returning to Mălīn's bed. "She probably wants to show me her latest 3D DNA sculpture. I have far more important business to tend to than her trifles."

"She rarely calls, though. I wonder what she wants. Perhaps you should go to Morgana today instead of going home," Mălīn suggested.

"I'm not ready to go back to Morgana," Maerora Ma said and then leaned in to kiss Mălīn on the cheek. "Do me a favor and get Katydid ready to go home. I need to do something important before we leave. I'll be back in a little while." Maerora Ma started to leave but then paused and turned around. "Mălīn, I'm sorry about what happened last night. I still trust you, but just remember what they say on Earth: 'loose lips sink ships.' A ruler must keep all her troubles inside. She can't have best friends nor trust her lover. It's part of the territory."

Maerora Ma then exited Mălīn's bedroom and ascended to her station. She leaned against her console and scrolled through recent military reconnaissance reports at random. She roamed through her immediate surroundings. No others were present, so she paused to look up at the sky through the ceiling windows. She stared at the dying star and then turned off her glasses' tracker and slipped away into the secured-communications room around the corner from her station. She applied a high-security lock on the door with her glasses and then sat at the desk, which was located in front of the official emblem of the presider of the second realm.

She called Roble. No response followed, so she called again. Still, nothing occurred and thus contacted Quercus. Moments later he appeared.

"Quercus, I'm unable to reach Roble. It's vital I speak to him."

"He's away in the realm somewhere. I too am unable to contact him," Quercus said.

"Look, Quercus, Roble may be your immediate leader, but *I* preside over the realm, and if we do not achieve communication in five minutes, serious consequences will befall you. I'm placing you responsible since Roble is unavailable."

"Maerora Ma, I apologize that you have not been informed about the change in our dynamics. Oaktobron can now obliterate Magenta in one fell swoop. Your threats are feathers floating in a storm."

A serious moment of silence ensued, and then Maerora Ma dashed the silence. "Quercus, connect me with Roble immediately."

"I will send him a message, but I cannot guarantee—"

"Hurry up, Quercus," Maerora Ma barked.

After a long moment, a graphic image of the seal of the leader of Oaktobron appeared in her glasses, and then Roble showed up, sitting in an over-stuffed armchair.

"Maerora Ma," he said in a charming yet complacent tone.

"What are your intentions, Roble?"

"Power transfer," he said with a mellifluous emphasis on each suffix.

"All right, Roble, let us make arrangements to that end. A peaceful transfer of power will be beneficial to your reign. You'll be respected and admired from the start."

"The condition of your eagerness alerts me of an emerging fraud," he said, scratching his beard.

"I'm not so much eager to lose power as I am to obtain a favor, and since I don't doubt you can destroy Magenta in an instant, I must bargain with the only means I have," she stated.

"You are astute in sizing up the situation, aren't you?" he said, laughing under his breath.

"Ah, such an odd feeling has just come over me. I don't think I've ever been complimented by an Oaktobron. I shall cherish this rare experience," she said.

"Thank you, Maerora Ma, for convincing me that I am, indeed, communicating with the real Maerora Ma, for no conversation with you is complete without a measure of sarcasm."

"Now, listen, Roble, would you prefer a treaty, incremental transfer, or a sudden replacement of the incumbent?" she asked.

"I don't know, Maerora Ma. Bypassing the gory battles and bloodshed of war has an emasculating effect. Plus, a peaceful transfer of power eliminates the chance to apply our new weapon."

"Roble!" Maerora Ma said in a scolding tone.

"Well, I suppose using it on the realm barrier will suffice. Anyway, what is this favor of yours that you've so overtly minimized?"

"I need an expert who can operate my rapid-healing machine, and he or she must come complete with manual in hand," she stated.

Roble chuckled aloud, revealing his long teeth. "I *knew* you were ailing. Oh, sick queen, you're really going to give away the store just to stay alive? Amazing, I say, if not a bit overwhelmingly selfish." He then leaned back in his chair, placed his hands on the armrests, jutted his chin out, and slowly rocked back and forth.

"What're you doing?" she asked.

"Savoring this mighty momentous moment. Do you realize the line of great Magentan leaders terminates right here? Do you realize what you'll be forfeiting—your inane plan to unite the first and second realms?" he said, leaning forward. "And *you do know* the MIC will be mine, and I won't allow anymore pathetic fawning over Earth. 'Earth is the source of all things . . . oh, my,'" he said, fluttering his eyelids in exaggerated mockery.

"Let us make arrangements," Maerora Ma said soberly.

"Well, there's a great many details to ponder here, Maerora Ma."

"Time, Roble, time. I don't have time for details. Let me suggest that I announce my resignation as ruler of the realm at your technology summit."

"This is so sudden."

"What's the matter? Is your brain not firing rapidly enough to process—"

"All right, enough with the sarcasm," he said, "I'll accept your resignation."

"Now, listen, Roble," she said in a softening tone. "I'll want to return once more for a death-acknowledgement visit."

"Hmm," Roble pondered. "Why bother with a

death-acknowledgment visit? The MIC and its history will matter no more once I fully reign."

"Roble, let me just have one more death-acknowledgment visit. I only want to honor my mother. After all, even you, yourself, adored Amora Ma," she said.

"Very well," Roble said. "For Amora Ma's honor, I will tolerate one last death-acknowledgment visit. Nonetheless, I will allow you to be accompanied by only a small detail. I wouldn't trust you otherwise."

"All right, Roble, I will travel with a bare-bones crew."

"Maerora Ma?"

"Yes, Roble."

"Please get some rest. I should like to have footage taken with me and the last leading lady of Magenta for posterity, and she ought to retain at least a hint of the once formidable Maerora Ma," he said and laughed.

CHAPTER 9:
THE MIDAS TOUCH

Two GUARDS carefully assisted me into Maerora Ma's air vehicle. My shoulder had especially started hurting during the long walk up to the hospital's roof. Maerora Ma recognized right away that I was in pain and stood over me to adjust my sling. Her chest was mere centimeters away from my face, and so I studied the insignia on her collar. She was wearing a Mao suit again, and this one had double rows of buttons that ran down the full length of the tailored tunic top. The proximity of her breasts caused a soft shockwave to run through me, and I was surprised within myself. How long were the effects of the aufillo going to last?

"Your arm was hanging too low. The excessive swinging was exasperating the torn ligaments," Maerora Ma said in a matter of fact tone. I thanked her, and she then returned to her seat and remained silent.

"Where's Mălīn?" I asked.

"She's working on a project at headquarters," Maerora Ma answered and then put on her glasses. "Forgive me, Captain Joan Jones. I must tend to business."

I turned to look at Katydid who was tugging at a loose piece of fabric on her seat, and when Maerora Ma noticed, she was quick on the draw and overly harsh in her scolding of her. Katydid started to cry, resulting in a further unpleasantness of the moment. Maerora Ma could barely restrain her aggravation, so I gently placed my hand on her arm, and she immediately relaxed in her seat as if my touch were potently powerful.

"Are you ok?" I asked, eager inside for her normal cordiality to return.

"I'm fine," she said, staring into her glasses. After a long while, she removed her glasses and caressed her brow and then turned to me. "I'd like to stroll through the Earth garden with you once we arrive home," she said.

"Oh, the garden . . . ," I said and couldn't readily think of an excuse to keep her out of it.

She then placed her glasses on her face and spoke in Magentan to a remote interlocutor, and I began to think about William and Porter. How strange the feeling was to realize that they would soon be mere meters away from me in the garden, hidden and deadly. Nevertheless, I felt a strong longing for them. I missed them because they were Earth, and Earth was Butterfly.

No sooner did we land atop Maerora Ma's home than she suggested walking in the Earth garden again.

"But walking may aggravate my shoulder," I said as we stood to exit the air vehicle.

"I'll have a chair brought out to the garden so you can recline and relax," she said, and when the door released open, a small group of Magentans, presumably household staff, clapped and cheered and parted themselves into a path for us. Katydid rushed out first and skipped happily through the path of people while Maerora Ma exited second and turned to see if I could manage myself down.

The light of day was bright and shined on the faces of everyone. The star, which I could not stop thinking of as a planet, was hugely present in the sky. The color magenta was no longer noticeable to me. I had fully acclimated to monochrome Magenta and only noticed the lack of colors when I forced myself to think about it.

At the end of the path, a male Magentan spoke in front of the crowd to Maerora Ma in a formal tone, I didn't know what he was saying until Maerora Ma told me he represented the group in expressing dismay about the Oaktobron attack in Morgana and that everyone had lamented her absence. The faces of the people clearly revealed genuine love for their leader. Maerora Ma then addressed them and received their embraces. All the while, I racked my brain for ideas of how I could prevent the seemingly inevitable walk in the garden of Earthly . . . well, not delight. We finally entered the large cylindrical lift and headed downward.

"How about if we drink aufillo and go to the museum where you can read Shakespeare to me from the book in the exhibit," I suggested.

"Mmm, I'd rather do that more than anything else in the world," she said, closing her eyes and smiling as if envisioning my suggestion in a reverie.

The lift ceased its downward motion and the door retracted. As we entered the foyer, Maerora Ma turned to Katydid. "Do you want to play with your friends?"

The little girl nodded, and Maerora Ma knelt down to hug her young daughter and remained in a sustained embrace. "Mama was too harsh earlier, baby. I'm sorry," she said and kissed her on each cheek. Maerora Ma then spoke into her glasses in Magentan. A few minutes later, a woman came to retrieve Katydid.

"I'm going to change into something more comfortable, and then I'll have a chair placed in the garden. In the meantime, you can wait in here," she said leading me through the set of doors that entered into the enormous observation area. We were in the same place in which I had first set eyes on her and her daughters. The room's wall of windows revealed the entire sphere of the dying star in the sky. Maerora Ma pulled a few pillows from one end of a settee and gestured for me to sit. She then adjusted the pillows behind my back, and once again her chest was in my face. She then headed towards a dispenser-like apparatus that was built into a distant wall and returned with a glass full of fluid. "I'll be back very soon," she said, handing me the glass.

"Maerora Ma, please don't bother with the chair. Just return and we'll walk in the garden together."

"All right," she said, exiting the room.

I then brainstormed heavily for an idea to prevent her from entering the garden but to no avail. How could I keep her from the killers in the garden? Frustrated at my lack of ingenuity, I stood up and walked closer to the windows to stare into the star. It mesmerized me, not merely because of its enormous size but because it represented a certain sadness. To have shined brightly in glory for a while and then to have advanced immensely on the path of petering out was no happy reminder to see in the sky every day.

"It's beautiful, isn't it," Maerora Ma said, re-entering the room.

"It's one of the most beautiful sights I've ever seen in all my life," I said, holding my gaze on the star.

"Come," she said, pulling on me gently. She had changed into a flowing garment that resembled an Indian sari, reconfirming my idea that a connection must have existed between her and the Indian goddess culture.

"Wait, I'm not finished with my drink," I said, breaking away to reach for my glass, which I then took a tiny sip from.

"Our ancient ancestors used to stare into the cracks of light on the star to scry the future. Sometimes I look at the star and wonder if they ever saw the very moment I was looking at it," she said with a languishing stare at the star.

"What do you mean by 'scry'?" I asked, trying desperately to delay our trip to the garden with conversation.

"Seeing the future. Did I not get it right in English?"

"I don't know. I've never heard the word. Your gown . . . it's very lovely," I said.

"Are you going to finish your drink?" she asked, moving well within my personal space. I backed away slightly enough to continue to see and admire her dress.

"The women in India wear clothing very similar to what you have on. Do you remember the goddess culture I told you about?"

She merely smiled then picked up my glass and handed it to me. Again, I took a teeny-tiny sip.

"Let us please go to the garden," she said.

"Maerora Ma, I need to know about the nineteenth mission."

"Not now, Joan," she said, and I paused to observe how the maroon drape she wore enhanced her natural air of majesty.

"Yes, now," I insisted and hated that I had to disturb her like this.

"Why did you come to Magenta, Captain Joan Jones?" she countered and moved to stand at the opposite end of the settee. I sipped my drink before I replied.

"Reconnaissance," I said, feeling regret over her withdrawal of intimate proximity.

"Does that mean we can expect a second mission to retrieve you?" she asked.

"No, the interpretation is such that if no returned communication ensues, Magenta will continue to be deemed hostile," I said.

"Well, let us send a signal right away then. We mustn't be considered hostile. We adore Earth. We seek it as the source of our own origin."

"Why'd you attack Earth then?" I asked.

She folded her arms over her chest and turned away from me. "If no one comes to retrieve you . . . ," she paused midsentence and then returned to fully face me. "Well, there's a deliberately tragic element to your visit then, isn't there . . . to not return home . . . to never be with your daughter again?"

I sipped my drink then sat down on the settee and held my bad shoulder, though it wasn't in pain at the moment, but I thought it would evoke the nurturing mother inside her. "How about if we remain here instead of going to the garden," I suggested.

"Captain Joan Jones, if you're not going to accompany me to the garden, it's fine. I'll go alone," she said then proceeded to exit, and I speedily jumped up to follow her. Suddenly, she stopped, and I nearly banged into her. She exhaled loudly and reversed her direction back into the observation room.

"What's the matter?" I asked.

"I forgot to rotate the building. I prefer the garden entryway to be in front of my bedroom so I can readily lie down after walking." She stopped before a huge shiny lever that stood in a far corner of the room, and before lifting the lever, she moved a minor lever, which activated a warning signal throughout the property. A moment later, the building began to roll, and she kept her back to me while the house slowly moved. I most definitely started to lose faith in my ability to keep her out of the garden.

"Won't you suffer from a lack of magenta in the garden?"

"That's one of the reasons I go there. I stay long enough for my excess energy to evaporate. Otherwise, I have trouble sleeping at night," she said.

"But it's not night," I said.

"It might as well be for me. I have to return to headquarters in a few hours, and after that I'm going to Oaktobron."

"Oaktobron?"

The building stopped moving, and Maerora Ma locked the levers and proceeded to walk out of the room.

"Why are you going to Oaktobron?" I asked.

"You know I have important business to conclude with the Oaktobrons," she said as we crossed the foyer and entered through another set of doors.

I didn't know exactly how close we were to the garden, but it didn't matter because we were close enough, and I still had not been able to divert her desire from it. We walked down a series of hallways, and the final one opened to a wall of windows where I could see the refreshing dominant green of the Earth garden, but there was also a mother and daughter in the hallway shouting in Magentan and waving their arms.

"What are they saying?" I asked. "Please tell them to speak in English."

"Speak in Earth English. Do you not notice that our guest from Earth is present?" Maerora Ma said.

"Ma'am, please stop. Do not enter the garden," each of them said in unison.

"It is shameful that you are out and about in my home. I should have . . . ," Maerora Ma looked at me and then prematurely ended her sentence.

"Please, Maerora Ma, Ma'am, please listen to us."

"Mălĭn informed me of your repeated spying. You proved me a

fool after I generously overlooked your first offense. What audacity you have now to call to me in shrill voices," Maerora Ma said.

I was surprised at how her rage rapidly ratcheted up with each sentence she uttered.

"Ma'am, please, there's danger out there," said the mother, pointing to the garden.

I then reached for Maerora Ma's arm, thinking my touch was still potent enough to calm her fury. It worked. Her rage subsided immediately. She took a deep breath of air and then gently wiggled my hand off her arm.

"Why are you preventing me from entering my garden?" Maerora Ma asked the woman and her daughter.

"There are things out there, animals or something that can kill, and we've waited here forever to save you from entering the danger."

"Oh, silly, fools, Mălīn is keeping pet animals in the garden, much to my chagrin I have to say. Anyway, this distasteful spectacle is repugnant." Maerora Ma then spoke in Magentan to someone in her glasses.

"No, Ma'am, please don't have us banished. Please listen to what my daughter heard, even though, yes, she was very wrong to have been spying. Please just listen to her."

"No," Maerora Ma said, "no second chances."

The girl started to speak anyway. "I heard DeNitor talking to Mălīn—"

As soon as I heard the name DeNitor, I knew this revelation had to be ended. "Maerora Ma!" I shouted. "There's movement in the garden. I saw two figures. I'll find out what's out there." I then rushed to the door, and Maerora Ma rushed behind me to pull me back.

"No, Captain Joan Jones! No!" Maerora Ma yelled, and the fervor in her momentum startled everyone. She wrapped her arms around me from behind and held me back with all her might.

"All right, it's ok. I won't go outside. It's ok," I said.

She released me and then struggled for a moment to

recompose herself. "I'll call Mălīn to find out about her animals," she said, panting.

Two guards then arrived.

"Take them away," Maerora Ma ordered, gesturing at the
mother and daughter. Maerora Ma then directed me to a set
of doors across from the garden's entryway. The two doors retracted, and we stepped into an elaborately decorated room,
which had large paintings that were like those you only see in
museums. Their gilded-gold frames dazzled my eyes.

"Is this another museum?" I asked.

"No, it's my bedroom."

"It is?"

"No, this is my bedroom," she said, opening another set of retracting doors and gesturing me through. I walked in, and noticed
an incredibly high ceiling. It was so high it could pierce Heaven.

"Dammit, Mălīn's tracker is off again," she muttered, staring
into her glasses.

"Is that unusual?" I asked.

"Unfortunately, it's becoming a habit with her," she said, and
then she turned and stood directly in front of me. "Captain Joan
Jones, don't ever take a risk like that again, please. I need you."

"Why do you need me?"

"I told you. We're going to unite the realms," she said.

"Well, Maerora Ma, we need to come to terms then, starting
with the nineteenth mission."

She removed the drape of her sari and then set herself on
her bed and leaned against her pillows, facing away from me.
"I ordered the nineteenth mission," she said.

"Why?"

"Retaliation."

"Retaliation for what?" I asked, even though I already knew.

She then turned her head towards me and said, "I can't
imagine with your rank in the military and the reconnaissance
mission you're on that you wouldn't be aware of the history of
your missions."

"The truth is I don't know about previous missions. They

were always conducted as covert operations."

"I see," she said and then seemed to drift off in thought. "I suppose it doesn't matter for you to know that I've agonized over the nineteenth mission and have regretted it."

"I sense your sincere remorse."

"Sometimes I don't believe I should feel remorse," she said, leaning back and looking up at the ceiling.

"Just tell me the reason you were compelled to retaliate."

"My daughter . . . ," she said, seemingly intending to say more, but then she remained silent.

"Morgana?" I asked.

"Please, Joan, just come lie beside me and help me fall asleep. I need to rest now," she said, patting the empty space on the bed beside her and still staring up at the ceiling.

"Maerora Ma, I need to know."

"I don't enjoy talking about my dead daughter."

"I assure you I don't enjoy asking you about her, but we must have an understanding of each other."

She then drew in a deep breath and exhaled very slowly and spoke. "An unexpected visitor from Earth dropped from the MIC. He immediately began firing his weapon. His bullets struck my daughter."

"Oh, God," I whispered, "how awful."

"She was a volunteer curator at the MIC museum located next to the MIC itself," she said, keeping her gaze fixed on the distant ceiling. "It may be easy for Earth mothers to detach from their daughters, but Magentan mothers never sever the umbilical cord, especially when it comes to firstborn daughters. Morgana was my beloved firstborn. I adored her. She . . . ."

I moved closer to the bed and sat at the end of it.

Maerora Ma covered her eyes with her arm. "Oh, my daughter," she whispered.

"I'm sorry," I said.

"She always reached out to hold my hand wherever we were, and she so readily shared the incredible contents of her deep soul with me . . . ."

As I listened to Maerora Ma speak, I didn't dare imagine what it would be like to lose a child because it would mean envisioning Butterfly as dead, and despite that Maerora Ma believed Earth mothers could easily detach from their daughters, I knew I could not withstand even the mere thought of Butterfly dead.

"She was terrible at Shakespeare, though," Maerora Ma said, removing her arm from over her eyes and smiling at me. I smiled back and then almost started to speak but yielded to her as she had more to share. "Every morning when I awake and remember she's dead, the electrical current of my reality shocks me . . . everyday, and it leaves me numb to joy. I can't truly enjoy anything anymore," she said, staring up at the ceiling again. I scooted up close to her and extended my arm to touch her, but she turned away and maneuvered out of reach.

"Maerora Ma, I honestly don't know anything about that terrible Earth mission. No one on Earth does. We received the Magentan attack, your nineteenth mission, as completely unprovoked," I said then reached again for her, but she didn't respond, and no gold sparkled where my hand landed on her skin. Her sadness was tightening my chest, and I lamented the loss of my Midas touch. "I wish I knew more about that mission. It's strange for there to have been only one crew member."

"You're the only crew member on *your* mission," she said.

Well, now, that wasn't true, I told myself and shuddered mentally at the thought of all the deception I was cloaked in. The thought of William and Porter poised in the garden to kill her caused me to feel inadequate and ill-suited to console her.

"Maerora Ma, I'm very eager to help you straighten out things between Earth and Magenta, and when you're ready, I'll do everything I can," I said. "I guess right now you should get your rest." I then walked towards the door.

"Joan, please stay," she said.

I then turned around and backtracked to the bed and lay down beside her. "I'm so sorry about what happened. I don't know why it happened," I told her.

"I just want go to sleep," she said.

I wrapped my arm around her despite a little discomfort in my injured shoulder. My forearm was mere centimeters away from her breasts, which were tucked under her midriff top, so I pulled my arm upwards and pressed into her breasts. The sensation of their warmth on my skin caused an arousing convulsion to start behind my heart and end well below my stomach. It was a pleasurable shock, and I craved to feel it again, so I cupped one of her breasts in my hand and let its nipple rise within my palm. When she vocalized a murmur of pleasure, my chest nearly burst from excitation, so I softly moved my hand in a circular motion over parts of her body, and she hummed in delight, and when I pulled her tightly into my belly with a hint of ravenous ardor, brilliant-colored gold flowed and shimmered under her skin and whirled in irregular swirls. She subtly weltered in the intimacy, and I then realized the chemistry giving rise to the gold was also amplifying the sensation of my touch. I felt so invincible with my Midas touch again and was so convinced that she was a goddess that I lost my worrisome self completely in the living fantasy at hand. I removed her underskirt and gently rolled her onto her back.

"Joan," she said, "will you not feel regret afterwards?"

"No," I whispered, elongating the ending of the word. I let the gold race down to her pelvic area with the direction of my hand, and it rushed in such a torrent that I lost control of it, which caused her to brace against me.

"Oh, Joan," she said, and then I watched her writhe in tormenting gratification, and when she settled down, her breathing rate lowered, and she slipped into a deep sleep.

I HAD LAIN AWAKE with a very sore shoulder for the few hours that had elapsed since she fell asleep, and finally when she awoke, she reached for her glasses and put them on. A few moments later, she removed them and pulled my hand and squeezed it gently. She then got up and picked up her sari and entered the room's bathroom. She didn't come out until an hour later when she was fully dressed in a turtleneck top under a tailored Eisenhower jacket, which bore significant insignia and symbols and other regalia. She looked like she was ready to lead us into war.

"Are you leaving now?" I asked.

"I am," she said. "I've instructed the household staff to attend to your needs. Katydid will be taken care of by her governess, and I will have Mǎlīn check in with you once I finally get a hold of her. You mustn't go into the garden. I'm sorry there isn't much for you to occupy yourself with here, but you're welcome to take the Shakespeare book from the museum and read it," she said.

I then stood up from the bed to hug her goodbye, but she gestured for me to halt and stay back.

"I'm sorry. I can't . . . ," she said and then walked towards the door.

"Maerora," I called, and she paused but didn't turn around.

"Don't speak anymore," she said. "I have to go."

"Are you ok?" I asked, but she didn't answer. She continued through the door into the antechamber, so I chased after her. "Please don't leave yet."

She then exited the antechamber and entered the long hallway that ran along the length of the Earth garden. I followed behind her until she stopped and turned towards me. The green foliage from the garden dominated the whole half of my eyesight, but I didn't avert my eyes from her for one second.

"I have serious business to take care of. I'll be back, and we'll spend proper time together then," she said.

"I'm worried. I mean, you know what happened in Morgana. They attacked you."

"I have everything under control. Now, please, go back and let me leave."

"What if something terrible happens?" I asked.

"If I don't return, please know that I am grateful to you for restoring my positive destiny and for tender moments," she said.

"Maerora—"

"No more!" she barked, and like a child, I obeyed and watched her leave.

CHAPTER 10:
GAMBIT TACTICS

MĂLĪN LAY ON HER BACK in bed sorting through information to which she formerly had no access. She searched for all the devices and techniques on how to cloak a weapon and to evade weapon detectors. As she looked into her pan-omni glasses, she received an incoming call from Noma.

"Where's your mother?" Noma asked.

"At home."

"Go get her for me."

"I'm not at home. I'm at headquarters."

"Why aren't you with her?"

"I'm working," Mălīn said.

"Working?"

"Uh-ha, on a special project."

"Whatever. Anyway, you need to have your mother come here to Morgana. It's very important," Noma said.

"I don't think she has time. She's heavily involved with the Oaktobron situation," Mălīn said.

"Ah, yes, of course, Maerora Ma becomes easily engrossed in the art of retribution. I'm certain she can't think of anything else right now."

"Just tell me why you need her to go to Morgana."

"No," Noma said with an abrupt end to the conversation.

Mălīn arose out of bed, bathed, and clothed herself. She then ascended to Maerora Ma's headquarters station and strolled through to an elevator and then descended a couple of stories. When the elevator stopped, she contemplated her security password into her glasses to open the elevator door, and when the door retracted, two guards stood with their weapons drawn and aimed at her.

"Whoa!" she exclaimed.

"Mălīn, never ever enter this weapons repository without your tracker on. We were unable to identify you. You could have been shot," one of the guards said.

"Oh, I forgot my tracker was off. I'll turn it on," she said, but she didn't. She walked on down the hall to a spacious room that had a barrier counter where a woman stood, an older woman who was staring into her pan-omni glasses and failed to acknowledge Mălīn, so after waiting patiently for a polite moment, Mălīn cleared her throat.

"I know you're there," said the woman without looking at Mălīn. A minute or two passed, and the woman spoke again. "I'm just on the last paragraph here." When the woman finally removed her glasses and recognized Mălīn, she went through the motions of looking abashed for neglecting Maerora Ma's daughter. "What brings Maerora Ma's beautiful daughter down here?"

"I need to be issued a VG WCD, please," Mălīn said.

The woman raised one of her eyebrows while putting on her glasses. "Well, we certainly have plenty of the VG WCDs on hand here," the woman said, removing her glasses and leaning on the counter. "That article I was just reading . . . it's the public report of what happened in Morgana. It was just released this morning. I certainly hope your mother wasn't too shaken by the incident."

"Well, she was, but she's not one to blither and blubber in public."

"Uh-ha, and what about the Earth woman?"

"What about her?" Mălīn asked.

"She really seems like something," the woman said.

"Yeah, she does, doesn't she? Now, what about that VG WCD?"

"So, you weren't in Morgana when it happened, were you?" the woman asked.

"No."

"That's unusual for you to have been apart from your mother."

"I'm not with her now. It's not *that* unusual," Mălīn said.

"Hmm, so, you probably can't verify the accuracy of the article, huh?"

"I'm certain whatever is in the article is the true story," Mălīn said.

"One never knows for sure. I hear on Oaktobron their articles are authored by a bunch of people, not just a select few like we have it here. It's better to have a multitude of points of view, don't you think?"

"I really don't know," Mălīn said.

"Yeah, you wouldn't know. You're too young and innocent. Now, don't be thinking I'm 'discontented,'" the woman said, gesturing with air quotes.

Mălīn politely smiled and patiently let the woman speak her mind.

"I like your mother, but, you know . . . ," the woman said, shrugging her shoulders.

"No, I don't know," Mălīn said.

"Well, you know, she's not quite the same as Amora Ma. You probably don't remember your grandmother, do you?"

"Of course I do," Mălīn said.

"Oh, right, you're the middle daughter. I mixed you up with the little one. Why do you suppose your mother is so stingy when it comes to death-acknowledgment visits? I think I can count on one hand the number of death-acknowledgement visits she's made since Amora Ma died."

"She doesn't handle magenta deprivation very well."

"Well, there's plenty of Magentan families still awaiting their visits. It's not like she has to go to Oaktobron, Birchron, and Pinovra all the time. She can at least visit Magentan families," the woman said.

"I will suggest that to her. Now, I truly hate to be rude, but I'm in a little bit of a hurry and need to transact with you, please."

"VG WCD, eh? Let's see here," the woman said, putting on her glasses. "All right, I'll bring one out to you in just a moment. You do know these WCDs require multiple clearance authorizations, right?"

"Of course they do and for good reason too," Mălĭn said. "If you'll observe, my clearance should be sufficient."

"Well, it's iffy at best," the woman said, rocking her hand horizontally in the air.

"Hmm, my mother was insistent on me having a WCD for my new weapon. How about if I bring my mother here? That way she can meet you and witness how enthusiastic you are about . . . oh, everything, I guess," Mălĭn said.

"Humph," the woman snorted. "You're not such a dumb girl, are you? And I always thought the one who died had all the smarts. So, the reason you need to carry a cloaked weapon is in case an Oaktobron jumps out and attacks you, eh?"

"Yes, that's exactly right."

"It makes sense to me," said the woman. "Now, I'll bypass the multiple-authorization requirement only because I was dumb enough to lead you into thinking I'm discontented. Well, I'm not. I just like to read. That's all." The woman then disappeared into the stockroom behind her and reappeared a moment later with a VG WCD.

A WHILE LATER, Mălĭn stood at the edge of the ground-level concourse of the headquarters hall, waiting for the nightshift-janitor supervisor to report to work. A plethora of sounds ricocheted off the smooth surfaces of the floors and windows, and the bustle of the many people stimulated ocular senses. Mălĭn looked up and squinted to see her mother's station high atop the large pillar-like structure that protruded two thirds up from the ground floor. The large balcony under her mother's station jutted out like a huge lower lip. It was where she and her mother had had their recent poignant conversation. When she returned her eyes back to the ground floor, she watched tens of guards wandering about. Two each were stationed at the multiple entrances of the concourse. Mălĭn clutched her large shoulder bag tightly as she moved closer to one of the entrances. Inside the bag was her new VG WCD.

"Mălīn, would you please turn on your tracker. It makes it easier for the guards to determine if you're leaving the building. You do realize that by recent order of Maerora Ma, you are to be accompanied by two guards whenever you exit headquarters," said a guard who had approached her from behind.

"Yeah-yeah, I know that," Mălīn replied, turning to face the guard. "I'm waiting for someone, and I'd like to have a little privacy if you don't mind." She then looped her shoulder bag over her head so that it hung in front of her.

"Ma'am, you do know that there's an inherent conflict between security and privacy, don't you?"

"Yeah-yeah, but, please, just let me kiss my new beau outside the door, and then we'll be right in."

The janitor then appeared, and Mălīn quickly popped herself outside and embraced him. "Hurry and slip your weapon into the WCD in my bag and kiss me while you do it and then walk away from me. We'll talk later."

"Ma-Mălīn, this doesn't see-seem right," he said. Mălīn pulled his face to hers and kissed him as seductively as she possibly could while he fumbled around in making the transfer. Two guards quickly stood beside Mălīn. One placed his hand on the janitor's shoulder to push him back, and Mălīn swiftly turned away to re-enter headquarters. She pulled her bag over her shoulder, and then two guards followed her in.

"You're dead meat if you tell my mother who I was kissing," she threatened then quickly worked her way back to the elevator. The guards chuckled and shook their heads.

A WHILE LATER, Mălīn, behind the locked door of her headquarters bedroom, handled the janitor's weapon and without firing it, practiced firing it to become familiar with it and to become one with it. She put on her pan-omni glasses and studied the weapon's performance specifications and user commentary. She then remembered to turn on her tracker and as she did, she received an immediate call from her mother.

"Where in the world have you been?"

"I've been here at headquarters."

"Dammit, what have I told you about your tracker?"

"Oh, Mama, I forget sometimes to turn it on."

"What kind of right-hand man are you if I can't get a hold of you when I need you?"

"I'm sorry. I'll do better."

"Mălīn, something strange happened at home."

"What?"

"The housekeeper and her daughter insisted I stay out of the garden," Maerora Ma said.

Mălīn quietly gasped.

"They said there were killer animals in the garden. What in the world is going on? What kind of animals are you keeping in there?"

"Mama, I don't really know what kind of animals they are. I just know they're there."

"They're not your pets?"

"No, not really."

"The report said you referred to them as your pets."

"I know. I just said that so they would leave the animals alone."

"Dammit, why do you have to be so difficult?"

"I don't know," Mălīn said, pausing for a moment. "Mama?"

"What?"

"Did you banish the spy girl and her mother?"

"Yes, I ordered a set of our household guards to carry it out."

"Thank you, Mama. We'll be much better off without them sneaking around all the time. I feel so much better."

"Just remember banishment mustn't be treated as a frivolous action," Maerora Ma said.

"Is spying frivolous?"

"Mălīn, just don't ever show such an eagerness for the banishment of your subjects. Now, tell me, do you have any new information about Yaylor Pi? Any clues?"

"There may be something in Morgana."

"Morgana? What in the world would Yaylor Pi be doing in

Morgana?"

"Don't you remember when he used to take us sailing?"

"Of course I do."

"His old sail boat was reported missing."

Maerora Ma released a quiet moan.

"Mama?"

"Mălīn, I'm going to Oaktobron—"

"No. There could be assassins. Please don't go. I beg of you."

"I don't have a choice. I have to go—"

"Why? Mama, why?"

"Don't worry about it. Nothing is going to happen to me there. Now, listen. I want you to return home right away to stay with Captain Joan Jones."

"Why?"

"Because she's very important, and I need for you to keep her safe . . . safe at all costs, Mălīn."

After the call ended, Mălīn placed her weapon in the WCD and then packed the WCD into her shoulder bag and headed down to the detention center.

"YOU'RE BACK!" said the jolly attendant guard who had received Mălīn previously. "Can't get enough of the schmuck, eh? Well, I got bad news for ya. We moved him to another location."

Mălīn's face turned the lightest shade of magenta.

"Na, just kidding," said the guard. "I'm sorry if that shook you. Let me go set things up for ya."

"Please restrain both his arms and legs. He's still very angry, and his anger frightens me."

"Alrighty, pretty lady . . . don't know why you choose to fuss over him."

Mălīn waited, closing her eyes and furrowing her brow as if imagining the next steps of action she was about to take.

"Ma-Mălīn," called the night-shift janitor supervisor.

Mălīn jumped seemingly two-feet off the ground and then placed her hand on her chest. "Oh, gosh, you scared me," she said, panting.

"Oh, I-I'm very very sorry."

"I'll come see you in just a moment. I promise. I just have to take care of something first," she said.

"Oh-ok, I thought you w-would be seeing me sooner, s-so I wanted to make sure everything was ok."

"It's fine. It's fine." she said.

"Ok, see you s-soon."

The janitor then exited, and the attending guard returned. "That's quite a shoulder bag there," he said. "Looks heavy. What's in it?" he asked, extending his arm to lift it from Mălĭn's shoulder.

"Uh, just personal things," she said, stepping backwards.

"Don't worry. I'm not going to look inside. I just want to see how heavy it is."

"It's not all that heavy. You'll be disappointed."

"I know a woman who wants a baby so badly that she carries around a diaper bag and says she's just practicing. Her bag's just like yours. I don't suppose you're practicing too, eh?"

Mălĭn quietly snorted and smirked.

The guard gazed at Mălĭn and snickered. "C'mon, I've got him all shackled up for ya." He then escorted her to the conjugal-visit room.

Mălĭn entered the room and momentarily looked at the wall mural.

"Gonna go get him right now."

Two minutes later the door opened and a writhing and defiant DeNitor was rolled in.

"I had to put him in this wheelchair. He didn't want to come," said the guard as he rolled DeNitor in and turned him around to face Mălĭn. "Good luck, ya'll."

When the door was shut and locked, Mălĭn faced a violently twisting DeNitor who wouldn't cease from constant motion.

"DeNitor! Stop!"

He wouldn't, so Mălĭn pulled her weapon out and pointed it at him.

He then screamed a defyingly loud screech, so she waited not a moment longer and fired the weapon once, twice, and three times. She then ran to the far side of the bed and called the guard through her glasses. In less than a minute later, the guard opened the door and walked in, and she fired once, twice, and three times then ran to shut the door and remained in the room, clutching her shoulder bag against her chest with the weapon grasped tightly in her hand.

IN A LARGE WINDOWLESS conference room located a couple of floors below Maerora Ma's station, Vysender and thirty strategical and tactical experts sat at a U-shaped set of tables. The experts were all clad in military garb with insignia galore covering their collars, and each of them had on pan-omni glasses. When Maerora Ma entered, they all stood up until she sat down at the bottom of the U.

Vysender formally opened the meeting by briefing the attendees about the Oaktobron situation. He then explained, "We've organized these proposals into three categories—active, passive, and hybrid. Shall we start with the active ones, Ma'am? The active strategies are your preference, correct?"

"Just proceed as you see fit," Maerora Ma said.

"After review of the proposals in the active category, I can confidently say they are all classically traditional, standard, and predictable. Although, one among them stands out because it ensures victory by means of strictly employing only gambit tactics, applied relentlessly and successively. Unfortunately, though, this is a most costly approach and thus is simply not justifiable. Besides, we're dealing with an enemy who has preemptive-strike capability; therefore, swiftness must be king in our choice of strategy."

Maerora Ma scanned through the abstracts of each proposal as quickly as she could. "Vysender, let us peruse the passive proposals. Diplomacy is a passive strategy and when facing the reality of a preemptive strike with no equal means, diplomacy may be our wisest choice," Maerora Ma said.

"A valid point," he said. "The only problem with diplomacy is that it too is costly. One might as well sell one's soul."

"We should be so lucky if our soul is worth our enemy's desire," she said.

Vysender squinted his eyes and tilted his head. "Roble will always desire the seat of the realm," he said.

"Which passive proposal do you find effective?" she asked.

"None. Roble wants one thing only—the seat of the realm, and that is simply not up for negotiation."

"So, then, perhaps our solution is among the hybrid proposals." she said. "Which proposal among the hybrids do you favor?"

"It's up for discussion," he answered.

"All right, then, let us discuss it after a brief break. Vysender, I need to talk to you. Please follow me," Maerora Ma said.

The two then exited the conference room and rode the elevator up to Maerora Ma's station. She then ushered him into the private room across from her console and locked the door with her glasses. "Vysender, you're a consummate military man. You're well respected, and you are the utmost citizen of Magenta. I heavily rely on you to keep my daughters and me safe and Magenta secure, and you do it so well."

"Please be direct, Maerora Ma."

"I miss how Yaylor Pi used to arbitrate between us—"

"Please, Maerora Ma, what is it you want to tell me?"

"I'm going to Oaktobron without security."

"Absolutely not!" Vysender said, ripping his pan-omni glasses from his face.

"There was a time when kings fought in battles," she said.

"You're a queen, not a king."

She laughed softly. "I'm still Supreme, and I shall invoke my Supremacy if you continue on this path of insubordination."

"Dammit it all!" he yelled. "You're a dead woman if you go to Oaktobron, and you won't need me. May I be excused?"

"Absolutely not, Vysender. We will resume our conference,

and we will select a strategy. After the conference, I will head off to Oaktobron as planned with only one assistant guard. Only you will be aware that I will be conducting a strategy of my own."

Vysender scowled and grimaced and then began to pace the room. Maerora Ma occupied herself by staring at the walls, waiting for Vysender to come to his senses. The room they were in was the very room in which Yaylor Pi had, not too long ago, tenderly consoled her and reassured her about making the right choice by ordering the nineteenth mission.

"I'm waiting for your acknowledgement, Vysender."

"I have a duty to protect you."

"I ordained that duty," Maerora Ma said.

"It's still my duty."

"I hereby officially suspend your duty to protect me for the purpose of this one mission," she said looking into her glasses. "The documented sanction is now issued and sealed for one year."

"Maerora Ma, do you think you can pull off some diplomatic stunt? You know very well, you have deplorable diplomatic skills, and Roble is vile beyond words," he said.

"'Let every eye negotiate for itself\And trust no agent,'" she said in English.

"Indeed," he said.

"Don't be insubordinate . . . ." She then paused to accept an urgent incoming call from Mǎlīn.

"Mama, please come help me."

"What's wrong, Mǎlīn?"

"Just come. Please hurry. Turn off your tracker. I'm in the detention center at the bottom of the building in the conjugal-visit room."

"I'm coming," Maerora Ma said. "Vysender, I'll be back in moment. Mǎlīn needs my help. Proceed with the conference. Choose a contingency proposal. I don't care which one it is. If I fail, you'll have the plan of your choosing."

Maerora Ma then exited the room to rush to Mǎlīn. Her stride indicated urgency, but she moderated it to prevent attention. When she encountered a slow elevator, she applied her high-priority status through her glasses to reverse the elevator's direction and ordered the elevator's passengers to exit at once. She rode down and exited the elevator at the bottom of the building, and when she passed by the janitorial office, the night-shift supervisor waved to her with such familiarity it caused her to pause, but she then quickly resumed her swift journey to Mălīn. Upon entering the detention center, she drew her arms into her body and squirmed at the filth and grime that adorned the place. She entered the seemingly desolate area tentatively and peeked inside each of the murky windows of the cells that lined the corridor. There were no prisoners, and there were no guards. She then called Mălīn through her glasses.

"I'm here," she said.

Mălīn opened the door at the end of the hall and called to her mother.

Maerora Ma entered the room and immediately saw dead DeNitor in a wheelchair and another body lying flat on the floor in a copious pool of blood that was dispersing steadily across the room. The bed's cover was hanging low and wicking some of the blood. Maerora Ma gasped and then noticed the weapon in Mălīn's hand.

Mălīn watched her mother's eyes. She watched her survey, estimate, and judge the scene.

"Where did you get that weapon?"

"The nightshift janitor."

"Does he know about this?"

"No."

"Are you hurt?"

"No."

"How did you get the janitor's gun?"

"I asked him to give it to me."

"Well, then, he knows too much. Call him here, and tell him to bring his best cleaning equipment. Make sure he comes alone," Maerora Ma ordered.

"All right," Mălīn said, calling the janitor through her glasses.

"Give me the gun. Does it have a cloaking device?"

"Yes," Mălīn answered, placing the gun in the WCD inside her shoulder bag and handing it over to her mother.

"The janitor must die. I will kill him after he cleans up," Maerora Ma said.

"Oh-no, Mama, let's not do that," Mălīn begged.

Maerora Ma grabbed at Mălīn's collar and crumpled it tight into her fist and then pulled Mălīn's face three centimeters in front of her own. "You don't say anything. You just figure out how to survive the consequences of your choices," Maerora Ma growled and then forcefully shoved Mălīn by her throat into the muralled wall."

Mălīn coughed from the impact on her throat. "Mama," she whimpered in shock.

The supervising janitor then entered. "Oh, gosh!" he exclaimed.

"I am so sorry to have to meet you under these circumstances," Maerora Ma said. "What is your name?"

"Lu-Lugee," said the janitor.

"Lugee, this is an unfortunate situation, one that we mustn't ever reveal. I need for you to exert your expertise in sanitation to assure that this mess will be completely eliminated from existence. I will reward you tremendously. You will live like a king, and I will be forever indebted to you," Maerora Ma said.

"Oh, Ma'am, I am more than plee-pleased to be of use to you. I will clean this up in n-no time."

"Thank you so much. We'll stay with you and even help you if you need it."

The janitor pulled his equipment from his large filth-encrusted cart, which he parked just outside the door. "What about the b-bodies, Ma'am? Have you con-contacted Medical yet?" he asked.

"Lugee, removal of the bodies will also be part of the clean up. I imagine this request seems horrible to you, but there are traitors among us, and every day we work to keep our society flowing with only wholesome Magentans such as yourself. It is never a lovely sight to witness societal maintenance in the works, but I'm certain in your wisdom you'll find understanding," Maerora Ma said.

Mălīn stood quietly watching her mother operate. She rubbed her throat where her mother had pushed it.

"Yes, Ma'am. I will follow your or-orders. I will need help to lift the b-bodies onto my cart," he said.

Maerora Ma gestured to Mălīn to help the janitor, and Mălīn moved quickly to avail herself. "Mama, my clothes."

"Lugee, do you not have an extra set of coveralls for Mălīn?"

"Oh, yes, of course, I do," he said, rummaging through his cart. He handed Mălīn man-sized coveralls. She slipped them on and over her clothes and tightly rolled up the excess sleeves and legs.

Maerora Ma received a call from Vysender. "I'll be there soon, Vysender. Just carry on without me for now."

Lugee and Mălīn struggled to raise the prison guard's body onto the cart. DeNitor's body was easier to lift since his arms and legs had been shackled, and he remained upright in the wheelchair. Mălīn looked over at her mother who had turned her back and appeared to be examining a portion of the mural or looking into her pan-omni glasses, so Mălīn touched DeNitor's face and lightly caressed his cheek with her thumb.

Lugee started to slop mop the floor and then stopped to fold the wheelchair. "Ma'am, do you want to save the wheelchair?" he asked, looking at Maerora Ma. She shook her head, and he then folded it and placed it on top of the dead bodies. When he completed the mopping, he started to dry the floor by hand with a huge towel. Maerora Ma then initiated her inspection of the crime-scene clean up.

"Take the bedspread, Mălīn, and toss it onto the cart," she ordered. "What's next, Lugee?"

"I'll go-go to the vaporizing incinerator and d-dispose of the contents of my cart," he said.

"All right, let us go," Maerora Ma said.

"Oh, Ma'am, the in-incinerator is not a place for the ruler of Ma-Magenta to go to."

"You're such a gentleman, Lugee, to think of me that way, but worry not. I shall enjoy the experience. Tell me, though, are there many workers down there?"

Lugee, checked the time in his pan-omni glasses. "Not at the moment, Ma'am."

"All right, let us hurry then," Maerora Ma said.

Lugee snatched the sheet off the bed and spread it over his cart, and then the three paraded down to the vaporizing incinerator. Lugee led the way. Maerora Ma followed directly behind, carrying Mălīn's shoulder bag, and Mălīn trailed behind, walking awkwardly in the oversized coveralls.

They arrived at the bottom of the building's absolute bottom, which was overly squalid and covered with fetid debris of indiscernible matter. Both Maerora Ma and Mălīn gagged, and then Lugee handed them each a small disposable mask.

There was a large square opening in the wall that looked like an evil, foul mouth. Two huge grime-covered metal plates, one suspended from the top and the other jutted up from the bottom, appeared like teeth ready to gnaw at a staple of refuse.

"I will pl-place the contents of the cart on the designated m-mark there, and then I will draw that lever on the wall there, which will f-force the incinerator to swallow the contents. The m-metal plates will shut, and the con-contents will be vaporized," Lugee said.

"Lugee, let us include the entire cart. Do you mind?" Maerora Ma asked.

"Whatever you say, Ma'am. I'm h-here to serve," he said.

"You're such a good man, Lugee. Stand back, Mălīn," Maerora Ma said, pulling the weapon from the shoulder bag. Lugee pushed the cart near the incinerator's opening, and Maerora Ma aimed the weapon dead center at his back and fired once. Lugee fell and hit his face on the corner of the filthy cart. Maerora Ma then hurled the weapon and the shoulder bag at the cart and rushed to pull the incinerator lever.

A strong ghastly gust of warm, putrid-smelling wind then rushed from behind them, drawing both Maerora Ma and Mălīn towards the gaping mouth of the incinerator. Maerora Ma grasped at and anchored herself on a rail near the lever as the force of the wind grew stronger. The torrent of wind ripped her pan-omni glasses from her face and whipped her hair all about her head, forcing her to shut her eyes.

Mălīn stumbled and fell onto the floor and immediately started to slide towards the wicked mouth. She desperately grasped at the floor to secure herself as parts and parcels smacked at her on their way into the incinerator.

Maerora Ma risked removing one of her hands from the rail to hold back her lashing hair so she could see Mălīn, but she couldn't effectively hold back her hair and couldn't fight her reflexes to protect her eyes, so she ripped the mask from her face and screamed out Mălīn's name but heard no answer. "My daughter," she uttered and then thrust herself from the anchoring rail and rolled across the slimy floor where she caught a glimpse of Mălīn, clawing the crud on the floor and slipping under the influence of the incinerator's powerful siphon. "Mălīn!" Maerora Ma yelled.

Maerora Ma was then in the same position as Mălīn and was forced to claw at the floor. She had not moved closely enough to Mălīn to reach her, so she released herself from a chunk of glue she had dug into and was sucked closer towards the incinerator's mouth. She managed to clamp onto another clump of matter, and when she checked her proximity to the mouth, her hair lashed viciously across her face and at her eyes.

Mălīn lost her grip from the floor and barreled past Maerora Ma. When Maerora Ma stretched to reach for her daughter, she gave up her own fix and was then swept away. The metal plates of the mouth vigorously started to vibrate while gutter-gunk gales pulled mother and daughter swiftly towards the incinerator. The plates then collided shut, and both Mălīn and Maerora Ma simultaneously careened into them. Subsequent knocks, clanks, and booms occurred while the horrid-smelling wind died down, and the incinerator room became eerily still and silent.

Maerora Ma shifted herself and reached out to Mălīn. Mălīn began to throw up in her mask and then breathed in chunks and globs of vomit, which caused her to snort, cough, and choke.

Maerora Ma ripped the mask from her face and pulled Mălīn's head against her chest. "Blow your nose hard," Maerora Ma said, blocking a nostril, "Harder!" she said, and then she blocked the other nostril and repeated her instruction.

Mălīn continued to hack and cough and gag. Maerora Ma then stood and grabbed Mălīn by the arm and fiercely pulled her up. "C'mon, let's get out of here," she said.

Mălīn buckled at the knees and cried, and her mother relentlessly pulled her and dragged her out into the hallway. She spotted a nearby restroom and hauled Mălīn into it. They both stumbled in loudly spitting, hacking, and gagging. Maerora Ma noticed an occupant in one of the two stalls and tugged at Mălīn to pull her into the adjacent stall. Maerora Ma gestured to Mălīn to be quiet, but Mălīn started to retch, and so Maerora Ma aimed Mălīn's face down at the toilet where she then only heaved unproductively.

The restroom occupant quickly vacated the stall and exited the restroom without stopping at the washbasin. Maerora Ma then flew out of the stall and moistened a towel and returned to dab the vomit and gunk from Mălīn's face and hair. Mălīn started to sob, and Maerora Ma stood her up, unzipped her coveralls, and held Mălīn steady so she could step out of them.

Maerora Ma's face was full of slime. Scum skids ran over the front, back, and sides of her Eisenhower jacket, and her hair was tangled and ratted. Blood had collected under the conjunctiva of both of her eyes, and her fingernails were broken and filled with filth. She approached the washbasin and attempted to clean the muck from her clothing and face.

"I don't have my glasses. Do you have yours?"

"No, they're gone," Mălīn answered.

"C'mon, let's go," Maerora Ma said.

"What about the coveralls?"

"Roll them up and bring them with you," Maerora Ma said.

The two then exited the restroom and rushed back to their dwelling by taking stairways and alternate hallways. Once inside their dwelling, Maerora Ma ran the shower, stripped her clothes off, and removed Mălīn's clothes too. With the showerhead set to its highest power, Maerora Ma rinsed Mălīn and herself as well. She profusely lathered her daughter with soap and vigorously scrubbed her. Mălīn stood lifeless while water pounded her head. Maerora Ma stepped out of the shower and returned with nail clippers and madly clipped Mălīn's fingernails down to the quick, and then cut her own. Maerora Ma then pulled Mălīn into her body and held her tightly. Mălīn's chin rested on her mother's breast while water poured over their heads.

"Go dry yourself off now," Maerora Ma ordered and then lathered and scrubbed herself. After she dried herself off, she called to Mălīn and asked her to bring her one of her suits, the one with military symbols.

Mălīn returned with the suit. "Your eyes," Mălīn said, semi-horrified at what she was seeing.

"I'm aware of it," Maerora Ma said, placing her glasses on her face and darkening their tint. She then finished dressing herself and ordered Mălīn to accompany her to the airdrome on the side of the building.

MAERORA MA PLACED Mălīn in a seat of an air vehicle and then kneeled in front of her. "Mălīn, I'm seriously disappointed in what you've done. It's not your right to kill; it's not even my right. Now, what just happened seems like punishment enough, but it's not over. You're going to tell me exactly why you killed DeNitor. However, I can't deal with it right now, so we'll talk when I get back."

Mălīn stared blankly into Maerora Ma's darkened glasses and remained docile if not catatonic.

"Oh, Mălīn," Maerora Ma said lowly, "now's the time to be strong, ok? Answer me. You're going to be strong, right?"

Mălīn nodded.

"I need for you to take care of Captain Joan Jones. She's going to do something *very* important for me soon. You don't know how important, Mălīn, so please make sure she stays safe.

Do you understand?" Maerora Ma asked.

Mălīn was slow to nod and did so nearly imperceptibly.

"Be strong, my girl." Maerora Ma then pressed her forehead against Mălīn's forehead and whispered, "'Doubt that the stars are fire,/Doubt that the sun doth move . . . /Doubt truth to be a liar,/But never doubt I love.' And I especially love you."

AFTER MAERORA MA watched Mălīn's flight depart, she contacted Vysender. "Vysender, I'm ready to leave."

"All right, transport to the MOC is ready. The MOC itself has been inspected, and both stations are expecting you."

"I'm sorry that I've had to—"

"Don't explain," Vysender interrupted.

"Listen to me. I'm attempting to perform a very surgical maneuver, and this trip is only preparatory. You must not respond to whatever happens."

"Whatever," Vysender said.

"Listen to me! I'm ordering you to block all communication channels to Magenta. I don't want anyone here to know what I'm doing, and if you can—without detection—block realm-wide outgoing communication transmissions. Intercept them if you can, but don't get caught. If what I do on Oaktobron gets out, it gets out, and I can then explain it, but I would rather not have to."

"Acknowledged. Have a safe trip," he said perfunctorily.

"Vysender, if I don't make it back, you're the one I trust to facilitate transfer of power to Mălīn. I believe you will treat her as if she were Amora Ma. I'm sorry you're unhappy with me right now and probably will be forever. Just don't respond no matter what happens to me on Oaktobron. Consider it a queen's gambit."

THE MAGENTAN MORNING shined across my room as I lay in bed. The light woke me up along with the pain in my shoulder. I couldn't remember when I last ate, but I wasn't hungry because an aggregate of heavy emotions was bearing down on my chest and stomach. I missed Maerora Ma, and a constant pining for her was only weighing me down more. To make myself feel better, I reminisced about making love to her, but the imposing fear that she might be killed on Oaktobron quickly obliterated anything pleasant in my mind. After all, I had fought the Oaktobrons first hand. They were strong and thick, and—worst of all—they hated her.

I felt like some sort of alkali of anxiety was crystallizing in my veins, leaving me tense and jittery, so I again refocused my thoughts on the pleasure of Maerora Ma—her shallow breathing when she slept, the amazing gold that streamed through her skin, her nurturing concern for my well-being, the stunning sight of her in her beautiful sari. Oh, how I longed to embrace her, and the sweet thought of doing so enabled me to slip back into a vision-filled slumber that made me feel as if I were pleasantly swinging in a hammock in paradise until an awful sneaking thought slithered into my reverie—the serpents in the garden. What was I going to do about William and Porter? Everything would be all right if they were gone, but I certainly wasn't going to kill them.

I finally got out of bed and stood at the wall of windows to admire the beauty of the distant Magentan landscape. The morning light was the promise of the day, and it made me feel optimistic despite the William-Porter menace that had to be dealt with plus the pain in my shoulder.

A knock on the door startled me. "Who is it?" I asked.

"It's me, Mălīn, and Katydid too."

"Wait just a second. I need to cover myself." I quickly put on a light robe then opened the door. Katydid rushed in and latched onto my legs.

"Mălīn, are you feeling ok? You don't look well."

"I'm tired."

"Mălīn slept in my bed last night," Katydid said.

"She did!" I said, crouching down to Katydid's level. I then poked her in the belly, and she giggled. I stood up and I looked at Mălīn. "What's wrong?"

"Nothing . . . I told you I was tired. That's all."

"How's your mother? Have you heard from her?"

"She's fine. She reached the MOC station a little while ago," Mălīn said.

"MOC station?"

"The Magentan-Oaktobron Conduit. It's like the MIC but there's no realm barrier to pass through, and the distance travelled is far shorter," she explained.

"What about magenta deprivation?" I asked.

"The stations on the two ends of the MOC are equipped to treat it."

"Hungry, Mălīn," Katydid whined.

"Come have breakfast with us, Captain Joan Jones," Mălīn said.

AFTER BREAKFAST, I played with Katydid on a life-sized checkerboard in the huge observation room. Naturally, I didn't play the traditional game of checkers. Instead, I taught Katydid how to turn the huge pieces onto their sides and then roll them off the board.

"Let's see who can roll all her pieces off the board the quickest," I told her.

We then conducted a zillion contests, and even though I had use of only one arm, I won every time, but she never gave up trying and played in earnest, so I finally rewarded her with a win. She then chose to invite a dozen of her friends in and show them how to play, and as the children played, I walked over to Mălīn and sat next to her. She was lounging on the settee, staring blankly out at the sky. The sky was bare without its huge dying star.

"Mălīn? Are you all right?"

"Gosh! You keep asking me that," she said impatiently.

"Well, you're acting like you've been lobotomized."

"I don't know what that means."

"It doesn't matter," I said.

"I killed DeNitor."

"Oh, Mălīn, how awful," I said, reaching to console her.

"You don't know the half it," she said, maneuvering out of my reach, "and I don't want to re-live it. I just want you to do your part now," she said.

"I told you I'm not going to kill my crewmates."

Mǎlīn closed her eyes and looked as if she were calming herself with meditation or contemplating a solution or something, so I took the opportunity to study her. She was well bred but still young, beautiful but not yet a woman, smart but not yet wise. She was clearly Maerora Ma's daughter but Densip Pi's daughter too. When she opened her eyes, she glared at me for staring too closely at her, and when she started to speak, I interrupted her.

"Mǎlīn, I have an idea. How about if I go out to the garden and convince them to go back home? We can send them through the MIC while your mother is away."

"Nothing goes through the MIC without the whole damn world knowing about it," she said.

"How did Densip Pi do it?"

"I don't know. It's too much of a huge undertaking. You need to kill your crewmates, and that's all there is to it. Everything else is just a waste of effort, so don't talk to me about anything else. Just hurry up and let me know what you're going to do."

"Even if I decided to kill them, I wouldn't be able to since I only have one useful arm," I said.

"I'll get you a weapon."

"Mǎlīn, I want to be liberated."

"What do you mean?"

"The truth, Mǎlīn! Let's just explain everything."

"No! Never!" she screamed, and all the children turned their heads to look at us but then quickly resumed in the fun they were having.

"I'm going to tell Maerora Ma the truth," I said.

"Don't you love her? You'll hurt her so deeply if she learns that I plotted to kill her. How could you be so heartless?"

I turned to watch the children play and to think about what Mǎlīn had just said. The answer was, yes, I did love Maerora Ma, but, no, I wasn't being heartless. The flow of life doesn't sneak and hide. It courses through the world like a river, and I wasn't going to lie to Maerora Ma anymore.

"I'm finished here. I'm going back to my room," I said, standing up.

"All right, Captain Joan Jones, but I'm going to have to confine you now that I'm aware of your former intentions to assassinate my mother. I'll restrict you to your room and let my mother deal with you when she gets back. I'm going to order that the Earth males be rounded up as well."

"Don't kill them, Mălīn."

"They have to die. They know too much."

"Then kill me with them," I said.

"I can't."

"Why?"

"Because my mother needs you."

"Well . . . ."

"Well, what?" she asked.

"Well, I'll do my best not to implicate you, but I'm going to tell her the truth, and it's going to include Densip Pi."

Mălīn dropped to the floor and placed her head in my lap. "I beg of you, please, I beg of you not to tell her anything, please, please, please."

"Mălīn, stop it! The children are watching us."

"Come with me then," she said solemnly, "and if you don't cooperate, I'll have the guards assist me."

I followed her as she led me back to my room. We didn't speak, and she never bothered to turn to check how far away from her I was as I followed her. When we stopped in front of my door, she opened it with her glasses.

"I'm beginning to hate Earth humans," she said. "They killed my sister and broke my mother. And we were so stupid to believe female humans were motherly and reasonable. Well, you'll never know what a truly phenomenal wonder my mother is. You'll never bear witness to a better mother in any of the realms." Tears streamed down her cheeks, and she then ordered the door shut and locked.

CHAPTER 11:
OAKTOBRON

SHE HAD crossed through the MOC then checked into the Oaktobron-side station and was now landing on Oaktobron. The Oaktobron airport was like any other airport, but Maerora Ma's arrival was extraordinary. Hyper ceremonialism covered every corner. A plushy laid carpeted walkway flanked by military-clad trumpeters stretched across the airport apron. School-aged boys sang ancient Oaktobron hymns of celebrated battle victories. Banners and flags rippled softly in a gentle breeze, and the vines of large-petalled flowers were laced through lattice barriers.

Though the dominant cast of light on Oaktobron was dull orange, Maerora Ma only saw magenta. She was expected to stroll down the walkway alone, but Roble instead walked out towards her once he saw that she appeared hesitant to step out into the open. Upon close proximity, he extended his hand to her and chivalrously gestured that he would lead the way. His bulk and size diminutized Maerora Ma's stature.

"Welcome, Maerora Ma. I'm grateful for your suggestion of a peaceful transfer of power. Few rulers, if any, would ever—"

"Please, don't remind me of the hara-kiri I'm about to commit," she said, looking warily out at the gathering of Oaktobrons. "Can we go inside as soon as possible?"

"I understand your distress. I'm told you've come with only one guard, and he remains at the station, is that right?"

"Yes, I have every intention to honor our deal. I hope you can say the same."

"Come, let's go inside. I've taken a great deal of precaution to protect you, but I can't help that you've allowed Oaktobrons to become so discontented during your reign as ruler of the realm," he said, placing his hand on her back to guide her down the carpeted path. Each trumpeter played a single sustained note in succession, a half step down then a half step up, as the two passed by. Hecklers in the distant could be heard while mordant murmurs rumbled through the nearby group of onlookers.

"There will be no peace if any harm comes to me."

"Let's not be disagreeable today," Roble said, stopping to lift her hand. He then started to kiss it, but she pulled it away.

"And let us not fornicate today," she said.

He chuckled and laughed and then gestured to her to enter an archway that led indoors. Once inside, Roble ordered a few camera operators to ready themselves.

"Come, I've arranged for footage to be taken of us. This day will be the most commemorated day of my life," Roble said.

The camera operators then directed Maerora Ma to stand in front of the great seal of Oaktobron as they adjusted their light diffusers and recorder settings before starting the actual footage. "Won't you remove your glasses, Maerora Ma?" A camera operator requested.

"I'd rather not," she said.

"And why is that?" Roble asked brusquely.

"It's better if they remain on."

"They'll spoil the footage," Roble said, attempting to snatch them off her face.

Maerora Ma grabbed his hand, and he retrieved it back immediately. She then moved in closely towards him to reveal her injured eyes.

"Oh, I've forgotten you're ill. You're right. It's best for them to remain on and darkened. I want no sign of an ailing ruler in my footage. I will have attained the seat of the realm without one drop of blood lost and will have gained it from a *formidable* ruler, not a sickly waif."

AFTER THE PHOTO SHOOT, Roble escorted Maerora Ma through to the greater part of the building, which was a

Romanesque-style coliseum and was open to the sky and held an over-capacity crowd. As they walked through the venue, entertainers on the main stage pacified the audience while just behind the stage, event organizers gave rein to chaos and scurried to and fro, yakking into their pan-omni glasses and exhibiting utter impatience when blocked or clipped by anyone in their path.

As Roble and Maerora Ma approached Roble's luxury box, he instructed her to pause and wait.

"Roble, I can't sit out there exposed without even a shield to protect me," Maerora Ma said.

"Don't worry. You're precious goods at the moment. You'll be protected by virtue of proximity to me," he replied.

Grating music then sounded, and all the Oaktobrons in the world were instructed to stand as Roble was revealed to the crowd. Roble then seated himself in a gaudy throne-like chair, and Maerora Ma was instructed to sit behind and to the left of him in an ordinary seat.

"Any one of the thousands of participants here can take aim at me," Maerora Ma said, leaning into Roble's throne.

"They won't with me present unless they're intending to commit suicide," Roble said.

"Very careless, Roble, very careless," she uttered and shook her head, and when she sat back, she discovered two individuals had sat next to her on the right. It was the leaders of Birchron and Pinovra.

"Maerora Ma, it's been ages since I've seen you," said the Pinovran, speaking in Magentan.

"Do either of you speak Earth English?" she asked.

They both shook their heads no.

"Too bad because I was going to share a line of Shakespeare with you, but what good would it do if it fell on deaf ears?"

"I think it would do neither good nor do bad," the Pinovran said as if answering a great legendary riddle.

"Yes, and words heard are just vibrations that travel through the air, no?" she said.

"You're very odd, Maerora Ma."

"Yes, as odd as the truth itself telling a lie," she said.

The music subsided, and an unseen speaker spoke in Oaktobron in meter and rhyme. Maerora Ma looked up at the sky and recognized the old dying star, which appeared only one-eighth the size she was used to seeing it at. She then adjusted the language translator in her pan-omni glasses and listened to the speaker finish reciting an elegy about a famous Oaktobron inventor. When the speaker finished the poem, he introduced Quercus, and Quercus then began his speech.

"I've discovered that once in a life time, something truly great happens, and this technology we are showcasing here today is truly once-in-a-lifetime great. It's so great, in fact, that it has astounded the highest cloud-occluded mountain-peak dweller of the entire cosmos, and she has actually vacated her plateau hermitage to be among us here today, breathing the same air, my fellow Oaktobrons, and walking on the same ground as you and I. The light of our endeavors shall shine in her face and reflect the future and illuminate the Oaktobron path of blessed expansion, for we have finally crawled out of the dark wilderness of sub-existence. The bolide of our liberation shall stream across the blessed sky because Oaktobron determination and will is the bright future of this realm and beyond." Quercus then paused for an applause that endured for many minutes.

Maerora Ma darkened the tint on her glasses and closed her eyes. She had now been out of magenta light for over an hour.

"Thank you, my fellow Oaktobrons," Quercus said. "Let us now acknowledge the ruler of Magenta for her wisdom in realizing the exact point at which we Oaktobrons surpassed all other realm inhabitants in knowledge, in capability, and in so many other ways. Yes, in her grace and dignity, she knew today was the day to stand down, and on this day with the release of Oaktobron desire, there shall be no war because Maerora Ma is the only Magentan leader capable of taking the bow of peace, and that, my fellow Oaktobrons, is the epitome of true wisdom, grandness, and grace for which we will always honor and admire her. Let her now stand here and speak to you, and you too shall witness—in the flesh—her extreme dignity."

Tepid applause ensued while Quercus offered his hand to Maerora Ma. She relied on his assistance to pull herself up. She then approached the podium and firmly grasped its frame.

"As the daughter of the beloved Amora Ma, I congratulate Oaktobron today. Its ever-bourgeoning technical prowess has led it to the victory of superiority. I bow . . . yes, I bow to Oaktobron superiority. If I did not, five-hundred-thousand deaths would prove Oaktobron superiority otherwise."

She paused and appeared reluctant to go on while the Birchron and Pinovran exchanged a dozen sidelong glances. The Oaktobron light of day was bright, so Maerora Ma adjusted her pan-omni glasses' tint even darker to the point that she probably could no longer see through them, but she could still read her speech within them, and so she continued.

"On this day—your day—I will refrain from recounting Magenta's celebrated past because this is *your* day. It is no longer our day. The shell of the sphere of night has rotated over Magenta. We now have our nighttime constellations to ponder, and our daytime sky objects to long for. In our ruminations, we'll find fortitude in the realization that our all-encompassing governance nurtured a thriving peace and enabled a wide and rampant period of harmony. Like a mother suckling her child, Magenta has nourished the world with provident care, and, now, like a grandmother in her rocking chair, she shall sit and dole out wisdom on which the realms might sustain themselves." She then engaged a pause and lightened her glasses to look at Magenta's loyal companion, the dying star. It was dark and none of its fissures of light glimmered. She then returned to her speech.

"Nevertheless, I shall grieve but little since we will have the fearless Roble ahead of us to endeavor the future. The future is a well-veiled lady and hope rests peacefully between her breasts, along with death and ruination, which are hidden from us now, but we all know they are there. A lady's man will fare well, so, let me now bow to Roble."

She then turned to face Roble and lowered her head slightly. He stood, approached her, embraced her, shook her hand, kissed her cheek, and then brought her back to her seat before he returned to the podium to speak.

"There are many ways in which to rule a mass of sentient beings. You can totally control every aspect of their lives, or you can ensure every aspect of their lives is free from control, or you can do a little of both, or you can do nothing at all. What is the best approach? We don't know," he said, shrugging like a Frenchman. "Civilizations rise and fall, and every one of them has a zenith and a nadir, but it is clear that total Magentan control is *over!*"

Applause rippled through the ocean of Oaktobrons as Maerora Ma looked over at the perplexed faces of the Birchron and Pinovran. She intruded upon them with a sustained glance, and they, in turn, looked at each other.

"We will no longer let the strongest among us be plucked away," Roble announced, "and we will no longer hear it explained as some sort of artificial societal maintenance. We will now live in the *wildlife* of desire and *thrust* our zenith through the sky and beyond. We will not backtrack into our ancient past; we will push forward into uncharted eternity. The third realm . . . ," he paused as thunder roared up from the ground floor of the coliseum. "There are no barriers we cannot overcome. The third realm is ready to receive us, and I here and now reveal to you the Effa-ray cannon."

A huge replica of the device was then wheeled onto the stage. Roble turned perpendicular to the podium to ogle it. It was a huge-barreled cannon that looked like the medieval Pumhart von Steyr. It had a protruding stubby barrel and wide-open cavernous bore. Roble demonstrated a hearty adoration for it while Maerora Ma looked down as if to pray, and the Birchron and Pinovran watched Maerora Ma with tentative expressions like kittens whose mother had just been switched with a jackal.

When Roble pulled a lever on it, the cannon blew a stream

of fire that heated the vicinity with a temperature high enough to sting the eyes of all those present within the coliseum. Some cried in delight while others clapped fanatically. Father's embraced their sons, and mothers gazed adoringly at the spectacle in the sky.

Roble's chest protruded as he stood and observed his people. He finally signaled an end to the ceremony and whisked Maerora Ma away down to a lower level of the stadium.

"Where are we going? I need to get back to the station. I'm beginning to feel shaky," Maerora Ma said.

"Must you so readily advertise your pathetic weakness?" he said, pushing her into a dark room.

"Why have you brought me here?"

The room was like an ancient dungeon that had crumbly cinder-block walls and a floor paved with concrete. A single large niche in the middle of the wall across from the door housed a huge wax candle that was consuming the room's oxygen and replacing it with the rank burning esters of fat.

"I intend to have a commemorative painting made," he said.

"How about if we do this when I return for the death-acknowledgement visit?"

"Death acknowledgements are such a waste of time."

"Roble, I really do need to get back to the station. I'm not feeling well."

"Would you shut up! I hate hearing that," he yelled. "I ought to poke you rough and fast against that wall right there."

"Roble! Why would you do that?"

"Because I can," he said.

"'Because you can'? Did you read that in your morning book of nursery rhymes?"

He suddenly struck her face firmly with the back of his hand, which sent her pan-omni glasses flying against the wall. "Your sarcasm is as pathetic as you are."

"I've just graciously handed over the realm. How could you—"

"Shut up! I won't be cheated of my commemorative painting.

Every great victory is commemorated in a painting that hangs in a museum to venerate the victor. Ask me what the title of my painting will be," he said, moving into her personal space.

She moved back a step.

"C'mon, ask me."

She refused to answer, so Roble grabbed her collar and pulled her face to his, and with a clenched jaw, he growled, "Ask me."

"What're you going to call it?" Maerora Ma whispered.

"Well, now, since you're curiosity is so charming, let me tell you," he said, releasing her collar. "I'm going to call it the rape of Magenta. You see, the artist will be up soon," he said looking down.

"Let us negotiate—"

"Shut up!" he yelled and then proceeded to undo his pants.

"I'm not well, remember? And I'm possibly contagious."

He froze for a slight moment and then said, "Bah! I have ten healing machines in my home. I use them regularly. I've probably had far worse in my lifetime than what you have, three times over too. You're lying anyway. You're just trying to stop me."

"We have contingency plans if any harm should—"

"Humph! I have the granddaddy of all weapons, and you mean to tell me that you have a few arrangements of toothpicks to flick at me," he said and then laughed wickedly.

"All I know is that the outcome of your assault on me will give rise to ramifications," she said.

"Mmm, I love threats. Threats enrage me, and rage gets the blood pumping, and blood fills the most important part of me, so keep the threats coming," he said, pushing her backwards into the wall.

"Roble . . . please. I'm ailing."

"Oh, bloody shit! Don't be pathetic. I hate pansies that blow limp in the wind and lose their petals with the faintest of puffs. You're weak, Maerora Ma, and that's why you've had to give up the realm. You're not strong like me. Shit! I could kill you with my bare hands right now, but you could never kill me with your bare hands, not in a million years. It's no wonder that you resort to plucking out the strong ones from Magentan society. You call them discontented, but the truth is you're not strong enough to withstand the force of growth, expansion, and change that they bear in their hearts. You're contagious all right. Just look at how pitiable all the men of Magenta are. They've all caught your wicked weakness as if it were a common cold. It is sick! Sick! Sick! Sick!" Roble said, exposing his long teeth with each successive sibilant s.

"Roble . . . please," she whimpered as he remained holding her to the wall with his large hand pressed up against the middle of her chest.

"Oh, dammit! Look at how uninspiring you are. I can't even get it up for you because you're so pathetic. The artist won't be able to come today."

He then hailed a few Oaktobron assistants through his glasses, and they readily appeared. "Transport her to her vessel and do so covertly," he ordered and then released her from the wall. "Each ounce of weakness she exhibits subtracts from the magnificence of my victory."

"Roble . . . the tech . . . ."

"I've honored the damn deal," Roble said. "The technician is already at the station."

Maerora Ma then moved to retrieve her glasses, and as she reached down for them, Roble set the top of his foot under her abdomen and rolled her over to the floor with a slow shove of his leg. One of the Oaktobron assistants gasped, and Roble then glared at him.

"I'll have that painting, Maerora Ma, and I'll expect you to be fit and ready for it upon your return."

CHAPTER 12:
MALCONTENT MALES

"Mălīn, we've scoured the garden and the rest of the grounds. The Earth males must be at large," reported a Magentan guard.

"What?" Her face significantly lightened in shade.

"We found feces in the garden. We're having it examined to determine how many days old it is—"

"Check again!"

"But—"

"Do it!" she ordered and then ran to Captain Joan Jones' room. She banged on the door and then unlocked and opened it immediately with her pan-omni glasses.

Mălīn ran into my room like a large cannon ball hurling into an old wooden ship. I was soaking in the bath because the pain in my shoulder had started becoming unbearable. I jumped up instantly.

"Mălīn! What the hell?" I yelled and grabbed a towel to cover myself.

"The Earth males are gone!"

"Oh, my God! They're deadly, Mălīn. We're not safe. Get Katydid. We've got to get out of here. Where can we go?"

"Headquarters," Mălīn said.

"Hurry!"

I was shivering cold from still having wet hair from my bath, plus I was sitting under the air vehicle's air-conditioner vent. My shoulder was killing me, and Katydid was fussing and constantly kicking her seat with her heels.

"Katydid, please stop it," I said.

"No, I don't want to go to headquarters," she whined.

"It's too late. We're on our way there," I said, and then the little girl whacked her seat with all her might in futile protest.

"Captain Joan Jones, what're we going to do?" Mălīn asked, sitting directly across from me.

"Shh, don't talk in front of . . . ," I said, pointing at Katydid behind one of my hands.

Mălīn, pushed back in her seat. She was unable to subdue her nervous energy and so remained in unending motion, crossing her legs, uncrossing her legs, folding her arms, unfolding them, etc.

Her restlessness was irritating me, so I closed my eyes to center myself, but doing so let a gorge of heavy, thick syrup fill my stomach, and it had the flavor of regret, the regret of failing to do the right thing. I should have told Maerora Ma about my mission right away, but instead I chose to pursue pleasure, the pleasure of Maerora Ma's attraction. At what point could I have told her about William and Porter? If I weren't going to kill her, why would I tell her about *them*? And now they were the menace of the hour, a fatal threat whose absolving had to be undertaken. A strong spasm of regret then shook me, and when I opened my eyes, Mălīn was watching me.

"Mălīn," I said, "are you able to reach your mother?"

Mălīn looked into her glasses. "No. It's strange . . . seems like a communications black out."

"When will she be back?" I asked, and then a sudden sharp pain struck my shoulder.

"I don't know," Mălīn answered.

"Mălīn, I'm in a lot of pain."

"I don't know what to do" she said.

"Can you call Bonson?"

Mălīn stared into her glasses and then handed them to me as a little ball floated in front of me.

"Bonson?"

"Yes, I see you Captain Joan Jones. How are you?"

"Not good. My shoulder . . . ."

"Come to the hospital." he ordered.

"The hospital—"

"No! We won't be safe there," Mălīn shouted.

"You and Katydid can be dropped off at headquarters, and then I'll go on to the hospital by myself," I suggested.

"No, I can't leave you," Mălīn said, "I promised my mother I would take care of you."

"I'll be in good hands with Bonson, Mălīn. Don't worry about me," I said.

"But I'm frightened to be here without you," Mălīn said.

"Mălīn, the guards will protect you."

"No! You don't understand. The guards won't be able to recognize the Earth males, neither will I nor anyone else. Earth people look like Magentans to us. They could easily steal the uniforms of guards and walk around freely until they find us. You're the only one who would be able to identify them quickly enough."

"What's this about Earth males?" Bonson asked.

"Nothing, Bonson, Mălīn's talking about some animals she saw in her mother's Earth garden. That's all," I said.

"Hmm, I thought I heard 'Earth males,'" he said.

"No, she said 'Earth garden.' Anyway, please just come to headquarters, Bonson, and please come soon. I can't handle this pain." I then pulled off the glasses and told Mălīn to terminate the call quickly.

"Why's Mălīn frightened?" Katydid asked.

"She's not *really* frightened. She just said that so I would play with you at headquarters. Would you like to play?"

Katydid nodded her head up and down exaggeratedly.

ONCE WE DEPLANED, Mălīn made a beeline to her destination. Katydid and I followed. The headquarters building was large and had huge windows at the upper levels where we were apparently headed.

"Mălīn, slow down," Katydid said, running as quickly as she could but trailing us by a few meters. I stopped to pick her up, which wasn't easy with only one arm. We then rode up on an elevator and emptied out onto a floor, which was essentially an island atop a huge column in the center of the building. We walked towards the middle of the floor, and then stepped down a small set of stairs where Mălīn stopped abruptly at a door. She then ordered a guard to check with infrared for anybody on the other side, and as we waited for the infrared sweep, Bonson appeared.

"What's going on here?" he asked.

"Mălīn's been uneasy ever since the attack in Morgana, so she's having the vicinity checked for Oaktobrons. Anyway, my shoulder, Bonson, can you do something?"

I set Katydid down and stood next to Bonson so he could examine my shoulder. The guard then reappeared and told Mălīn all was clear.

"It's impossible for Oaktobrons to be in headquarters," Bonson said as we all walked into a luxurious abode.

"C'mon, let's play now," Katydid said.

"In a minute, Katydid," I told her.

Katydid then ran out to a large balcony area, and Bonson directed me to a settee while Mălīn remained standing, watching me. I grimaced as Bonson pressed my shoulder and moved my arm about.

"You have failed to keep your shoulder immobile, Captain Joan Jones," he chided me, "and I'm hesitant to give you anything for fear you'll have an adverse reaction."

"I can't bear the pain," I said and felt my eyes begin to water.

"If you go to the hospital, we can apply an electronic apparatus that will help reduce the discomfort you're feeling."

"No!" Mălīn shouted like a demon-possessed lunatic.

"Good God, Mălīn," I said.

"Bonson, you can go now," Mălīn ordered. "When my mother gets back, we'll bring Captain Joan Jones to the hospital."

Bonson shook his head but obeyed Mălīn's orders anyway, and before leaving, he brought me into a sumptuous bedroom and had me lie down on top of the plush covers of the bed. Large oil paintings hung on the wall and had ornate golden borders that framed ancient Magentan scenes of naked statuesque goddesses and nymphs. When Bonson left, Mălīn entered the bedroom.

"What's our plan?" she asked.

Katydid then stomped into the room with her arms akimbo. "Are we going to play or not?"

"Get out!" Mălīn screamed viciously at her little sister.

"Mălīn," I said, attempting to admonish her.

Katydid started to cry, so I got up from the bed to console her despite the intense pain in my shoulder.

"We need a plan," Mălīn said.

"I haven't changed my mind about what I'm going to tell your mother." I said, sitting back down on the bed with Katydid still in my arm.

"And what you're going to tell her doesn't include me," Mălīn said.

"*Of course*, Mălīn. We've discussed this already," I said, rocking Katydid gently. "Whose bedroom is this?"

"My mother's," Mălīn said. "Now, listen to me. You can't mention anything about Densip Pi. She'll immediately be suspicious of me."

"It's essential that your mother know about Densip Pi."

"I ought to rip your damn arm out of its socket right now."

"I don't think your mother would appreciate that," I said, still rocking the now sleeping Katydid. "I've been thinking we might be able to soften the blow if we find out about the Earth male who killed Morgana."

"Oh, yeah, that makes real sense. Just go ahead and remind her of her dead daughter right in the middle of explaining how her middle child plotted to kill her," she said.

"Mălīn, your mother bears such a burden of guilt about the nineteenth mission. If we can absolve her of killing hundreds of humans, it can only help." I gently set Katydid down on her mother's pillows and covered her with her mother's covers. Mǎlīn had been leaning against the wall during the entire conversation, so I asked her to sit beside me on the bed. She shrugged and exhibited reluctance but finally relented to do so.

"Is it possible I can use your glasses to research our internet? Your mother told me that Magentans had downloaded the entire contents of our internet at one point. I may be able to find something about the unknown Earth mission," I said.

"You won't be able to do much with my glasses. They're tuned to my neural-wave patterns, but I *can* patch them into one of my spare glasses and let you watch everything I do. You can then tell me what to search for," she said.

"All right, let's do that," I said.

We then left Katydid asleep in Maerora Ma's bed and sat out on the balcony in lounge chairs. The windows overhead revealed a dark sky, which must have been overcast with clouds since there were no stars in the sky, and the huge dying star itself was out of sight.

Mǎlīn had retrieved her spare glasses along with a warm pad for my shoulder. She even checked and tightened my sling. I guess she wasn't going to pull my arm out of its socket after all.

I placed her glasses on my face and could then see a seamless and infinitely large computer screen. "Is there footage of the Earth male dropping out of the MIC?" I asked.

"My mother forbids anyone to view the death of Morgana. I don't think *I* can even access it."

"Well, try," I said and she did. I could then see inside my glasses her attempting to find the footage, and then suddenly I could see the horrible moment of Morgana being shot to death. "Oh, my God." I pulled off the glasses and turned to look at Mǎlīn.

She was frozen.

Mǎlīn?" I called, but she didn't answer. I waited for her to process the horrific imagery, and then I thought about Maerora Ma herself. How long was it before she could even eat food after losing Morgana? Could she ever again truly enjoy seeing a puppy play or a kitten suckle or a butterfly flit about without remembering how Morgana might have enjoyed puppies, kittens, and butterflies? Oh, God, poor Maerora Ma.

"Mălīn, I feel bad that you had to see that," I said, "but we have to keep researching. Can you please zoom in on the face of the Earth male?"

She remained quiet as silent little tears trickled down her cheeks.

"I'm so sorry, Mălīn," I said, moving to embrace her.

She cried and nestled her head into my neck.

"I'm sorry. It's horrible, I know," I said, stroking her back.

She moved out of my embrace and wiped her eyes and nose with the sleeves of her shirt. "I didn't cry when Morgana died. I never cried for her until just now," she said. "I'm cold-hearted."

"Ah, Mălīn," I said, holding her hand.

"I was always worried my mother would be mad, but, lucky for me, she never noticed that I hadn't cried. You probably think I'm cold hearted, don't you?"

"No, not at all," I said. "There's just no way in the world anyone would ever be prepared for the way Morgana died. It seems maybe your mother was shipwrecked on top of the raging sea while you were submerged below in a suffocating submarine."

She repeatedly sniffed and wiped her nose.

"Mălīn, we really have to continue researching. Can you wear your glasses again and zoom in on the Earth male?"

She put on her glasses and then viewed the Earth male's face closely, and I could then see that the Earth male was of Indian descent.

"Zoom in on his name tag," I said, and then I read his name aloud, "Shri Durga."

"Do you know him?" she asked, still congested from crying.

"No. His uniform is not U.S. military issue. My guess is that he may have been a member of one of the study cooperatives that took up residence at the mouth of the MIC. Can you search the Earth internet for 'Shri Durga'?" I requested.

Too many results then appeared.

"Search again. This time enter 'Shri Durga magenta goddess.'"

"Earth has a magenta goddess?" Mălīn asked.

"Well, India has a lot of goddesses," I said while noticing an interesting headline. "Select the last one, please . . . no, Mălīn, the one on the bottom that says, 'Mother Matriarch of Matrifocal Khasi Banishes Son.' Give me a minute to read this article."

While I read the article, Mălīn removed her glasses and went into the abode. She returned later with two glasses of fluid.

"Was there anything useful in the article?" she asked, handing me a glass.

"Maybe," I said. "Tell me why Magentans claim that Earth is the source of all things? Where did that come from?" I asked.

"It's an ancient notion," she said.

"'Notion'? Why do you say '*notion*'?"

"Because it's not scientific. Only fools believe it," she said.

"But where does it come from? How did it originate?"

"An ancient archeologist proposed it. She claimed that Magenta, Oaktobron, Birchron, and Pinovra all followed a pattern of goddess worship and that at the core of their beliefs was the notion that Earth is the source of all things."

"Interesting," I said.

"Yeah, but what makes it hokey is supposedly the goddess that these four planets worshipped was magenta colored."

"Was the archeologist Magentan?" I asked.

"Yes, but—"

"Well, that explains it, right? I mean, you know, Magentans can only see magenta." I said.

"And gold," she said. "But, don't you see what a major flaw that is? Her work has always been considered overly biased and never accepted by serious scholars," Mălīn argued.

"So, I guess if you're from Earth, you can't postulate anything about Earth, and if you're a man, surely you wouldn't have anything useful to say about men, and if you were a woman—"

"I get your point, but it doesn't change anything. Only stupid people believe Earth is the source of all things."

"Does your mother believe it?"

Mălĭn shrugged. "I don't know. All I know is that she always protests the discussion of it and claims it's not polite to talk about it, but I understand why she does that. It's because the whole idea of the MIC is based on the notion that Earth is the source of all things."

"Well, I'd say she believes it whole heartedly then."

"That's embarrassing. Why do you think that?"

"Because she desperately wants me to help her unite Earth and Magenta."

"I didn't know that. When did she say that?"

"She announced it at the banquet, and she's told me privately too."

"Hmm, I guess that's why she insists I protect you while she's away, and I thought it had something to do with Oaktobron," she said then paused. "So, you're The Great Liaison, eh?"

"'The Great Liaison'?" I asked.

"My mother didn't explain The Great Liaison?"

"Well, she mentioned it."

"Oh, gosh, I hate having to think of my mother as stupid."

"Mălĭn, you're committing a logical fallacy."

"A what?"

"It doesn't matter. Now, listen, Shri Durga's mother's name is Monisha Durga, and I met her briefly before I came here."

"So, you *do* know him then," she said.

"*No, I don't.* I just found out about him right now. I never knew of him, and I had only just met his mother before I came to Magenta. I told you."

"I don't care. Just tell me why he killed Morgana?"

"I don't know why he killed Morgana, but his mother banished him for rebelling against community-accepted norms, and, like you, he insisted the idea of a magenta-colored goddess was *unscientific*. He was determined to destroy the goddess culture that he grew up in. He wanted his community to rise up and become a technologically advanced society, and somehow he managed to access the MIC."

"How is all this going to make my mother feel better?"

We then both heard a loud knock on the door, which caused Mălīn to jump from her seat and cling to me from behind.

"The Earth males," she said.

"Can't you check who it is with your glasses?" I asked.

"Their tracker is off. I'm trying to get a camera aimed on them. They look like guards, but I can only see their backs. Can you recognize them from behind?"

"No," I said. "We need to identify them. Talk to them through your glasses."

We both then headed closer towards the door behind which they were standing.

"Turn on your trackers and state your names," she ordered in Magentan, and when they started communicating back to her in Magentan, I felt tremendous relief.

"What do they want, Mălīn?"

"Vysender sent them here to ask me about the feces that was found in the garden," she said.

"Feces?" I asked.

"Excrement," she said.

"I know damn well what feces is, Mălīn. You didn't tell me about it earlier."

"The guards want to come in," she said.

"What did you tell the guards at home about me?" I asked.

"Nothing."

"We can't trust them. They might lock me up since I'm associated with the Earth males," I said.

"We can't let that happen. You're the only one who can identify them," she said.

"Call your mother."

"Long-range communications are down."

"Call Vysender then."

"Do you trust him?" she asked.

"Mălīn, don't you have authority over him?"

"Well, yes, technically I do since my mother is not available."

"Invoke your power."

She then called Vysender, and spoke to him in Magentan.

I couldn't understand what was being said, but they seemed to be arguing intensely, and I wondered if Mǎlīn was any match for him. I hoped she knew how to wield her power.

"Captain Joan Jones, we need to go to the MOC's Magenta-side station right away." Mǎlīn said.

"Why?"

"Vysender is going to inform my mother about the Earth males as soon as he can, which is right when she hits the Magenta-side station. We have to get to her before he does, so hurry. Let's go."

"But what about the guards at the front door?" I asked.

"You're right. Ok, I know a secret way out of here. C'mon, let's hurry. Can you get Katydid?"

"Mǎlīn, I can't carry her anymore . . . my shoulder."

"It's ok, I'll get her."

WE ARRIVED at the MOC's Magenta-side station relatively quickly. Maerora Ma was still in transport through the MOC. The station was cold, and the coldness made my shoulder ache, but I felt safer at the station than I did at headquarters because William and Porter, resourceful as they were, would never be able to get to this place. Nevertheless, Vysender and his guards could capture me at anytime. We were somewhere between Maganta's mesosphere and thermosphere. Less than ten Magentans were present at the station, which was a mostly empty sphere the size of a football field. We sat in a small transparent enclosure and huddled together to keep warm. Katydid was shivering severely, and I then began to feel more frightened about what Maerora Ma would do to me for letting her baby freeze rather than what she would do when she heard about William and Porter on the loose, so I removed my sling and wrapped it around her head to keep her ears warm. A handful of other transparent enclosures were scattered throughout the sphere, and I could see each was filled with a Magentan or two.

"How much longer is it going to take until your mother

arrives?" I asked.

"I don't know."

"It's freezing in here," I said. "Can you contact the others in the enclosure across the way and ask them for spare blankets?"

"No."

"Well, why not? It's way too cold for Katydid."

"Because seals are taken very seriously here. You're expected to enter and exit an enclosure only once."

"Well, lay yourself on top of Katydid then. We need to keep her warm," I said, curling up into the little girl and wrapping myself around her. Mălīn did the same.

"Captain Joan Jones?" Mălīn called.

"What, Mălīn?"

"Vysender told me something strange."

"What?" I asked.

"He said my mother sold her soul to Roble. Why do you think he said that?"

"I have no idea," I said and wondered what Maerora Ma was up to. After a short time, though, I had fallen asleep.

AN ETHEREAL SOUND, like soft chimes and light bells, entered my slumber. It was a jingling sound that one might imagine would be accompanied by someone throwing fairy dust. I opened my eyes and the inside of the sphere was slowly filling in with iridescent-like plasma. I really thought I was dreaming, especially when Maerora Ma appeared walking through the plasma like an apparition. I shook my head and rubbed my eyes, and then Katydid and Mălīn untangled themselves and ran to their mother.

"Mălīn, what in the world are you doing here?" Maerora Ma said, picking up Katydid. She was wearing dark glasses, and I noticed a bruise on one side of her face. As all of the plasma started to evaporate and the fairy music began to fade, a single guard and a single Oaktobron then emerged from behind her.

"Captain Joan Jones," she said, wrapping her free arm

around my waist and pulling my body into hers. I was still freezing, but I melted within her embrace. Her glasses then signaled an incoming call. "Vysender," she answered, releasing me to focus on her call.

"Mama, no!" Mălīn shouted.

"What do you mean, Vysender?" she said, waving off Mălīn.

"Mama, please!" Mălīn yelled, attempting to pull off her mother's glasses.

"Good grief, Mălīn," Maerora Ma said and then told Vysender she would call him back.

"Mama . . . ," Mălīn said and then paused as if in that instance she had become paralyzed.

"What in the world has gotten into you? And, dammit, it's too cold in here for Katydid," Maerora Ma said. "C'mon, let's get into the transport vessel right now."

A loud streaming noise sounded as a seal was broken, and when it broke, we were able to enter a transport pod. The single-chamber pod was small, and we all sat squished against each other, including the guard and Oaktobron.

"What is it you wanted to tell me, Mălīn?" Maerora Ma asked.

"I can't tell you now in front of the guard."

"Captain Joan Jones, you haven't said a word. Are you all right?" Maerora Ma asked, reaching for me.

"She's in a lot of pain. Her shoulder is hurting her really badly," Mălīn quickly said.

"Well, let's get your sling back on." Maerora Ma then removed the sling from Katydid's head and leaned towards me to set my arm into it. She tied and tightened it perfectly and as she did, radiant gold sparkled on her skin where it touched mine. She then whispered into my ear, "I brought back an Oaktobron machine technician for you. You're going to be better in no time. I told you I wouldn't let you suffer, Joan."

AFTER THE POD landed at headquarters, Maerora Ma engaged in officiating in Magentan in her darkened glasses. Mălīn grabbed at her mother, and Maerora Ma gestured to her to leave. Katydid and I stood waiting a few meters away on the tarmac of the open airdrome. I scanned the area for William and Porter while Mălīn continued to gesticulate madly in front of her mother, trying to convince her to avoid talking to Vysender.

Two guards showed up and escorted the Oaktobron technician away, and then Vysender appeared and grabbed me from behind. Katydid ran to her mother, and I squealed when Vysender pulled my injured shoulder back and applied restraints on my wrists. When Maerora Ma became aware of Vysender's manhandling of me, she launched a fusillade of Magentan sentences at him. Swarms of soldiers then invaded the airdrome.

Vysender and Maerora Ma volleyed an argument back and forth, and the intensity of their passion doubled with each exchange. The faces of the soldiers matched the rhythm of their rally. Their expressions reflected confusion then conflict and then confusion again. The only Magentan words I recognized were names: 'Roble' and 'DeNitor' and 'Densip Pi' and 'Yaylor Pi.'" Vysender held a tight grip on me, and it was killing my shoulder.

"What's happening?" I shouted to Mălīn and simultaneously grimaced in extreme pain.

"It's really bad," she said.

"I need to know!"

"My mother abdicated her position as ruler of the realm."

I felt my heart sink severely as if it were an uncooled nuclear fuel rod melting through to the planet's core. "Tell me more, Mălīn. Are *you* the ruler now?" I said.

"No, Roble is."

"The leader of Oaktobron?"

"Yes and Vysender's trying to take over Magenta."

"Like a coup?" I asked, and she nodded yes.

Many of the soldiers then aimed their weapons at Maerora Ma, and Katydid started to cry. Maerora Ma stooped down to pick her up, and Vysender's grip on me then loosened, so I instantly dropped to the ground and knocked his legs out from under him, and as he fell, guards loyal to Maerora Ma pounced on him and restrained him while others dove on top of Maerora Ma, Katydid, and Mălīn, covering them entirely with their bodies. A dozen skirmishes then rippled through the mass of soldiers, and I heard Maerora Ma scream something in Magentan. A moment later, two soldiers grabbed me and placed me in a little delta formation, and we darted off into the headquarters building. They had no mercy for the pain I was in, and I was convinced my arm was now attached to my shoulder merely by my skin, and I was worried the healing machine would not be able to repair it, if, in fact, I'd ever get the chance to be healed by the machine at this point.

"What's happening?" I asked. "Do you speak English?"

The soldiers refused to answer me while they marched me upwardly inside the building.

"Is Maerora Ma safe? Please! Tell me her daughters are all right." I shivered in fear that they might be harmed or killed in the ensuing tumult that I had just been removed from. I was nervous about William and Porter too. They had to be around here somewhere, locked in their mission aim with point-of-no-return momentum to kill Maerora Ma. The throbbing soreness in my arm then pierced my thoughts. "Son of a . . . ," I cried.

These soldiers didn't give a damn about the pain I was in as they continued to direct me forward by grabbing the arm of my injured shoulder. Uncertainty about whether they were taking me to prison or to safety was my sustaining thought, and when the familiar island floor came into view, I had a feeling I was going to be safe. The soldiers opened the door to the sunken abode that I had been in earlier with Mălīn and Katydid. They let me walk inside, and without removing the restraints on my wrists, they closed the door and locked it. I was in so much agony that I couldn't take one more step, and so I crouched down onto the floor and writhed, wailed, and cried in pain.

CHAPTER 13:
NOMA

"I KNOW you're in there," I heard a familiar voice say. "All my equipment tells me so."

"Bonson?"

"There she is!" he said.

When I opened my eyes, Bonson's friendly face was staring at me. It seemed waking up from unconsciousness and seeing Bonson was becoming a habit.

"Where's Mălīn?" I asked.

"I think you mean Maerora Ma, don't you? She's right here, waiting for you," Bonson said.

"Mălīn?" I called.

"No, Captain Joan Jones, it's me, not Mălīn. You've been unconscious for a few days now, and we've just taken you out of the rapid-healing machine. How do you feel?" Maerora Ma asked, petting my forehead. Gold glistened.

"Where's Mălīn?"

"She's down the hallway. I'll get her in a moment. Perhaps all your memories haven't filled in yet," she said, looking at Bonson.

"Well, Maerora Ma, I didn't want her to go into the machine unconscious as you insisted we do," Bonson whined.

"Bonson, leave us alone for a few minutes," Maerora Ma said.

Bonson exited the room, and Maerora Ma set herself next to me on the bed. She was wearing civilian clothing, a pullover sweater and tapered pants.

"Joan?" she called softly. "You do remember *us*, don't you? The meadow? The gold?"

"Yes, I know. I'm sorry. I just don't remember what

happened after you arrived in a vision I was having. I was with Mălīn and Katydid, and we were freezing. Mălīn and I needed to tell you . . . ." I then paused.

"That's right, Joan. You and Mălīn had something you wanted to tell me. What is it? Do you remember?"

"No, I don't," I said, reaching for her hand. "Why do you have sunglasses on?"

"I injured my eyes before I went to Oaktobron," she said.

"What about that bruise on your face?"

"Don't worry, Joan. I will be healed by the machine next," she said, leaning down to kiss my lips. "You saved my life *again*, Joan."

"What do you mean?"

"You don't remember Vysender?" she asked.

"I know Vysender," I said, and then I remembered the danger of William and Porter. "We're in danger!" I warned.

"No, it's ok now. Vysender's been executed," she said.

"I'm not talking about Vysender—"

Mălīn suddenly barged into the room along with Katydid.

"Mălīn! Knock before entering a room," Maerora Ma said.

"Captain Joan Jones, I'm so glad you're back," Mălīn said, kissing me on the cheek and then mumbling, "keep your mouth shut," in my ear.

A WHILE LATER Mălīn, Katydid, and I sat on the floor in the hallway next to the door of the hospital room that contained the rapid-healing machine. Maerora Ma had just been placed inside it after I had passed a physical. I was one-hundred percent restored again, and we were now waiting for Maerora Ma to have her eyes healed.

Mălīn insisted I guard the door since William and Porter were still at large. Mălīn was once again momentarily in charge of Magenta since her mother was unavailable. We hadn't been able to speak about William and Porter to each other and couldn't do so now in front of Katydid, so we tried to lull her to sleep but without success. Noma, of all people, then appeared down the hallway. She walked towards us and hollered something in Magentan.

Mălīn jumped up. "Noma! What are doing here?"

Noma fired out a hostile reply in Magentan, which included Vysender's name.

"How do you know about Vysender?" Mălīn asked in English.

Noma looked at me and then began speaking in English. "Don't you know Magentans are parading in the streets, lauding the greatness of your mother and defaming Vysender?"

"That's good," Mălīn said.

"Oh, heir apparent, Magentans can march and dance around their flowered floats all day long, but that's not going to enable Maerora Ma to sit her ass back down on the seat of the realm. If you ask me, Vysender was our only hope."

Mălīn looked down.

"Your mother's a fool and has left you with less than a pinky finger full off power to inherit. She has permanently damaged your pedigree."

Mălīn remained silent, and Noma then snorted smugly.

"Why's Maerora Ma in the hospital?"

"She's undergoing surgery to excise that tumor that oozes out kind regard for you," Mălīn said.

"You're just like your mother. I'm so glad I missed out on your upbringing. Why are you all sitting here on the floor like the dregs of society?"

"Why are you here, Noma?" Mălīn asked.

"I have something very important to tell your mother," Noma said, "Why don't you get some chairs?" Noma asked.

"Oh, yeah, and obstruct the hospital hallways," Mălīn said.

Noma glared at Mălīn and remained standing.

I stood up and announced that I was going to the restroom.

"Wait, Captain Joan Jones. You can't leave us here without guards," Mălīn said.

Noma squinted her eyes at us as Mălīn called for guards

through her glasses. Six guards then appeared, none of whom were William or Porter.

"Why so many guards?" Noma asked.

Mălīn ignored her aunt and then attempted to speak to me cryptically. "Are these fine Magentan guards or not?" she said.

"Yes, Mălīn, they're Magenta's finest," I replied.

"Good. I'll accompany you to the restroom," she said.

As soon as we entered the restroom, Mălīn embraced me tightly and thanked me for saving her mother's life. "If you hadn't have knocked over Vysender, he would have ordered the soldiers to execute all of us on the spot," she said.

"Why, Mălīn? Why did Vysender do that?"

"Because my mother handed over the rule of the realm to Roble."

"And why did she do that?" I asked.

"I don't know. She won't tell me, but she was up to something. She had an intense hidden agenda going on. She was corresponding with Roble behind Vysender's back. I even accidentally spoke to Roble myself," she said. "He's a real jerk."

"Mălīn, do you think it's possible she gave up the seat of the realm for the machine technician?"

"That's crazy if she did," she said.

"Oh, God," I said, feeling deeply disturbed by the thought that my welfare could have been the impetus of Maerora Ma's downfall.

"Don't worry, Captain Joan Jones, I have immense faith in my mother. It's going to be all right," she said, patting me gently on the back, "and the best part about it is that Vysender and his posse are all dead now. There's now no one who knows about the Earth males, so we don't have to tell my mother about them. And *we won't*, of course," she said, eyeing me advisedly.

"But they're out there somewhere, Mălīn. We can't live our lives in constant fear of them."

"I'll figure something out."

A sudden intense fear of disagreeing with Mălīn on this subject paralyzed my normal righteous impulse. After all, Mălīn, at the moment, was the ruler of Magenta—a young, volatile, and unreasonable ruler.

"All right, I won't say anything to your mother, but it's not easy for me to be deceptive, especially towards Maerora Ma."

"Don't worry, Captain Joan Jones. You're better at it than you think."

MANY HOURS had passed, and we were still sitting on the floor, waiting for Maerora Ma. Finally, Bonson and a couple of nurses walked down the hallway towards us.

"It will be just a few minutes," he said. He and the nurses then walked into the room, and the door slid shut behind them.

"Mălīn, I demand to speak to Maerora Ma alone," Noma said.

"No, I won't allow that," Mălīn told her.

"In a few minutes, you won't be able to *allow* a fly to land on a piece of shit!" Noma said.

"I just love your Earth English, Noma."

The door retracted, and I could see Maerora Ma right away. She was standing and raring to go. Her eyes were uncovered and sparkled in violet, and the bruise on her face was gone. I held Katydid in my arms and felt a passionate eagerness for Maerora Ma.

"Noma!" Maerora Ma said, looking at Noma and retrieving Katydid from my arms. She kissed her little daughter and kissed me all the while focusing on Noma. "What in the world are you doing here?"

"You know damn well I've been trying to get a hold of you. We need to talk," Noma said.

Maerora Ma kissed Mălīn and then set Katydid down and reached to put on her glasses. "No, Noma, I'm in a hurry. Captain Joan Jones and I are going to Oaktobron right now," Maerora Ma said and then reached to pull me to her side. Gold flickered on her skin.

Noma eyed the gold while Mălīn took a few steps towards her mother.

"You can't go there. It's not safe," Mălīn said.

Maerora Ma then spoke in Magentan to someone in her

glasses, and after she finished, she ordered Mălīn to take care of Katydid and told Noma she'd talk with her upon returning from Oaktobron. She then pulled me along with her as she exited the room.

Noma then rushed out into the middle of the hallway and shouted, "What about Yaylor Pi?"

Mălīn and Katydid followed Noma into the hallway.

Maerora Ma stopped and turned around to face Noma. "What did you say?"

"Yaylor Pi—"

"Yaylor Pi, Mama!" Katydid shouted. "He's here! He's here!"

Maerora Ma walked over to Katydid, picked her up, kissed her, and handed her to Mălīn. "Take her to the waiting room," Maerora Ma ordered.

"Mama, don't you think I should know about Yaylor Pi," Mălīn said.

"Do what I say."

Mălīn carried Katydid down the hallway while Maerora Ma turned to glare at Noma. "You delight in other people's misfortune, don't you?"

"Only in yours, Maerora Ma," Noma said.

"Is he dead?"

"Yep, he committed suicide . . . couldn't handle the cold," Noma said.

"Where are his remains?"

"In Morgana," Noma said.

Maerora Ma then spoke into her glasses in Magentan while I studied Noma's face. A residue expression of perverted joy lingered on her face as her sister stoically suffered.

Maerora Ma then reached for my hand, and her skin turned brilliant gold as she led me down the hallway.

"Sister," Noma shouted, "you have a turncoat at hand? There's no other explanation for her visit from a tortured Earth."

CHAPTER 14:
SEESAW

"Maerora Ma and I hadn't spoken since leaving the hospital. She had spent most of the time speaking in Magentan through her glasses. There were probably more officiating details for her to cover now that Vysender was gone, and I figured she, herself, had to be involved with some of the arrangements for Yaylor Pi.

In a small detached structure at the airdrome, she dressed into a military uniform, which had only half the insignia that I had seen before. She then fitted me with a parka for our layover at the MOC station and then embraced me tightly for a long moment.

"Joan, there's something very serious you have to do for me on Oaktobron," she said.

"Of course, anything, Maerora," I replied softly in her ear.

"I've been playing a risky game with Roble and have already sacrificed my soul, so now we're going to Oaktobron to reclaim it," she said, pushing out of the embrace.

We then walked over to and climbed inside of the small MOC-transport pod, and as it launched, she continued to explain what she wanted me to do.

"I'll convince Roble to meet with us alone, and then all you have to do is break his neck. I've already arranged for our safe escape from Oaktobron."

"Ok," I said, but a feeling of apprehension then invaded me. Interfering with the affairs of this realm was well beyond my authority as an officer in the U.S. military, but I had already abandoned that role, hadn't I? So, what did it matter this trespass if it helped Maerora Ma? I watched her look at me through a small expression of relief that was on her face, and it fulfilled me. "I'm so very sorry about Yaylor Pi," I said, reaching to touch her.

"He didn't commit suicide," she said. "Those Oaktobrons that were in Morgana killed him and made it look like a suicide. Roble ordered it. I've been talking with residents of Morgana. It's likely that that's what happened. He needed the tension between our nations to reach the tipping point, so he would have an excuse to use his new weapon of extreme mass destruction on us. He's a gravely dangerous male. At the least, he's a disrupter of balance; at the worst, he's a destroyer of life," she said, placing her hand on mine. Gold sparkled.

I then placed my hand on top of hers.

"Oh, Joan, all I truly want to do is restore my grandmother's dream," she said. "For well over a hundred years, it has been the mission of Magenta to return to its source, but when Earth killed Morgana . . . ,"

"I know. It's ok. Everything will be all right," I said.

She then cuddled into my side, which caused a bolt of electricity to discharge from the center of my body.

"Maerora, there's something I need to tell you."

"Tell me later," she said, "we need to stay focused right now."

"No, I need to tell you now."

"Oh, Joan," she said, pushing back into her seat.

"Listen to me, Maerora, I didn't come to Magenta on a reconnaissance mission."

"Ok," she said.

"I came here to assassinate you, and you should know that Densip Pi visited Earth and convinced us that you were preparing to destroy us."

Maerora Ma crossed her arms. "Let's stop talking please."

"No, Maerora, there's more I need to tell you. I didn't come here alone."

"What do you mean?" she asked.

"I was accompanied by two crewmates—"

"Where are they?"

"I don't know."

"What do you mean you don't know? What about my daughters?" she said, and then she called Mălīn through her glasses. "Mălīn, where are you? Where's Katydid? Listen to me. There are Earth males on the loose. Are you at headquarters? . . . Oh, good. Just stay there. Don't let anyone in . . . What do you mean how do I know? Captain Joan Jones just told me . . . I'm fine, Mălīn. Don't worry about me. Just stay safe. I'll be back so very soon, daughter. I love you, Mălīn. Please kiss my baby for me."

"I'm sorry, Maerora," I said, reaching for her hand.

She retracted her hand and scooted as far away from me as possible in the tiny transport pod.

"Captain Joan Jones, I need for you to carry out the task I've explained."

"I will," I said, and I reached for her again, but she rejected me.

"My daughters are in peril. I can't reconcile with you until I know they're safe, and I do need for you to kill Roble."

"Of course, Maerora, I'll do anything for you. Please don't change," I begged.

"I don't want to talk to you right now," she said, turning away from me in an obviously uncomfortable position.

"But I have more to tell you . . . better news," I said.

"No more!" she barked with the authority of a mother indistinguishable from that of an autocrat.

WE TRANSFERRED through the MOC, and once we were inside the Oaktobron-side station, we readied ourselves for the Oaktobron mission. Maerora Ma minimized her interactions with me and limited all discussion to my task of killing Roble.

I hadn't mentally practiced the skill of breaking necks in a while and was too upset about Maerora Ma's withdrawal from me to be able to do it now, but I felt confident about killing Roble since I knew what to expect of an Oaktobron neck.

"Captain Joan Jones, I will first attend a death-acknowledgement gathering—"

"Death acknowledgment?" I said.

"Yes, my grandmother insisted we personally acknowledge those who died while building the MIC. While I'm at the gathering, you'll remain here."

"Ok."

"I will then call Roble, and once I've convinced him to meet us, I will call for you. Now, I expect you to do exactly as I tell you. Do not worry if you see me suffering from magenta deprivation. You just break Roble's neck when I tell you to do so. Ok?"

"Yes, Ma'am," I said, saluting her in earnest.

"I'm leaving now. The pod is programmed to return here, and once you've boarded it, it will automatically launch and head down to Oaktobron. I'll be waiting for you."

"Maerora, before you leave, can we please—"

"Captain Joan Jones, a Magentan woman obviously cannot conceal her love nor can she force it," she said, touching my arm to show me the absence of gold. She then exited the pod.

MAERORA MA had completed her death-acknowledgement visit that had taken place in the home of a large Oatktobron family, which Yaylor Pi had selected randomly when he originally planned the visit. As she exited the home, a huge single stream of fire, many kilometers above, seared the sky in a single hissing pulse. Maerora Ma studied the blazing streak for a moment, and then she hurriedly started to contact Roble through her glasses but was interrupted by a young Oaktobron woman who was passing by.

"They're testing the Effa-ray today," said the woman, speaking in Magentan.

Maerora Ma smiled and nodded and then proceeded with her call to Roble.

"I knew you would be here today," the woman said.

"Are you a member of this family?" Maerora Ma asked.

"No."

"Well, if *you* know, then others know, and I won't be safe for long. I don't mean to be rude, but I need to talk into my glasses," Maerora Ma said.

"'Are not you moved when all the sway of earth/Shakes like a thing unfirm? O Cicero,/I have seen tempests when the scolding winds have rived the knotty oaks . . . .'"

Maerora Ma discontinued her call and looked at the woman with extraordinary interest and then continued the passage the woman had started. "'And I have seen/Th'ambitious ocean swell and rage and foam/To be exalted with the threatening clouds . . . .'"

"'But never till tonight, never till now,/Did I go through a tempest dropping fire./Either there is a civil strife in heaven,/Or else the world, too saucy with the gods,/incenses them to send destruction,'" the woman said then resumed speaking in Magentan. "I knew you wouldn't be able to resist finishing a line of Shakespeare. You're a slave to Shakespeare as I understand it, plus you're Magentan, and Magentans are very obedient."

Maerora Ma smirked and snorted lightly. "How do you know Shakespeare?"

"The free press," the woman answered.

"Ah!" Maerora Ma acknowledged.

"I dreamed of meeting you one day, but of course I'll admit I did my due diligence in finding you here today, so I don't mean to imply that there was any divine intervention, although there's always that whisper in our minds . . . ."

"I'm not divine," Maerora Ma said.

"Oh, I know that. Oaktobrons aren't as gullible as Magentans. We don't believe in gods or goddesses."

"I recognize that the word 'Magentan' is a pejorative in your vocabulary. There's something inauspicious about that."

"Not every Oaktobron hates you, you know," she said.

"I'm not so worried about every Oaktobron, just the one in front of me."

"You worry well, Maerora Ma, for I have sharp objects on my body, and I am prepared to use them on you," she said.

"Your head in my hand presented to the masses of 'knotty oaks' would land me a ton of respect and admiration, enough to be pleased for a whole lifetime and then some."

"Well, I'm mighty vulnerable right now, but still I have an army of soldiers at my command," Maerora Ma said.

"Are they invisible?" the woman said, laughing.

"Intangible for sure," Maerora Ma said. "Here are a few for you now: First, the very act of slicing my head off won't be as easy as it seems. It will shock you to pierce my skin, and then there's the thick and full-of-tough-gristle spine that you'll have to contend with unless you're carrying a guillotine on your back. Second, your fearsome leader is expecting me, and, at the moment, I am more valuable to him alive than dead. I doubt he is someone you want to reckon with."

The woman smiled and retrieved a carving knife from behind her back. "I dreamed of this blade slipping past your skin and through your flesh to cross-section your carotid artery."

"You're quite a dreamer," Maerora Ma said. "Roble will be calling me soon. Is it worth it? And what was the reason to kill me again?"

"Oppression!" the woman shouted.

"Oh, I thought it was for respect and admiration. Who exactly has been oppressed?"

"Oaktobrons!"

"Yet, you have a free press, and technological advancement, and you, yourself, exude a dash of esprit," Maerora Ma said.

"You oppress Magentans," the woman said.

"But Magentans are gullible and obedient. They beg to be led."

The woman drew her knife back to full kinetic potential and then released it at Maerora Ma. Maerora Ma used her hand to deflect the incoming knife, causing the serrated edge to cut a gorge through her palm. The woman ran off, and Maerora Ma bent over, pressing her uninjured hand into her wounded hand to stop the bleeding. She then called Roble, grimacing and cringing in pain physically but otherwise in control of the sound of her voice.

"Maerora Ma," Roble said, "have you already been to the death-acknowledgment visit? You were supposed to have checked in with me first."

"I wanted to get it over with so that there would be more time for the painting," she said.

"The painting?" he asked.

Maerora Ma remained silent and held her bleeding hand above her heart just under her chin.

"Ah, yes, the painting. That was just a metaphor. I don't have time for that now. My son's just finished his Peri-Oakbrawn, and I've been participating in efforts to prepare the Effa-ray for its debut session."

"All right, Roble. I'll go back home, but I did bring someone you may be interested in meeting before I leave."

"Who?"

"An Earth woman."

"Ah! *Ménage à trois*," he said laughing. "Yes, bring her to me. Bring her now," he said.

"All right, but we'll need guards to protect us. I've already been attacked by a very confused Oaktobron."

"Oh, don't whine so much, Maerora Ma. It's not my fault Oaktobrons hate you."

I LANDED at the Oaktobron airport in the small pod, and Maerora Ma was there waiting for me.

"Captain Joan Jones, c'mon, let's go," she said. Magenta-colored blood was smeared all over the top of her uniform.

"Oh, my God, what happened?" I asked.

"A knife-wielding Oaktobron attacked me," she said and then showed me the deep stripe of maroon in the middle of her palm.

"Maerora, you need get that cleaned right away. It'll become infected."

"I told you to remain focused. Now, just follow my directions."

"Why'd the Oaktobron attack you?" I asked.

"They've all been brainwashed by their free press," she said. "C'mon, Roble's waiting for us. Now remember, Captain Joan Jones, please act when I tell you to do so."

AFTER WE WERE TRANSPORTED to a huge palace made entirely of triangular-shaped marble wedges, guards escorted us into a waiting room that was decorated in amazing technological ornaments and art. The full visible-light spectrum was free to range here on Oaktobron, but a dominant dull-orange overcast ruined the true vibrancy of colors that I was used to seeing on Earth. Still, though, the electronic art captivated me, and I stood and concentrated on the beauty of each piece.

Maerora Ma sat on a settee, holding her injured hand. She apparently hadn't forgotten our conversation in the pod and seemed far removed from regarding me with any leniency. I didn't want to look at her in this light, but I missed her warm regard, and I worried about her hand and her sensitivity to a lack of magenta.

"Are you ok?" I asked, still holding my gaze on the scintillating art.

"Don't worry about me," she said.

An Oaktobron male, acting like a butler, then appeared and spoke in Magentan. Maerora Ma told me he was here to escort us to Roble. We followed him up a flight of stairs. I remained one-step ahead of Maerora Ma and one-step behind the Oaktobron butler. The butler then stopped and activated an electronic door that retracted open and revealed a tall, wide, buff, and bearded man who was standing at a large window. The outdoor light from the window landed on his curvy physique at an angle that enhanced the definition of his muscles. I quickly reminded myself of the purpose of my presence, and I then let my glance drop from his face to his neck.

The butler announced us to Roble and then exited the room and let the door slide shut.

"Maerora Ma," Roble said with a slight smile.

Maerora Ma then spoke to Roble in Magentan and placed her hand in the middle of my back and gently nudged me towards him. He responded with a few words in Magentan and then pointed to a little boy who was sitting in a big overstuffed chair in the room.

Maerora Ma looked at me with concealed consternation and then said to me, "That's Roble's son."

He appeared to be no older than ten and still retained that precious innocence that always results in the softening of muscle tissue around the hearts of adults. He held a small object in his hand, which looked like a puzzle or a toy game. He smiled at Maerora Ma and then looked back down at his toy.

Roble walked over to his son and patted him on the back, exhibiting genuine pride and joy. He then spoke, and Maerora Ma translated for me. "His son just finished his Peri-Oakbrawn. It's an Oaktobron rite of passage."

"Congratulations," I said, and Maerora Ma then conveyed my sentiment to the two.

"Joan, get ready," she said, "while he's near his son."

I moved close to the boy and gestured interest in his toy. He then handed it to me, and I then felt sick. Oh, God, I was seriously sick.

Roble smiled at me as I stared at the boy's toy in my hand, but it was my hands that were in focus, not the toy. Oh, God, is my mind going to let my hands kill in front of a child?

Maerora Ma then moved in and took the toy out of my hands. "Now, Joan," she ordered, and I then watched my hands rise up. One landed on the top of the base of Roble's neck and the other just under his ear. One and two immensely sharp and sudden whips amidst eighty wallops of self-defense from Roble's showcase muscles ended all vitality in the juggernaut who then dropped to the floor in a blunt thump.

Maerora Ma had held back Roble's son's arms, but she failed to cover his eyes, and what he had just seen, no doubt, dashed all innocence. The boy began to scream, and Maerora Ma then ordered me to break his neck. The momentum of my skill was ahead of me, and my hands were landing on the boy's neck, and then a petit sort of replay of what I had just done to his father took place.

When I looked over at Maerora Ma, she had her back to me and was speaking into her glasses in Magentan. She then gestured for us to leave the palace.

WE WERE BACK in the transport pod, headed to the Oaktobron-side station of the MOC. Maerora Ma had a single loyal Oaktobron who safely enabled our escape. We sat in the pod across from each other, and I concentrated on holding back the vomit that was in my throat. I hated Maerora Ma, and the weight of my hate made it impossible for me to lift my head to look at her.

"Joan?" she called, but I didn't answer.

"Oh, Joan," she said softly.

Once we landed at the Oaktobron-side station, a station attendant treated Maerora Ma's hand wound while I avoided any acknowledgement of her existence. She informed me that we would be remaining at the station for a while until she had absorbed enough magenta to carry on through the MOC.

IT HAD NOW BEEN several hours since I killed the little boy, and we had just arrived at headquarters. Maerora Ma had given up on trying to talk to me, and the last thing I wanted to do was spend more time in close proximity to her. We were still at the airdrome when she asked me to follow her to her abode up in the building.

"Is there somewhere else I can stay?" I asked.

She looked at me with a multitude of complexities welling up in her eyes. "What am I supposed to do with you, Joan? Do I lock you up or keep embracing you as a member of my family?"

WHEN WE entered the abode, Mălīn aimed all her resentment at me in a caustic glare while little Katydid eagerly grabbed at my legs and jumped up and down for me to pick her up, but I just stood in place. Maerora Ma then reached for Katydid and carried her to the settee and sat with her in her arms and quietly wept.

Mălīn then glared at me ever severer and sat next to her mother and leaned lovingly into her. I then walked over to the far end of the settee to sit and stare out at the balcony.

Maerora Ma received an incoming call and spoke in Magentan, and Mălīn then took the opportunity to speak to me.

"What happened on Oaktobron?" Mălīn asked me.

"Let your mother tell you," I said.

Mălīn then began to listen to her mother's conversation.

"Roble's dead?" Mălīn asked, looking at me with a tilted head.

"Yes," I answered.

"Did *you* kill him?"

"Yes."

Mălīn kept one ear on her mother's conversation and one for her conversation with me. "Thank goodness my mother's once again the ruler of the realm. She really had things under control, didn't she?"

I continued to stare out at the balcony, even though my neck was getting sore from being fixed in one direction, but it was my only refuge. I couldn't ease the misery of regret from the heinous act I had just committed and knew ultimately there would be no escape from it ever. I could imagine in the future I'd be able to feign normalcy while in public, but in private I might as well be condemned to Hell. Ah, yes, Hell. This was just par for the course in Hell. Why did I think I was anywhere else?"

"You don't seem too satisfied with the outcome. How come?" Mălīn asked.

"Let your mother tell you."

Maerora Ma then ended her conversation and carried sleeping Katydid into her bedroom.

With Maerora Ma now out of earshot, Mălīn asked, "Why in the world did you tell my mom about the Earth males?"

"Because it was the right thing to do," I said.

"Did you tell her about Densip Pi?"

"Yes."

"Did she show any suspicion about me?"

"No."

Maerora Ma then returned. "Mălin, it's late. You should go to bed now."

"All right, Mama." She then kissed her mother on the cheek.

After Mălin had gone into her room and shut the door, Maerora Ma sat at the middle of the settee and faced me. I remained silent and aloof.

"Please come to bed with me."

"No, I'll sleep here on the settee. Is there a blanket and pillow I can borrow?"

"Joan, Roble's son was collateral damage, and those types of events come with the territory. You know that. You're military," she said.

"He didn't need to die. I could have prevented it, but I was such a stupid mindless robot to have followed your command."

"And since you *did* follow my command, the responsibility is *mine, not yours*. I had just cause to prevent Roble—at whatever cost—from using his weapon of extreme mass destruction."

"I agree. You had just cause in regards to Roble's death, but we didn't have to kill his son!"

"His son's death was collateral damage. It wasn't my intention . . . his screaming was a threat to our successful escape."

"Our escape was no justification for killing an innocent little boy. I'm a soldier and am always prepared to die."

"And I'm a ruler, and a soldier is expected to protect its ruler."

"I'm from Earth. You're not *my* ruler . . . thank God."

"All right, you're not obligated to protect *me*, but you'd better—to the death of you—defend my daughters. After all, half of your lethal contingent is running around my planet," she said, and then she retrieved a blanket and pillow and unfolded the blanket and tucked it under the settee's cushions, and then she plumped up the pillow and set it at against the arm of the settee.

CHAPTER 15:
CONTINGENT UPON MAGENTA

MAERORA MA had left her bedroom door open all night while I lay on the settee. It was now morning, and she had received a call and was speaking in Magentan. She sounded happy, relieved, and pleased.

I hadn't slept all night because Roble's son haunted me. I got up and washed in the abode's guest bathroom, and as I exited the bathroom, Katydid ran to me, grabbed my hand, and led me to the dining room.

"Mălīn's fick," she said as we sat at the table.

Maerora Ma then entered the dining room. "What did you say, Katydid?" she asked. She was wearing a thick bathrobe. Her hair was unbrushed, and her eyes were puffy.

"Mălīn's fick," Katydid repeated.

"Katydid, just be quiet and mind your own business," Mălīn said, entering the room.

"Mălīn, are you sick? You don't have a fever, do you?" Maerora Ma asked.

"No, Mama," Mălīn said and stood unsteadily as if on the verge of crying. "I know what you're thinking."

"It's all right," Maerora Ma said, reaching to pat her on the back.

"Mama, what if when I see her, she reminds me of DeNitor?" Tears then trickled down Mălīn's cheeks.

"You'll love her no matter what. Trust me."

"But I won't love me," Mălīn said. "She'll remind me of what I've . . . ." She looked at me then began to speak in Magentan.

I left the dining room and wandered out onto the balcony. The huge dying star was so immense in the sky. It seemed like it had two long arms grabbing my face and preventing me from looking at anything else. While I gazed at it, I considered what Maerora Ma had said about protecting her daughters. I was in alignment with her about that, and I most certainly would commit to protecting her daughters. Perish the thought they should become collateral damage. After all, had I followed through with my mission orders at first opportunity, the two innocent siblings would not be in danger now. If only I hadn't seen Butterfly when I first met Katydid, I could have carried out my orders.

The balcony door retracted, but I didn't turn my head to look. I just crossed my arms and continued to stare at the star.

"Joan, please return to have breakfast with us," Maerora Ma said.

"All right," I said, "Is Mălīn ok?"

"She's pregnant."

"Is it good or bad that she's pregnant?" I asked, turning to face her.

"Daughters are always wholeheartedly welcomed here on Magenta no matter what."

"But what if she's pregnant with a boy?"

"We only conceive daughters," she said.

"Well, if that were the case, then there would be no male Magentans on Magenta, and without males . . . ."

"Other Magentan women have sons all the time . . . more sons than daughters in fact," she said, "but my mother and her mother and so forth were biologically matrilineal."

"So, you don't have any sons, brothers, or uncles? How far back does that go?" I asked.

"All the way to Mother Earth."

"But Mother Earth produces male, female, and otherwise."

"Yes, she does. Earth is the source of all things."

I smirked and snorted subtly then turned back to look at the star.

"Joan, please, what can I do? I can't stand to lose you. You're The Great Liaison, and together we have work to do," she said, clutching at my arm.

I was on the moon, far away from her sentiment and thus had no impulse to respond.

"Please, Joan," she said, lifting my hand in front of my face to demonstrate her gold skin. "I'm sincere."

"Oh, hey, look at that. It's back in all its glory," I said.

"Don't be derisive," she said. "It's hurtful."

"Are we finished? I have no more civility to contrive."

"Joan, please . . . please tell me what I can do."

"Send me home," I said.

"To Earth?" she asked.

"Well, yes, that's my home, Maerora Ma."

"No," she said, "I can't let you go back home. My daughters need your unique protection."

"I know. Your daughters are in the forefront of your mind in each waking moment I have. But what about *my* daughter? Butterfly needs me too, and you know what? I desperately need her. I need to hold her just like you hold Katydid."

"I'll have her brought here, Joan . . . safely, and she'll be a beloved member of our family," she said, trying to hold my hand.

"No," I said, moving ten steps away from her to the balcony's edge.

"If you leave, who will protect my daughters?"

"Surely you can figure it out. After all, you're far more technologically advanced than we are. How about a DNA-identification system or something? My crewmates left excrement in your garden, so there's plenty of DNA to be had. Maybe even Noma can help you since she's so good with DNA."

SEVERAL DAYS had gone by, and I dutifully stayed on guard to protect Mălīn and Katydid. We all remained at headquarters, and I slept nights on the settee. Maerora Ma worked early and late at her console, and we barely spoke to each other.

One morning at the breakfast table, Mălīn mentioned Shri Durga. "Mama," she said, "Morgana was killed by an angry Earth male who misrepresented Earth humans. Captain Joan

Jones and I researched it. So, maybe we can explain to them the huge misunderstanding by distributing flyers written in Earth English. We'll scatter the planet with the flyers, and when they inevitably read it, they'll understand why you did what you did, and they'll forgive you, Mama. Please can we try this, Mama? Even Captain Joan Jones thinks this is a good idea, don't you?"

I didn't answer. I just subtly shrugged and watched for Maerora Ma's reaction, but Maerora Ma didn't say a word. However, our eyes captured each other, and when they did, I realized how much I missed her. I could feel faint creaks crack through my hardened heart, and it hurt.

"Come with me," Maerora Ma said, gesturing me to her bedroom. I followed her inside, and she then let the door slide shut. "You can go home now . . . today if you'd like," she said.

"What about my crewmates?"

"I have it all under control now."

"Did you find them?" I asked.

"We're very close," she said.

A sweeping wave of relief then flowed through me, and the realization that I'd be holding my daughter in my arms soon lightened me. "Did you say I could leave today?" I asked.

"If you wish," she said. "It's the right thing to do . . . for you to be close to your daughter. Everything is going to be all right. You don't need to worry about us."

"Well, if I can leave today, I would like to," I said.

HOURS LATER, Maerora Ma had me say my goodbyes to Mǎlīn and Katydid, and then she brought me to the MIC. Being there reminded me of the horrible footage of Morgana's death. Dozens of guards and MIC operators filled the area while Maerora Ma escorted me over to the dangling opening of the Magenta-side sack. She stopped then turned to face me. She had on her familiar military Mao suit, which bore more insignia than ever before. Some of her hair had slipped under her collar on one side while a few spiraling curls waved in a gentle breeze on the other side.

I felt like I was wearing a wet sweater in the thick of a snow-storm, cold and frozen over by the galing winds of guilt. The dying star in the sky was pale and non-luminous, barely present except for its enormous size.

"What should I tell my superiors?" I asked.

Maerora Ma then stared into my face with a weak smile. "You'll have to recite a little Shakespeare for them. Tell them, 'If you prick us, do we not bleed? if you tickle us, do we not laugh? if you poison us, do we not die? and if you wrong us, shall we not revenge?'"

"Well, you know my Shakespeare's not very good."

"Then just recite the last sentence," she said, losing her smile.

"And what should I tell the goddess culture? They believe in you."

"Well, I do exist, Joan, so confirm to them that Earth really is the source of all things."

"Is there anything you want me to say to Butterfly?" I asked and then reached to move her hair from under the side of her collar. She immediately rested her cheek on my hand, and gold then flowed under her skin.

"Tell her I eagerly await for the both of you to return. I'll have the landing pad permanently installed in anticipation of—"

"Oh, my God! Maerora!" I screamed and pushed her from under an airborne William, and then I felt the two hands of Porter land on the side of my neck, and . . . ."

Maerora Ma stood in her garden with her daughters. The three stood hand in hand in front of Morgana's plaque, and next to Morgana was Captain Joan Jones' plaque, which had been set in freshly upturned earth. Maerora Ma let go of Mălīn's hand to put on her glasses and then spoke into them. "Prepare the twentieth mission," she said. "We're going to retrieve Butterfly Jones."

CONTINGENT UPON MAGENTA

NOTE FROM THE AUTHOR:

Thank you for reading my debut book. I hope it added a little something to you as reading books can often do. If you enjoyed the story, please rate and review it on Amazon or any other sites you prefer. Thank you.

www.ingramcontent.com/pod-product-compliance
Lightning Source LLC
Chambersburg PA
CBHW070917180626
46817CB00003B/1093